25953

Spa Vacation

Books by Theresa Alan

WHO YOU KNOW

SPUR OF THE MOMENT

THE GIRLS' GLOBAL GUIDE TO GUYS

GIRLS WHO GOSSIP

THE DANGERS OF MISTLETOE

GETTING MARRIED

SPA VACATION

Published by Kensington Publishing Corporation

Spa Vacation

THERESA ALAN

KENSINGTON BOOKS
http://www.kensingtonbooks.com

KENSINGTON BOOKS are published by

Kensington Publishing Corp.
850 Third Avenue
New York, NY 10022

ISBN-13: 978-0-7582-0998-6
ISBN-10: 0-7582-0998-3

First Kensington Trade Paperback Printing: June 2008
10 9 8 7 6 5 4 3 2 1

Printed in the United States of America

Spa Vacation

Chapter 1

The Tuesday before the trip

Amy Harrington had never been the kind of woman who was consumed by lust. Desire was a messy and fickle thing. Amy didn't act recklessly or hastily. She wasn't a big fan of spontaneity. She liked making rational decisions based on the best information available. She was a sensible girl, always had been.

That was why what was happening to her now was throwing her world into a frenzied, baffling orbit. She had never experienced such an immediate carnal reaction to anyone before, and the feelings were making her thoughts blurry and confused.

Amy couldn't focus on what he was saying. She watched his lips moving as he sat behind his desk in his tastefully decorated office, but she couldn't seem to actually put together what the words coming out of his mouth *meant*.

He was good looking, certainly, but that wasn't enough to explain what was causing this reaction in her. She'd encountered hundreds of sexy, handsome men in her life, and none of them had turned her insides into quivering mush like Brent Meyer did.

Amy's friend Caitlyn, the poet, would be able to find a turn of phrase that could explain exactly what it was about his smile that was so captivating. She would have the words to describe the precise bright green shade of his eyes. Stoplight green maybe? No, that conjured traffic and headaches, not beautiful, brilliant Oz-emerald eyes. Amy didn't have Caitlyn's gift with words, that was obvious.

Amy's friend Leah, the scientist, would be able to explain the exact chemical and physical reactions that were happening in Amy's body. They involved an increase in adrenaline, probably, and maybe something about pheromones, but Amy didn't know about that sort of thing. She knew about financial planning and making budgets and ensuring that all the numbers at the bottom of the spreadsheet added up. Love? Attraction? Lust? These simply weren't her areas of expertise.

Amy imagined that their meeting would run long and he would ask her to dinner. The meal would go on for several hours and many drinks. She'd have a little too much alcohol, and he would offer to drive her home. She would say that was very generous of him. She would get in his car and relax in the comfortable leather seats. He would say he needed to stop by the office for just a moment. She would accompany him in. In the empty office building of the software company he'd founded, they would sit beside each other on the comfortable gray couch in the reception area. He would put his hand on her leg. She'd pretend to protest, but only for a moment. He would slide his hand up her leg, beneath her skirt . . .

Amy realized suddenly that he'd asked her something, and she had no idea what, since she had been too busy fantasizing about an illicit tryst with him. "I'm sorry, what did you say?" she asked.

"I asked when you're getting married."

He gestured to her left hand. She followed his gaze and saw that she'd been spinning her engagement ring around and around with her thumb.

"Two months."

"Still getting used to the ring, huh?"

"Yeah, I suppose so." *And still getting used to the idea of being married, apparently.*

Amy suspected that it wasn't a good sign to be daydreaming about having sex with other men when she wasn't even married yet.

It's just a fantasy, Amy assured herself. She could *think* about anything she wanted. She just couldn't *act* on those feelings. And she didn't *want* to act on the feelings anyway because she loved Eric. He was the love of her life.

Right?

Amy and Brent continued discussing budgets and economic forecasts for another hour or so, with Amy struggling to focus on doing her job and trying to keep her lust for a man she'd met only a couple hours ago in check.

When the meeting with Brent was over at last, Amy put on her winter coat and her leather gloves. She picked up her briefcase, gave Brent a big, confident smile goodbye, and exited the Meyer Technology building into the cold March air of the Colorado Rocky Mountains.

She got in her car, turned the ignition on, and sat for a few minutes as the car warmed up, staring blankly at her dashboard in a daze of confusion.

What was wrong with her? She *never* fantasized about hurling a strange man across his desk and doing X-rated things to him.

Amy just didn't do things like that.

Maybe that was her problem. Maybe that was why things had fallen into such a rut at home. Sex between Eric and her was so . . . *polite*. It hadn't always been like that. When they first dated, she thought of him as clitoral heroin. They used to have sex for hours; there had been a time when they couldn't get enough of each other.

That time was long gone.

It wasn't that she was having problems with her husband-to-be. Not exactly. On the surface, everything was perfect.

They'd moved in together eight months ago, and they rarely fought. They were comfortable financially and lived within their means. Neither of them gambled or drank to excess. In other words, their lives were unbelievably boring. And Amy had no idea what to do about it.

Lately, Amy's life felt hollow, empty. A husk. A shell. Something barren of substance. Her life was a memory. An aftertaste. Something that could be imagined but was not actually there.

She knew this was not how a bride-to-be was supposed to feel. The truth was that even amid all the hubbub of planning her wedding, her days were gauzy.

As she pulled out of the parking lot and into traffic, she thought for the millionth time of how much she was looking forward to her trip, to getting away from the prewedding insanity.

Amy had arranged to meet her college girlfriends, Caitlyn and Leah, at a spa in Mexico for two weeks. She wanted some sort of Aerobic Dominatrix to force her to get in shape for her wedding pictures. This way, she could get in shape while catching up with her two best friends. Caitlyn and Leah were going to be her bridesmaids, but she knew they wouldn't have any time to talk at the wedding. Things would be much too crazy for that. They'd been drifting ever since graduation when Leah took a job as a biologist in Portland, Caitlyn returned to Chicago where she'd grown up, and Amy accepted a position as a financial consultant in Denver. Amy supposed that there was no way to help the fact that they weren't as close as they'd been in school, but that didn't mean she liked it. On this trip they'd be able to relax and catch up and become skinny, sexy vixens while they were at it. It would be great.

Sun. Exercise. Friends. She would be feeling like herself again in no time.

When she got back to work, Amy dropped off her coat and briefcase and went to the kitchen to heat up a low-calorie, taste-free frozen meal. She brought it back to her office in time to hear her extension ringing. She figured it was her wedding planner calling yet again to ask her about yet another detail. Amy had done the financing on major corporate mergers that were less stressful and time-consuming than planning a wedding. It was just one more reason she couldn't wait to get away.

"Hello?" She sat in her chair, setting her lunch on her desk in front of her.

"Hey, babe." Eric's voice sent a jolt of guilt through her.

"Hi. What's up?" She attempted to sound casual; she wondered if she was pulling it off.

"Christine and Adam want to know if we want to go to dinner Thursday night before you leave for your trip."

"Oh," Amy said, disappointed. It wasn't that she didn't like Christine and Adam, she did; it was just that every time she and Eric got together with them, they talked about their experiences sky diving or hang gliding or deep sea diving or engaged in some other life-threatening activity. Amy had no desire to do any of the potentially deadly or injurious things they did, but it made her feel dull by comparison. All Amy could add to the conversation was, *Well, this weekend we ordered in pizza and watched NetFlix so we didn't have to leave the house even once. It's not quite as thrilling as parasailing, but we live a full life anyway as you can plainly see.*

"Sure, that would be fun."

"Great. I'll let them know. How's your day?"

"My day? Oh, you know, the usual. And you?"

"It's going well. Do you want me to cook tonight?"

"Cook? Yeah, that'd be great."

"Okay. I'll think of something good. I love you."

"I love you, too."

"See you tonight, hon."

"Tonight," she repeated dumbly before returning the receiver to its cradle. She stared at the receiver for a moment as her heart thumped painfully, as if Eric could somehow psychically know all the traitorous thoughts she'd been having.

Exhaling, she turned to her computer and opened an Excel file. Listlessly she took bites of her chicken and vegetables, luckily not tasting any of it. When she dropped a sliver of a carrot into her keyboard, she turned the keyboard over and banged on the back of it as if she were attempting to make a baby burp, watching the food go flying out from her technological Heimlich maneuverings.

She tossed the rest of her lunch into the garbage and swiveled in her chair, her eyes taking on the glazed look of someone drooling at the asylum.

That glazed look was replaced with bright, alert eyes when her e-mail pinged to let her know she had new mail and she saw the name on the FROM line. As she read the e-mail, her heart raced.

To: amyharrington@attbi.com
From: meyer@meyertechnologies.com
I really enjoyed meeting you this morning. You're an incredibly beautiful woman. And smart, too! Can I take you out for a drink after our meeting on Friday? Strictly for pleasure, no business.

She blinked. Then, tentatively, hit REPLY.

To: meyer@meyertechnologies.com
From: amyharrington@attbi.com
Thanks for the offer, but I don't think my fiancé would appreciate me going out for drinks with a handsome entrepreneur.

Before hitting SEND, she stared at the word handsome. She knew she was being deliberately flirty and provocative. She was never flirty and provocative. But just now she didn't want to be herself. She wanted to be daring. She wanted to be a risk taker. As adrenaline surged through her veins, she hit SEND.

She stared at her computer screen for a full minute. Oh, God. Had she stepped over the line? Had she . . .

Her e-mail pinged again.

To: amyharrington@attbi.com
From: meyer@meyertechnologies.com
   Your fiancé doesn't have to know.

Amy swallowed and tried to get her breathing to return to normal. She clearly wasn't cut out for a life of crime or high adventure if sending a few e-mails nearly gave her a heart attack.

To: meyer@meyertechnologies.com
From: amyharrington@attbi.com
   It's tempting, but I'm leaving for Mexico on Saturday and I need to pack.

She was already packed; the truth was that she didn't trust herself alone with Brent and alcohol.

The ringing phone made her jump. She'd been so focused on watching her computer screen for a reply from Brent that the shrill of the phone made her feel like a burglar who'd been caught and the alarm was signaling the police. It was the reaction, she knew, of a guilty person. She wondered if it might be Brent calling her.

"Hello?"

"Amy, hi." It was Gretchen, her wedding planner. "Listen, have you made any progress on the dress?"

Amy exhaled. "I told you, I'll make my decision just as soon as I get back from the spa. I want to lose a few pounds before I make my final choice."

"Amy, you know how important the dress is. The seamstress can always take it in when you lose a few pounds. I just don't get you. You searched for three weeks straight so you could find the perfect periwinkle blue shade of tablecloths, but when it comes to something as vital as the dress, you leave it to the last second. I've never had a client with more exacting taste than you. I like it, I'm a perfectionist myself, so I appreciate a woman who knows what she wants. I'm just saying . . ."

"Gretchen, I appreciate your concern, I really do. I've narrowed it down to two dresses. I promise I'll pick one just as soon as I get back." One of the gowns was simple and conservative. It fit Amy's personality and body perfectly. She felt comfortable in it. The other dress wasn't Amy at all—it had elaborate beadwork and showed off Amy's ample cleavage—Amy never showed her cleavage. But she'd fallen in love with the dress when she'd tried it on. Maybe it was that when she tried the dress on, she felt like the woman she wanted to be instead of the woman she was. "Look, Gretchen, I really . . ."

"Wait, wait, I need to ask you about—"

Amy's e-mail pinged. "Sorry, I need to go. I'll talk to you before I leave for Mexico, I promise."

To: amyharrington@attbi.com
From: meyer@meyertechnologies.com
　A rain check, then?

"Bye Gretchen." Amy hung up the phone, and before she could think, she wrote back.

To: meyer@meyertechnologies.com
From: amyharrington@attbi.com
　We'll talk on Friday . . .

Chapter 2

On the way to the spa

Caitlyn looked at the digital clock blearily, not understanding what she was seeing. How could it possibly be 6:32 when she remembered very clearly setting it for 4:55 A.M.?

She bolted out of bed, screaming obscenities at her alarm clock, even though technically it had done nothing wrong. It had gone off when it was supposed to; it was Caitlyn who had shut it off and promptly fallen back to sleep.

"Shit, shit, shit!" she yelled, hopping around the room. She hadn't done her laundry or packed yet, and if she didn't haul ass, she was going to miss her flight. She hadn't meant to stay out so late the night before. She'd spent the night with Sean. His ex had the kids, so he and Caitlyn had been free to stay up into the wee hours of the morning, romping themselves senseless, which was exactly what they did. After five orgasms, Caitlyn had been ready to say goodbye to Kyle and Reg and declare her undying devotion to Sean. Then the orgasmic haze wore off and she came back to her senses and remembered that she and Sean didn't have anything in common outside the bedroom, and the only thing she really wanted to commit to with Sean was many more hours of obligation-free screwing.

What was the deal with flights leaving so damn early in the morning anyway? Caitlyn had searched for a flight that left at a reasonable hour, but everything she could find departed at the crack of dawn. It was so unreasonable to expect people to finish up their last-minute packing when they had just been woken from slumber in the middle of the night and were stumbling around groggily and still half asleep. Honestly, how could you not forget vitally important things under such trying circumstances?

Caitlyn put on a black push-up bra that matched her thong underwear and fished out of her laundry basket an outfit that was barely dirty. She slipped on a pair of clear plastic high-heeled shoes with hot pink heels and pulled her highlighted hair back into a ponytail. She opened her suitcase and laid it on the bed and threw whatever clothes weren't filthy inside. She tossed in her bikini and a few pairs of shorts and some T-shirts and declared herself done. She was forgetting something. She knew she was forgetting something. But what? A toothbrush! Make-up! A hair dryer! Oh, how calamitous it would have been if she'd found herself in the remote mountains of Central Mexico without her hair dryer or lip liner!

She sprayed herself in a cloud of Lancôme Miracle perfume, put on some ruby red lipstick, brushed mascara on her eyelashes, and rubbed lotion over her arms and legs. The lotion was a special blend she'd concocted at the lotion store where she worked. It was made especially for a Pisces to help improve her concentration and heighten feelings of well-being. With suitcase in hand, she raced to the elevator, waited impatiently as it descended eighteen floors, and bounded outside where she was promptly blasted by an arctic chill from which her thin blouse and skirt did little to shield her. She had already mentally been in Mexico and had forgotten that she was still in chilly Chicago in the middle of winter. She turned around, sprinted back inside, went back up eighteen endless stories, unlocked her apartment, set her suitcase down, threw on a winter coat, picked the suitcase back up, and struggled to get outside without walloping her suitcase into the walls too much (without success). After running the three blocks to where her car was parked, she turned the ignition over and was about to pull out when she remembered that she had no identification or money. Oops. That might be a problem.

"Shit!" She turned off her car, raced back to the apartment, went up the eighteen stories, and then began the mad dash to find her passport.

Where the hell had she put her passport? Oh God! Oh God! She didn't have time for this. She blazed through her house opening drawers, riffling through them, and then slamming them shut again.

"Think, Caitlyn, think!"

When was the last time she used her passport? Was it when she flew to Paris with the married man? Was it when she went to Madrid with the race car driver to watch him run with the bulls? Yes. That must have been it. That meant her passport would be . . . in her adorable tangerine-colored beach tote bag! Ah-ha!

Now. Where was that bag?

The hall closet! Yes!

Caitlyn charged triumphantly to the closet. Behind the never-used vacuum cleaner, wedged into the corner, was her tangerine tote bag. Inside she found sunglasses (she'd forgotten about this pair! They were so cute! What a find!), a linty, moldy, half-eaten candy bar, and her passport. Phew! She was now ready for her trip.

As long as the plane didn't leave without her . . .

Caitlyn made it on board the plane with only a few minutes to spare. The flight was crowded with people cranky from having to wake up at such an unfortunate hour, and no matter how hard she tried, Caitlyn couldn't seem to keep her suitcase from ramming into every seated passenger she tried to make her way past. "Sorry, sorry, sorry, so sorry, sorry about that," Caitlyn said as she made her way down the aisle.

At last she came to her seat. When she tried to swing her suitcase into the overhead bin, the weight of it made her topple backward into a man's lap.

"Oops. I'm really sorry about that," Caitlyn said.

He chuckled. "Can I help you?"

"Yes, absolutely, thank you."

The man unfastened his seat belt, stood, and struggled to fit her suitcase into the tiny space available. After great effort, he managed to do so. Caitlyn thanked him again and again and then took her seat, throwing him her trademark smile. He smiled back, stupidly, caught in her snare. Caitlyn was used to having that effect on men.

As had been her habit since she'd been a little girl, she studied the man's features to look for any similarities to her own. Any male who looked to be at least fifteen years older than her was subject to her scrutiny. She knew the odds that she would find her nose or eyes or smile on some strange man's face were about a jillion to one, but that didn't stop her. Her mother might forever refuse to give her the slightest hint about the true identity of her father, but Caitlyn was determined to find out the truth somehow. She'd read that women tended to marry men who were like their father. Was it any wonder Caitlyn couldn't settle on one guy? How was she to know what kind of guy to marry if she didn't know what her father was like?

This man looked to be about forty, tops, and Caitlyn seriously doubted that an eight-year-old had knocked up her sixteen-year-old mother thirty-two years ago.

With that fruitless exercise complete, Caitlyn settled into her seat, able to relax at last.

"Where are you from?" the man who helped her asked.

If the man had been cute, she would have loved to chat with him. Unfortunately, he was gangly and weird looking.

She didn't date men whose arms were as thin as hers. He wore glasses and had large diamond posts in each ear—it was a rare man who could pull off that look, and he wasn't one of them. He looked like a dull engineer who was attempting to pass for someone hip and failing spectacularly.

"I'm actually from Chicago originally. I moved around a lot, but here I am again."

"Oh, yeah? Where else have you lived?"

While talking about herself was always interesting, she was tired and not remotely interested in him. She had three cute guys she was dating; why should she waste her time on a geek? "Well, my mother married a man . . ." (Or four, but she didn't feel it was necessary to mention that.) "We were transferred to Ohio, then California, then Texas, but we always came back to Chicago. I went to school in Iowa but came back. This place seems to have a magnetic pull on me."

"Why Iowa?"

"Iowa has one of the best writers' workshops in the country. I'm a poet."

"A poet? Really? You don't meet many of those these days. What got you interested in poetry?"

Caitlyn smiled. If they had a twenty-two hour flight around the world, she wasn't sure she could fully explain it. Writing had been her therapy since she'd been a kid—poor person's therapy, she always called it. She would express her hopes and fears and sorrows onto the page—she didn't have anyone else to talk to since her mother was always too busy getting married or divorced, and they moved around so much, Caitlyn had a hard time making lasting friendships.

To the man sitting beside her, she said, "Oh, you know, I've always just loved the art form."

"Are you published?" he asked.

She nodded.

"Wow. That's very impressive. You're so young."

Caitlyn liked telling people she was a poet because there was no such thing as a stupid poet. Caitlyn knew that when people looked at how she dressed and did her hair, they immediately assumed she was a bimbo. When she told them she was a published poet, particularly if she mentioned the awards she had won or that she had three books out, they had to adjust their assumptions about her. She liked the apparent contradiction: she could be smart, talented, and successful, and still wear slutty mini skirts . . .

The "magnetic pull" Chicago had on Caitlyn was her mother, Bridget. Caitlyn hadn't wanted to come back to the Windy City after college, but her mother had needed her. Bridget was going through divorce number four at the time. When Bridget called Caitlyn two weeks before Caitlyn was due to graduate, she told Caitlyn that Number Four was gone for good and she was going to have to declare bankruptcy. Bridget sobbed and ranted and raved.

Caitlyn yawned dramatically. "Sorry, they make these flights so damn early. I think I'm going to take a nap. It was nice talking to you."

She flashed him another smile and then sank deeper into her chair, closed her eyes, and pretended to sleep.

She had been looking forward to this trip for months. Two weeks of massages and facials and manicures sounded heavenly. Plus, she never needed an excuse to get away from Chicago in the winter. And you didn't have to twist her arm very hard to get her to take a break from her low-paying day job at the lotion store. Of course, her poetry was her real job, but she earned a pittance publishing her work in literary journals. The job at the lotion store didn't exactly challenge her intellect, but it was a big step up from being a cocktail waitress or working as a receptionist for a power-hungry letch or getting screamed at all day answering complaints of unhappy customers at the cable company.

Caitlyn's mom had helped her land the job. Bridget had been friends with the owner, Frank, for years. Frank was the most flamboyant gay man Caitlyn had ever seen outside the movies, and Caitlyn adored him. He'd been dating the same

man—a reserved high school history teacher named Byron—
for eighteen years. Frank couldn't pay Caitlyn much, but he
was a great boss, and when things were quiet at the store, she
was free to write. At least, she told herself that was why she
stayed at a low-paying job rather than pursuing an actual career. Unfortunately, it had been years since Caitlyn had done
much writing. The acclaim she'd earned for the work she'd
done in her early twenties was slipping away.

Maybe two weeks away from reality would inspire her
once again. When Amy had first suggested the trip, Caitlyn
had no clue how she could possibly afford it. Because the spa
was located in Central Mexico, it was a bargain compared to
most health spas, but Caitlyn couldn't afford a trip to the
suburbs, let alone a trip to a foreign country. Then she thought,
as she often did, *The hell with it, what's a little more credit
card debt?*

Plus, the important thing in life was friends and loved ones.
Though Amy, Leah, and Caitlyn stayed in touch by phone
and e-mail, it was never the same thing as seeing each other
in person. Was Amy still as sleek and demure as ever, the
chronic good girl? Was Leah still the same nature girl intellectual, her mind too crowded with questions about science
and nature to bother with important things like dating and
make-up and clothes?

Caitlyn couldn't wait to find out.

Chapter 3

On the way to the spa

L eah carried her suitcase out to her eight-year-old Saturn, started up her car, and pulled out into traffic. This time of year was always gray and rainy in Portland, and today was no exception. It would be nice to get some sun, and even nicer to see Amy and Caitlyn again. In some ways, Leah couldn't be more different from her friends. Caitlyn changed her hair color and style constantly, while Leah wore her dark hair in the same short style she had back in college. Amy was always impeccably kempt, her blond hair was always sleek, her clothes ever stylish. Amy and Caitlyn loved make-up and perfume and impractical footwear; Leah was wary of using too many chemicals and wore only orthopedic-friendly shoes. Instead of using antiperspirant that blocked pores with powerful astringents such as aluminum salts, Leah used a natural alum crystal instead. All of her soaps, toothpastes, shampoos, and detergents were natural and odor free. She knew she'd probably get cancer anyway, but it was worth a shot.

Leah had become instant friends with her roommate, Amy, and their next-door neighbor, Caitlyn, the day before school began in their freshman year of college at the University of Iowa. Leah was from a small town in Iowa called Boone,

Amy was from Dubuque, and Caitlyn was from the Chicago area.

On the day she met her future best friends, Leah's stomach had been a tangle of nerves. When she walked into her dorm room with her suitcase that day, one smile from Amy had made the knot of tension disappear.

"Which bed do you want? I've been using this one to hold my suitcase and stuff, but I can switch; it's not a problem," Amy said.

"This one's fine."

Amy was wearing a preppy pink polo shirt, pressed khaki shorts, and leather sandals. "Are you sure?"

Leah nodded, wondering if Amy thought her Birkenstocks, cutoffs, and oversized T-shirt were grungy.

As they unpacked they spoke in stilted bursts: Where are you from? What's your major? What classes are you taking? Leah had been thrilled to learn that Amy was a math and science geek just like she was.

They'd left the door to their room open—everyone in the hallway did—and as they were putting away their underwear and socks in their institutional dressers, Caitlyn, who at the time had dyed her hair flaming red, came streaking into their room screaming, "Fuck! Fuck! Fuck! Fuck!" She slammed the door behind her and went diving onto Leah's bed. She buried her head in her arms and let out an anguished moan. After a moment, she looked up. She glanced from Leah to Amy. "Who are you?" she said.

"Who are you?" Amy said.

"I'm Caitlyn Blake. Why are you in my room? This is 718, right?"

"This is 716. This is our room," Leah said.

"Oh. Sorry. I'm still trying to figure out my way around."

"No problem. What are you freaking out about?"

She sat up, exhaling dramatically. "I'm all crushed out on this guy who lives in on the ninth floor. I saw him coming down the hallway, and I was staring so hard at him that I didn't notice this box that someone had left in the hallway. I tripped over it and I went *flying*. I was *airborne!* I went sailing over the box and then landed in a crumpled heap. I ran away as fast as I could. I'm hoping he didn't recognize me."

"You have Kool–Aid colored hair," Amy pointed out. "It's not the color of hair that blends in with a crowd. It looks good on you, I'm just saying . . ."

"Shit. You're right. Oh, my life is over! This is not what college is supposed to be like." Caitlyn lay back on the bed with her hand on her forehead like a swooning starlet. "Do you hear that sound?"

No one said anything for a beat. "Are people fighting?" Amy asked.

"No, that's my roommate talking on the phone. That's her natural volume. I'm never going to make any friends. My roommate is going to scare them all away. I'm just dreading having to go to the cafeteria all by myself tonight like some loser . . ."

"Do you want to join us for dinner?" Leah asked.

"Really?" Caitlyn said. Her eyes brightened.

"Sure."

"Do you mean it?"

"Definitely," Amy said.

From that moment on, their friendship was forged. Caitlyn had been responsible for dragging Leah and Amy out to parties and for teaching them the truly important things in life like how to drink tequila shots without puking and how to give such an expert blow job that it was over in seconds and you could get on with what really mattered—like getting oral sex yourself. In turn, Amy and Leah forced Caitlyn to study so she wouldn't flunk out of school. It wasn't that Caitlyn wasn't smart. If anything, she was too smart. She had so many thoughts, she was scattered and unfocused. She had trouble remembering mundane things like when her essays were due and what time she was supposed to show up to take her midterms. Amy and Leah kept her on track.

At the airport, Leah pulled into long-term parking, got her suitcase, and walked through the parking lot to the terminal. After shuffling slowly through the security lines, she found her gate and sat in an empty seat to wait to be called for boarding. She rooted through her backpack for the articles she'd printed out on influenza A. She was writing an article on the topic for the magazine she worked for.

She had originally been hesitant about coming on this trip at all. It was true that as a writer she could make her own hours and work from anywhere, but the pressure of constant deadlines kept her working twelve-hour days, six days a week. It was only after a guilt trip from Amy and Caitlyn that Leah changed her mind and agreed to come. Amy pointed out that there was nothing more important in the world than friends and family. Leah had to admit that was true. She herself had even written an article about how women with strong female friendships lived longer than women who didn't have that support network. Though Leah was looking forward to catching up with them, she couldn't go two whole weeks without doing any work at all, so she'd brought her research with her.

After she'd quit her job as a researcher for the Oregon Fish and Wildlife department, she'd taken a position with *Our World*, a science magazine for the layperson.

When a man sat next to her, she quickly glanced up at him and did a double take. He looked an awful lot like her college boyfriend, David. Leah pulled her folder out of her backpack and snuck another quick glance. The resemblance was just uncanny. David had been the best-looking guy she'd ever dated, and the man sitting next to her looked just like him, only a little older, of course. His face had filled out.

She hadn't thought about David in years. They'd met thanks to Caitlyn and alcohol.

It had been a hot, humid September night. Caitlyn, Amy, and Leah were sophomores. They'd done a few shots before leaving for the bars as a cost-saving measure. When they got into the club using their laughably bad fake IDs they headed straight to the bar. Heat and humidity drenched the September night. Leah had been wearing a tank top and shorts, an outfit that showed off the well-defined muscles she'd earned from years of playing volleyball and basketball.

Just in front of the bar, Caitlyn stopped at a high, round table with a cluster of guys sitting around it.

"I know you," Caitlyn had said to David.

"You do?" David was tall. He gelled his black hair into tousled waves and he wore an extra-thick black watch on his left wrist. Silver rings adorned three of his fingers. A small silver earring looped through his left ear.

"You were in my creative writing class last semester."

He looked closely at her, trying to place her.

"I had pink hair then."

"Ah, the pink-haired girl. I remember her. You, I mean."

"What does it take to get a beer around here?" Leah said, draping her body across the bar. She pounded her fist against it, feigning indignation.

"You look like a woman who shouldn't be messed with," David had said to her. "Not many women have biceps like you. Let me feel a muscle."

"Which one?"

"What are my options?" he said, grinning.

Leah smiled and flexed her biceps. He gave her arm a quick squeeze.

"Very impressive."

"Let me feel one of yours."

He flexed. He was tall and slim.

"You going for the musician/heroin addict look?"

He laughed. "I'm secretly a math geek. I just play the guitar to get women."

"Does it work?"

"Sadly, not really. You like music?"

"Some. Rock. Blues. That sort of thing. I'd rather take my eye out with a fork than listen to country."

"I asked if you liked music, not noise. Country is the devil's work."

For the rest of the evening, David paid no attention to anyone but Leah. At the end of the night he invited her to see his band play that weekend. She dragged Amy and Caitlyn with her. In between sets, David sat with Leah, and they talked about music and science and politics and life. He told her that he'd taken a year off from school and lived in the mountains of Colorado and Wyoming with only a tent and a sleeping bag to protect him from the elements and only his poetry and his guitar for company. She told him that she spent her summers working as a nature guide in Utah in a program for high school students called Outward Bound. They traded war stories about sleeping in the wild and hiking through rain and snow.

At the end of the night David admitted he had a thing for smart women who weren't afraid of getting dirt under their nails and he'd like to see her again. She told him she had a thing for sexy poetry-writing guitar players and she'd like to see him again, too. He toured a lot of weekends, leaving Leah at home with Caitlyn and Amy, but when he was in town, he was a regular fixture at the apartment Amy, Caitlyn, and Leah shared.

Leah and David were together for the next three years. At graduation, he hit the road with his band, and Leah took a job with the Oregon Fish and Wildlife Department in Portland, where she worked for the next five years before becoming a writer for *Our World.* Breaking up had been hard, but their chosen professions made staying together impossible. Since David, she'd had one serious boyfriend named Chuck, a smattering of semiserious boyfriends, and more crappy first dates than any one human should have to live through. Since she'd broken up with Chuck two years ago, the dates had gone from bad to worse. They were so awful, celibacy and eternal loneliness were looking pretty good. At least she didn't have to shave or put on lipstick for dates with her couch and remote control.

Leah turned her attention to the article she was reading, but she just couldn't focus. She glanced over to the man again. Obviously, he could feel her gaze on him, and this time he looked up from his newspaper and met her eyes.

Shit! Leah froze. She'd been caught; there was nothing else to do but talk to him. "David?"

"Yes?"

Her heart flipped. Was this really him? Her first great love? "David Richardson?"

"Yes?"

"It's me, Leah."

He smiled. "I'm just kidding. I'm not David."

Leah's nerves rattled like a tambourine. She giggled nervously. She never giggled. She simply wasn't the giggling type. "Oh. Sorry." She pretended to turn her attention back to the article she was reading.

After a minute or so "David" said, "Did we date?"

"Excuse me?"

"You and me, David Richardson, did we date?"

"Ah, yes."

He nodded and smiled a smile that was disarmingly sexy. "Good. My name is really Russ, by the way. Russ Evans."

"Nice to meet you."

"Nice to meet you."

Russ went back to his paper and Leah pretended to go back to what she was doing.

"So, Leah," he said after a few beats, "watcha working on over there?"

"Uh." She wanted to think of a witty response, but nothing came to her, and her pause grew awkwardly drawn out. He broke the silence for her.

"It's early, I understand."

"I'm doing research for an article I'm working on. I write for a science magazine called *Our World*."

"Ooh, a smart girl. I've always liked smart girls."

There it was again. That damn schoolgirl giggle. What pod person had overtaken her body?

"Hey, would you like to go out sometime? I'm in Portland several days each month on business."

"Oh, I don't know . . ." Would it be too creepy to date a guy who looked eerily like her first serious boyfriend?

"Think about it. Here's my card. My e-mail address is on there. Like I said, I have a thing for smart girls. I'd better get going. That's my flight."

Leah hadn't even heard the announcement. She just nodded dumbly. She wasn't used to guys flirting with her. Leah watched him as he got in line. Just before he walked down the gate, he turned and gave her a little wave. She returned the wave and then studied the business card he gave her. *Russ Evans, Recruiter.* She knew she should just throw the card away right now. There was no point in keeping the card. Things never worked out with the guys she dated. She should just throw away the card right now.

She put it in her wallet instead.

Chapter 4

On the way to the spa

An empty, microscopic bag of pretzels, a plastic glass with melting ice, and an unread paperback novel lay on the tray in front of her. Amy stared out the window, thinking of her meeting with Brent the day before.

She'd taken extra care getting ready to meet with him. She'd even traded her glasses for contact lenses. When she'd arrived at his office and his brilliant green eyes looked at her as he flashed a smile, Amy's breath caught in her throat. She found herself strangely disappointed when he didn't comment on how good she looked. Amy wondered where the Brent who had sent her flirty e-mails a few days earlier had gone. Though she would never admit it to anyone, she wanted that Brent back.

As they wound up their meeting, Amy wondered if Brent had changed his mind about finding her attractive.

They scheduled their next meeting for two weeks after she got back from Mexico. As Amy packed her briefcase, she was disappointed that his offer for a drink was apparently no longer on the table. She had planned on telling him she couldn't go, of course, but now that he hadn't tried to persuade her to join him for a cocktail, she found herself feeling oddly rejected.

"I don't suppose I could interest you in that drink?" Brent said.

Immediately Amy's mood lightened.

"Oh, I should probably get going. My flight leaves in the morning." Even as she said the words, she silently hoped that he would try harder to persuade her. He did.

"Just one quick drink. Come on. Don't make me go home to spend my Friday night alone without at least one drink in me."

How could a man so handsome and successful possibly not have a date? Amy smiled. "Okay, but just one."

He took her to a crowded bar. Though he was handsome and rich, he didn't strike Amy as being a player.

There had been only two barstools left and they were packed so tightly together that when Amy and Brent turned to look at each other, their knees grazed.

"Oh sorry," Amy had said.

"It's *really* not a problem."

The way he said "really" was charged with so much sexual tension, it took Amy off balance.

She couldn't stop thinking of that moment. Their knees had barely touched, but the feeling was so electric it had been like getting zapped with a taser.

Abruptly, Amy realized what she was doing. What was wrong with her? She was getting married soon. She loved Eric. Things had just been a little hectic lately. After the wedding, everything would go back to normal.

Last night, after "just one drink" had become three, Amy had come home to an especially affectionate Eric.

He'd wanted to make love before she left for Mexico for two weeks. It was hardly an unreasonable request considering they hadn't had sex any time in recent memory, but Amy had no desire to make love whatsoever.

Amy knew there were lots of things that could lead to a low sex drive—stress and fatigue were two factors—and with the long hours she was putting in at the office and the endless hours of work planning the perfect wedding, it had been months since she'd gotten a good night of sleep. Stress had long been her constant companion. Whatever the reason her sex drive was on vacation, the fact was that she hadn't been in the mood to make love to Eric or to anyone else for a long time. That was why her attraction to Brent had in some ways been almost welcome. At least it let her know that part of her was still alive.

Chapter 5

Day One

Leah, Caitlyn, and Amy had planned their flights so they would arrive at the airport in Mexico within a couple hours of each other. Caitlyn arrived first. The airport was abuzz with conversation and overhead announcements and people rushing by. It was a little unsettling to be on her own in a country in which she didn't speak the language. Caitlyn had taken four years of high school Spanish, but she had cheated her way through the whole thing, and the few words and phrases that had somehow managed to penetrate her brain had long been forgotten in the years since graduation.

She took her luggage and set her suitcase down on the floor by the wall. She sat on her suitcase and watched the teeming throng of people. She thought Leah was supposed to have arrived before her. What if Leah was here but was someplace else in the airport? Leah had e-mailed Amy and Caitlyn her flight itinerary, but Caitlin hadn't thought to print it off. Hell, it was a miracle Caitlyn had managed to make it here herself.

Then a terrible thought occurred to her: could she have flown into the wrong airport? *Oh, God, I'm going to be stranded alone in a foreign country. I'm going to be kidnapped, raped, and then murdered. Some vacation this turned out to be. Ooh, he's cute . . .*

Caitlyn's eye's followed the dark-haired hottie. He was probably a little too young for her, but she'd always had a thing for Latin men with their dark hair and smoldering smiles. Of course, she also had a thing for Italian men. And Greek men. And Australians and New Zealanders. Oh, and Native Americans with their long dark hair . . .

When Caitlin saw Amy come through customs, a wave of giddy expectation flooded through her. A smile exploded on her face, and she leapt up to greet her friend.

Amy looked fabulous as always. Her pale blond hair was straight and shoulder length. She wore a long brown skirt, a cream-colored top, and sumptuous leather boots with heels. Her dark brown eyes were outlined by delicate silver-framed glasses. Amy usually opted for glasses rather than contacts because as a naturally busty blonde, she used any props she could find to remind men that she was more than just a pretty face.

They hugged.

"It is so good to see you," Caitlyn said. "You look great. Same as always."

"You look fabulous, too." These days Caitlyn was wearing her light brown hair with blond highlights that brought out the green in her hazel eyes.

"My God, that ring, it's gorgeous." Caitlyn grabbed Amy's left hand, where a stunning sapphire ring was mounted in a platinum band. Tiny diamonds lined either side of the sapphire. The ring had had to have set Eric back at leat $15,000. Looking at Amy's ring, Caitlyn felt a strange flush of . . . something. Jealousy, perhaps.

"Where's Leah? I thought her plane was supposed to get here before mine. Did it get delayed or something?"

"I was wondering about that, but I didn't want to leave

this spot to look because I was terrified one of you would get here and I'd miss you."

"I'll go check it out. You stay here. I'll be back in a few minutes."

Caitlyn nodded and resumed her watch of passengers coming through customs with a much lighter heart now that Amy was here.

After several minutes, Amy returned to announce that Leah's plane had been delayed. Unlike Caitlyn, Amy remained standing. "It should get here in about twenty minutes."

"That's a relief."

"So, what's up with you?" Amy asked. "Any serious guy in your life these days?"

"Nope. I'm dating a lot, but nothing serious."

"Thank God I don't have to date anymore." When the words were out of her mouth, she felt a slight pang—it wasn't exactly true. She actually sort of missed dating.

Caitlyn smiled. "I think dating is a blast. I love how you're a blank slate. He doesn't know anything about you. You can become anyone you want. Like I went on a date with a father. You know I've never wanted kids. But suddenly I thought it would be kind of cool to get to know about that whole world of kids and raising them. Maybe I could become a different person. Maybe I could become patient and nurturing and motherly, who knows?"

"Do you like his kids?"

"I haven't met them yet. Sean doesn't want to introduce me to them unless we decide this is a long-term deal. But when I do meet them, all my latent maternal instincts will come bursting through."

Amy smiled. Caitlyn the Chameleon they'd called her. Caitlyn always seemed to be experimenting with men, jobs, and hairstyles to define who she really was. Was she a sexy blonde with long tresses who wore see-through blouses? Was she sporty and sophisticated, with short, trendy dark hair? Was

she a witty, zany redhead? Was she a partier? A poet? A waitress? A sales guru? Who was the right guy for her? A sexy
musician? A sensible doctor? A sensitive English professor?
When exactly would the day come when her hairstyle and
job and boyfriend and life would all come together and she'd
finally figure out who she was and what she wanted from
life?

When she'd dated the liberal vegetarian, she'd stopped
wearing nail polish and hid her leather jacket beneath a blanket in the closet. When she dated the pilot who spent all his
free time golfing, she pretended she'd always been desperate
to learn the sport herself. Now she was dating a father and
pretended she actually liked kids. It was no wonder she could
never make a relationship last—a person could keep up the
façade for only so long.

"Don't you ever want just one guy?"

"I don't know. If I could find a guy who was as good in
bed as Sean, as generous and fun as Reg, as intelligent as
Kyle, maybe. Until then, I'm having fun." Caitlyn like dating
several guys at once. It kept things exciting. Her life was like
a choose-your-own-adventure novel.

"Do these guys know about the others?"

"Not exactly."

"Don't you think that's a little unethical?"

"Why? Guys do it all the time. Hey, look who's coming
this way!" Caitlyn pointed in Leah's direction. At five-foot-
ten, Leah's height and pale skin made her stand out, like a
neon green home in a planned community, amid the shorter,
darker-skinned Mexican people who dominated the halls.

"Leah! It's so good to see you!" Amy embraced her friend.

"My turn!" Caitlyn said.

Leah pulled away from Amy and hugged Caitlyn. The
three friends stood in the middle of the bustling airport smiling stupidly at one another for a moment until Amy said, "At

last! We're here in Mexico! Let's find our taxi and let the relaxation begin. Leah, you speak some Spanish, don't you?"

"Very little. I haven't used it since high school."

"Well, I took French, so you've got to know more than I do. All I know is *cerveza*."

"That's really the only word you need to know."

The automatic doors whooshed open; the warm air and bright sun were a shock from the air-conditioned gloom of the airport.

Cabs snaked along the curb outside the airport. Amy went to one and told the driver the name of the spa. After haggling over the price, Amy, Caitlyn, and Leah climbed into the backseat. The reddish brown vinyl was so worn it almost gleamed.

"Did you guys fly in an airplane the size of a toaster?" Amy asked her friends. Amy had snagged a window seat. Though Leah was the tallest of the three by several inches, she took the middle—she was used to roughing it. "My plane was so tiny it would have been safer to fold up a piece of notebook paper into a paper airplane and fly that into Mexico. I was worried that if I sneezed, I'd set the plane off course. The slightest gust of wind shook us like a baby rattle. You're always hearing about small planes going down. If you think about it, small planes are the mobile homes of the aviation world."

"I had a normal plane," Caitlyn said. "I just popped a Vicodin and had myself a lovely little flight. God, Amy. Getting married. Tell us everything. How are the wedding plans coming? I've got my dress. Gorgeous. Good work."

"Thanks. If you don't mind, the last thing I want to talk about are wedding plans. On this trip, all I want to do is take off a couple pounds, get into shape, forget all about my life, and catch up with you guys. Caitlyn, how's your writing going?"

"Well, I applied for a grant to write a series of poems on the work of the artist Tamara de Lempicka. The grant will allow me to live in France for a while and see a lot of her work firsthand. She lived in Paris for several years, and I thought that if I followed her footsteps, it would help inspire me."

"Wow, Caitlyn, I hope you get it. That would be so cool. How fun. When do you find out?" Amy asked.

"It could be any time now or it could be months. Sometimes these things can take a while."

"You're going to write an entire series on the art of just one person?" Leah asked.

"It's a solid body of work. Her pieces are erotic, and they celebrate the materialism and decadence of the 1920s. What's not to like? Those are my fondest ideals." Caitlyn paused a moment, squinting her eyes at Leah. "What's up with you? You're glowing. You pregnant?"

"No! God no!"

"So? What's up?"

"It's so stupid. It's nothing." Leah's cheeks flushed. She couldn't hide her smile.

"Tell us!" Caitlyn urged.

Leah recounted the story of her initial embarrassment in mistakenly identifying a guy at the airport as her ex.

"Ooh, Dave, he was a hottie." Caitlyn nodded.

"So cute," Amy agreed.

"We just sort of flirted and talked. I'd forgotten how nice it feels to have someone find you attractive." Leah paused.

"Are you going to see him again?"

"He gave me his card and I took it, but . . ."

"Good for you!"

"Well, he doesn't even live in Portland; he just travels there for work a couple times a month."

"Still, it would get you back in the dating game," Caitlyn said.

Leah said nothing. She'd had only one major boyfriend since David. Chuck was an associate biology professor at the University of Oregon she'd met while researching an article for *Our World*. Chuck had been working furiously for tenure, which meant that in addition to his grueling teaching and lecturing schedule, he was always doing research and writing articles to be published in academic journals. The saying in academia went, *publish or perish*. With Chuck so busy with his teaching and research, Leah was able to drown herself in work without guilt. The only problem was that with both of them working so much, they had little emotional energy left to nurture their relationship, and eventually Chuck managed to find a doting undergraduate who put his career over her personal ambitions, and he left Leah for the fawning twenty-two-year-old. Since then Leah had focused even more on her work—it helped her distract herself from the fact that it had been two years since she'd had sex or been in love or made out with a hot guy. She'd done such a good job making her work her whole life, she rarely even thought about what it felt like to fall in love, the giddy high of making love and holding hands and having someone to kiss and hold. Seeing the David lookalike had brought all memories to the forefront.

"Oof," Caitlyn said as she was catapulted into Leah's lap when the driver pulled off the main road into a small town with narrow cobblestone streets that had likely been constructed many hundreds of years earlier. The roads were so bumpy that even with the driver going slowly, his passengers were jostled about as if they were in a martini shaker. Run-down houses and stores lined the rickety streets. Paint-cracked off the sides of buildings, and shutters hung askew from windows. Stray dogs loitered on every corner. Merchants sold grilled meats, fruits, and juices in hutlike constructions or if they were ten-year-olds with lemonade stands.

The driver pulled off the road, primitive as it was, and began bounding along a narrow dirt road. They couldn't see where they were in relation to town or anything else because their view was obscured by the tall grass in the fields around them.

"Isn't it beautiful here?" Leah said.

"I wouldn't know," Amy said dryly. "I'm a little busy trying not to shit a brick to be able to enjoy the view. I'd like to speak to the planning committee of this community on the state of their roads."

Amy had chosen this particular spa because it had been a bargain compared to other places she'd researched. Now she was beginning to question whether going to a bargain spa was such a good plan after all. Money wasn't an issue for her, but she knew a deluxe spa would have been a stretch for Caitlyn and Leah. Amy had paid for their bridesmaids' dresses for the wedding, along with their shoes and plane tickets to Denver. She's offered to pay for their tickets to the spa as well, but they'd both turned her down. She'd anticipated that they would, which was why she'd chosen this place. Besides, the pricey spas let guests consume only a thousand calories a day. Amy wanted to lose weight, but she wanted to do it in a healthy way, not by starving herself.

They rumbled down the dirt road for so long, Amy was beginning to worry that maybe they were lost.

Then, like the sun coming out after a long and dreary storm, the driver pulled up to a gate that had the words *La Buena Vida* painted on it. He got out of the taxi, opened the gate, and drove them into paradise.

Leah stared wide-eyed at the lush landscape. The area was rich with verdant trees and flowers in brilliant shades of fuchsia and tangerine. Palm trees stood beside cactuses and other trees and plants that Leah couldn't identify.

The taxi driver dropped them off at the front office, and Amy paid him.

"Here, let me give you some cash," Leah said.

"Yeah, hang on," Caitlyn echoed.

"You guys, don't worry about it." Amy, take-charge as ever, marched into the office. "I have a reservation for three under the name Amy Harrington."

"Yes, of course, welcome to *La Buena Vida*," the man behind the desk said. He was a short man with silvery hair and a large smile. "My name is Raul." He slid a small pamphlet across the desk. "This will let you know the schedule for the hikes, yoga classes, meals, and workshops."

"Thanks," Amy said.

A young man of nineteen or twenty with dark brown skin came out from behind the desk. "This is Gabriel," Raul said. "He will take your bags. Leave them here. Follow me."

They followed Raul outside. "That is the dining room," he said, pointing to a rectangular building. "Over there are the pools, steam room, and treatment centers."

"Treatment centers?" Leah asked.

"For the massages and facials," Amy explained.

"Ah."

All of the cottages were painted a light peach color with burnt sienna trim and barrel-tile roofs. Bright flowers adorned every cottage and pathway.

"On your Web site it said there was a computer with Internet access? Where could I find that?" Leah asked.

"Leah! You are not going to do work when we're on our spa vacation!" Caitlyn said.

"No, I'm not going to do work . . . *much*, but I can't go without Internet access for two weeks. Be reasonable. Imagine life without e-mail. It's unthinkable!"

"It is in the building beside the dining room," Raul said.

"Great. Thanks."

Raul stopped in front of one of the cottages. "This is your room." He unlocked the door and handed over two sets of keys to Amy.

"Be sure not to drink the water from the sink or shower," Raul said. "Not even to rinse your mouth out when you brush your teeth. We will bring you fresh water every morning." He showed them where a pitcher of water was kept in the bathroom, along with three clean glasses. "If you need more, you can buy bottled water at the office or you can get water from the dining room. Any questions?"

No one had any, so with a wave goodbye, Raul left them on their own.

Their room was a simple affair. There was no phone, television, or clock. There were three small single beds with colorful, hand-woven blankets. The stone floors were painted a reddish brown. Colorful bark paintings decorated the walls. The patio offered a view of the mountains that surrounded the spa on three sides. The mountains were part of a vast national forest thickly blanketed by trees.

"It's not exactly the Hilton," Amy said, "but it's nice. I like it. I absolutely love that there is no phone. I love the fact that my wedding planner can't get hold of me for two whole weeks. I told her that if she has any emergencies, she's just going to have to go to Eric. I think Eric is a little terrified about that. I think he thinks if he makes a decision I don't like, I won't go through with marrying him. Of course, he's probably right." Amy smiled.

"How's Eric's mom?" Caitlyn asked. "One of my girlfriends in Chicago got married last year, and she said the most stressful thing about planning the wedding was dealing with her mother and her mother-in-law."

"Eric's mom is great. I think she's just so thrilled to see her only child get married she wouldn't care if we got hitched in a cave wearing sackcloth." Amy didn't need to mention that her own mother wasn't participating in the wedding at all. Since Amy's parents divorced and her father took custody of her, and her mother took custody of her brother, Bill, Amy's mother had been in the sidelines of Amy's life.

"I think this place is adorable," Leah said. "You did a great job picking the place."

"Thank you, thank you."

They took turns washing up and finding spots for their luggage.

"Let's go for a swim," Leah said as they settled in.

"Let's go after dinner. They stop serving in an hour, and I don't want to miss it. I'm starving," Amy said.

"I'm ravenous," Caitlyn seconded.

They walked up the rocky path to the dining room, a large, open space with wood floors and rustic wood tables and chairs. At the head of the room was a long buffet-style table. A young Mexican girl in an apron asked, *"Sopa?"* gesturing with her ladle to the pot of soup.

Amy scanned the table for more substantive fare. All she saw was a large platter of mixed green salad and a bowl that was marked "Stewed Fruit."

"Do you think this is the appetizer course?" Amy asked Leah and Caitlyn hopefully.

Leah shrugged. "I have no idea."

They each took a bowl of soup along with a slice of hearty whole grain bread. They fixed themselves salads that were comprised only of healthy vegetables and nothing tasty like croutons or cheese, and they made their way to a table. As they ate, Leah flipped through the pamphlet Raul had given them.

"It says here that because you digest meals more slowly at night, dinner is intentionally light," Leah said. "Breakfast and lunch are the big meals of the day."

"Oh." Amy frowned.

"You said you wanted to get in shape," Caitlyn said.

"You're right." Amy nodded. "It's good soup."

"It says they grow all their vegetables in an organic garden here at the spa," Leah said. "That explains why they have lettuce."

"What do you mean?" Caitlyn asked.

"Lettuce just isn't eaten in Mexico—not with the poor water quality. Lettuce is almost all water."

"Oh." Caitlyn mouthed the word silently. She scanned the room, observing the other guests. The majority seem to be women in their fifties. There was one cluster of three women in their early forties and a couple older men. "I feel very young here. It's good for the ego. Unfortunately, there don't seem to be any hot guys here. *Mucho* bummer."

"Sorry," Amy said, feeling responsible, even though there had been no way for her to know the spa would primarily attract older women. She wanted to make sure Leah and Caitlyn had a fabulous time.

"Speaking of boy-crazy women," Leah said to Caitlyn, "how's your mom? Any weddings in the future?"

Caitlin smiled. "None that I know of, although I think it's safe to say there will be another wedding at some point. She's been dating the same guy for the last few months, and she keeps pestering me to come out with the two of them so I can get to know him better. I met him once at a dinner party, and afterward she kept asking me what I thought of him. I told her he seemed nice, but what I wanted to tell her was that he seemed just like all the other guys she dated, and what's the point of bothering to get to know him anyway? Even if she marries him, if history is anything to go by, she'll just end up divorcing him."

After dinner they helped themselves to "dessert" of stewed fruit. Amy didn't normally crave sweets, but this meal had seemed unnaturally healthy, and suddenly she wanted cake and ice cream. Maybe a nice crème brûlé. There was something about eating this healthfully that made Amy feel denied and wanting to gorge on fattening foods.

"It's so good to see you guys," Caitlyn said, spearing a pear stewed in cinnamon. "What would I have done in college if I hadn't met you two?"

"If we hadn't met you, Leah and I would have remained nerds forever. Remember what we would do with ourselves on the nights Caitlyn had a date?"

Leah laughed. "We were such geeks. Every Friday night that we weren't out with Caitlyn, you and I would get a slice of pizza, go to Dairy Queen for Snickers Blizzards, then come home and play geography on your computer."

"Friday nights with pizza and geography. How pathetic." Amy shook her head. "You saved us, Caitlyn. We would have never left our dorm if it weren't for you. And I may never have discovered the joys of alcohol if you hadn't gotten me drunk all those nights. If you hadn't forced me to try that vibrator, I may never have learned the full joys of sex."

"It took you long enough to freakin' get around to having it."

"I was waiting for the right guy. Twenty isn't *that* old."

When they were done with what passed for dessert, they walked back across the spa grounds to their room. Leah whipped off her clothes without a thought and paraded around the room naked as she fished her suit out of her suitcase. Leah was the type who would pee with the door open, strip in front of nearly anyone, and go skinny dipping with half a dozen strangers without blinking. With her background in science, Leah saw nothing shameful about the human body and how it worked.

Caitlyn was also comfortable with her body—she loved showing it off—and she put on a barely there bikini with a push-up bra top and high-heeled sandals.

Amy, on the other hand, had always been painfully shy about her body. She put on her modest one-piece suit in the privacy of the bathroom and covered it with a matching cover-up dress.

When she'd been little, she had colorful wallpaper with smiling lions, giraffes, hippos, and monkeys on it. Amy thought the animals were watching her when she changed with the lights out. She didn't grow out of the habit until she was eleven years old, and even then there were times she was sure someone had rigged a secret camera in her room to spy on her. As a teenager, Amy hid behind her glasses and baggy clothes that were much too big for her. In the locker room before and after gym class, she perfected a method of being able to change without ever getting completely naked—her over-sized shirts would cover her underwear when she changed from jeans into her gym shorts, and she could put on a shirt in a flash before anyone could get a glimpse of her bra.

Amy emerged from the bathroom fully dressed. "You guys ready?"

Leah held up the stack of towels she was holding. "I've got towels for all of us."

Amy locked the door behind them.

Darkness blanketed the grounds, but there were enough lights that they could easily see their way.

"Do you think the water is going to be cold?" Caitlyn asked.

"No," Leah said. "The brochure said that the spa is located in the center of natural hot springs from a volcano that's been dormant for several hundred years. The springs feed the pools and the steam room."

There were two kidney-shaped pools side by side in a sort of elongated yin-yang way. Caitlyn dunked her toe into one of the pools, and instead of cool, refreshing water, it was nearly as hot as a Jacuzzi.

"Damn, that's hot!" She walked to the other one. "This one is more like bathwater."

Leah dipped her toe in. "I'm not really sure if you can swim in water this warm. Your organs might melt."

Caitlyn went to the hotter one and walked down the steps into the water. "It feels *good.*"

Amy and Leah stepped into the pool after her, slowly acclimating to the temperature. A sheen of sweat broke out on Amy's face, chest, and neck. She found what effectively served as a seat—a concrete shelf around the edge of the pool—and sat on it.

"Remember the last time we traveled together?" Caitlyn said.

"South Padre Island, Texas!" Leah said as she found a place to sit beside Amy. She traced her fingers over the water's surface as if stroking a bolt of silk.

South Padre Island had been the obvious choice because Leah's older sister had moved to South Texas a year earlier to take a job as an elementary schoolteacher. Leah, Caitlyn, and Amy had driven twenty-five hours to get to South Texas from Iowa, surviving on a diet of chocolate-covered Oreos, Pop Tarts, Cheetos, and Diet Coke.

Caitlyn found a new guy every night, which was de rigueur for spring break. Amy had been dating a guy at the time, so she just looked on as Caitlyn worked her voodoo magic on the guys. Leah had never been good at flirting, so she usually ended up having intellectual discussions with the nerdy male friend leftovers of Caitlyn's conquests.

"Remember that night we were with those guys?" Amy said. "We were waiting in the parking lot of the hotel for them in your sister's car?"

"No, I don't remember that," Leah said.

"I remember." Caitlyn sank deeper into the pool so the water came over her shoulders, wetting the bottom of her hair, turning her highlighted blond hair dark and silky at the ends. "There was that one guy that I met at the bar who I had the hots for—"

"Yeah, that narrows it down."

Caitlyn ignored Leah's remark. "And they needed to grab more alcohol from their room, so we were waiting for them. Your sister had these little stickers in her car that she would use to decorate her students' papers when they'd done well."

"Little smiley faces," Amy added. "And everyone kept asking us how much we wanted for them."

"Oh, yeah." Leah laughed, remembering. "We couldn't figure out why there was such high demand for little smiley face stickers. Someone finally said something about wanting a hit of acid, and we finally figured out that they thought we were drug dealers."

"We were just three sweet girls from Iowa," Amy said, smiling and fluttering her eyelashes in mock innocence.

"What ever happened to those guys? I don't remember the rest of the night." Caitlyn sat next to Amy on the underwater bench.

"Like idiots, we waited for them for an hour," Amy said. "Security was really tight because the hotels didn't want drunk spring breakers destroying the rooms, so we couldn't get in to check on them. So you went screaming outside their window until that four-hundred-pound security guard came storming out and threatened you with grievous bodily harm."

"Oh, yeah! I ran screaming and shrieking back to the car, and we took off like bank robbers." Caitlyn laughed.

"I'm pretty sure those guys we'd been waiting for had passed out or something," Amy added. "But it ended up even better because we met those cute guys with a boat. And of course, Caitlyn, being your ever charming self, you talked them into letting us on and giving us a ride."

"That was a blast," Leah said.

They continued to reminisce, laughing and interrupting each other until their fingers looked like Raisinettes; then they returned to their room, showered, and got ready for bed.

When the lights were off, Amy pulled the soft sheets and scratchy blankets to her chin and wondered how Eric was doing. Then an image of Brent smiling at her popped into her mind. He was the last thing she thought about before drifting to sleep.

Chapter 6

Day Two

The curtains of the room were so thick, not a ray of morning sunlight was able to creep through. Caitlyn and Leah might have slept till noon if they hadn't been awoken by Amy screaming, "Ga!" as she toppled over a wood chair that came crashing to the ground with a deafening *thunk!*

"Huh?" Caitlyn cried, bolting upright. "What?" She turned the light on, her eyes blinking, never fully opening, squinting in the light.

"Ouch!" Leah shielded her eyes from the sudden spotlight of brightness.

"Sorry, sorry." Amy sat on the edge of her bed, rubbing her bruised shin. "I was trying to quietly sneak to the bathroom in the dark. Didn't quite work out."

"What time is it?" Leah reached over to the bedside table and picked up her sports watch, squinting at the numbers. "It's already eight. We've got to get up anyway so we can get breakfast before the hike." She swung her legs over the side of the bed, closed her eyes for one last moment, and then forced herself up to stagger over to her suitcase.

"Aag!" Caitlyn buried her head in her pillow. "It's too early."

"We went to bed at ten last night. That's ten hours of

sleep," Amy pointed out, bringing her clothes into the bathroom so she could change in private.

"Maybe it's jet lag. Or maybe we got too much sleep," Caitlyn moaned. Turning over on her back, she forced her eyes open. At last she threw off the blankets and managed to stand on unsteady legs. She wore a ribbed tank top that clung to her pert breasts and red silk boxer shorts that some ex had left at her place. She pulled the tank top off and put on a bra, T-shirt, and shorts. At the mirror, she brushed her hair, then took her make-up bag and began applying her mascara in the over-the-top, tarantula-leg style she loved so well.

"Caitlyn, why are you putting make-up on? We're going hiking." Leah pulled her gym socks on.

"I need just a little or I feel naked." Caitlyn's make-up bag was splattered with dried foundation. Her mascara was so old it was probably toxic. Her lipstick had nothing left to it but a small nub of color—it was really more like a hint of lipstick, an *idea* of it.

Amy emerged from the bathroom fully dressed as Caitlyn took one last appraising glance in the mirror.

They both took their hiking boots and sat on the edges of their respective beds. As Caitlyn lifted one boot to put it on, she thought she heard something in her right boot. Figuring it was a pebble, she turned the boot upside down and shook it. When the one-and-a-half-inch long scorpion fell out and began skittering across the floor, Caitlyn screamed the blood-curdling scream of a horror movie actress being attacked by a knife-wielding villain. Amy, who had been bending over to tie her shoelaces, nearly fell off the bed.

"What? What? What?" Leah said.

"Monster thingy! Monster thingy!" Caitlyn screamed, pointing in the scorpion's direction as she leapt up onto her bed.

"Monster? Are you talking about the scorpion?" Leah asked.

"Those things are deadly! They're poisonous! They can

kill you!" Caitlyn plastered herself into the corner, which was as far away both in height and in distance as she could get from the fiendish creature she was certain wanted her blood.

"Caitlyn, calm down. I'll kill it," Amy said.

"No! Don't kill it! This kind of scorpion isn't poisonous. He's a good kind of scorpion," Leah said.

"There is no such thing! Are you mad?" Caitlyn said.

Leah took a short water glass from the bathroom and, using one of her magazines for a lid, scooped up the offending creature with little fanfare. "Amy, get the door for me, would you?"

Amy, wearing just one shoe, hobbled awkwardly over to the door and opened it. Leah walked outside several feet away from their door and let the scorpion loose in the grass. When she returned, she and Amy exchanged glances and chuckled.

"It's just going to come back in!" Caitlyn said. She'd let her arms drop from their defensive pose, but she was still up on the bed, cowering in the corner.

"Caitlyn, yes, it might come back in. But if you keep the plugs stopped up in the sink and the shower and keep the doors closed, scorpions and other creatures will have no way to get in. Anyway, you should always check your shoes before putting them on in this sort of climate," Leah said.

"Nobody told me that. About the shoes or the plugs in the tub and sink," Caitlyn said. "Check that the sinks are plugged. Please?"

With a sigh, Leah checked the bathroom and assured Caitlyn that all was safe. Caitlyn made Leah put her hand in Caitlyn's hiking boots to be extra sure no other poisonous beasts were lurking. Even after Leah did so, Caitlyn cringed as she put on her boots. Amy and Leah, now ready, stood by the door waiting for her to finish up.

With day bags stocked with cameras and bottles of Evian, they went to the dining room for breakfast, where the smell of fresh coffee and ripe papaya filled the air. They loaded their

plates with fresh fruit from the buffet—papaya and grapefruit and pineapple and banana. The fruit was so rich in
color it was like surveying a jeweler's selection of rubies and
sapphires and yellow amber stones. Amy thought about her
own grocery store back home where it seemed most of the
time as if the produce had been grown in Chernobyl. By comparison, the spread here was quite a treat.

They sat beside a window that offered a terrific view of the
mountains around them. Simple bird feeders hung from the
trees outside the window. Small, colorful birds ate the fresh
fruit that the *La Buena Vida* staff served. The room buzzed
with guests clattering their plates and silverware.

"What's that stupid smile on your face for?" Caitlyn asked
Leah.

"Hmm? Nothing. You know, it's just great to be here with
you guys."

"Bullshiteroni. What gives?"

"I just was remembering how funny the incident with the
guy in the airport was, that's all."

"Still thinking about that guy. Huh. Very interesting,"
Caitlyn said. "Methinks you have the hots for him."

"That's not it. It's just that he brought back some memories, that's all." Seeing someone who reminded her of her
past love brought back memories of just how nice it had been
to be in love. When exactly *was* the last the time she'd been
on a date? After Chuck had left her for the twenty-two-year-
old, she'd become wary of everything a man said to her. But
that didn't mean she'd given up on the idea of love. She was
merely being cautious.

It was very easy to be cautious when you worked from
home alone. Leah did almost all of her interviews via phone
or e-mail. The only time she got out of the house was to go
grocery shopping or visit friends. Going to lunch with a girlfriend wasn't exactly the best opportunity to meet men, and
even at parties, most of the men were married. The tricky
thing about dating in your thirties was that most single men

were divorced, which often meant there were complex cus-tody arrangements to deal with, as if dating and romance weren't hard enough. On the rare occasions that Leah did agree to go out on a date, she was inevitably disappointed. It was easier just to let her work consume her. Her work never let her down.

"We'd better be going if we're going to have time to sign up for manis and pedis," Caitlyn said.

Amy and Leah nodded. They walked over to the front of-fice where the sign-up sheet was and took turns signing their names in open slots for the various treatments. Amy man-aged to schedule a mud wrap for after the hike. She'd never had a mud wrap before, but she hoped the description in the pamphlet about its transformative powers was true. She wanted to look drop-dead gorgeous at her wedding. The wedding had to be perfect. Amy had no doubt that it *would* be perfect.

As long as she was marrying the right guy.

Eric *had* to be the right guy. She was running out of time to find someone to marry and start having kids. For the past two years, she would look at the children she saw at the gro-cery store or at restaurants with such envy it was like a phys-ical ache. One time she'd been waiting to meet a client for lunch and she'd seen a boy who was about a year and a half old with his mother. The boy kept pointing to something he wanted outside. His hands would flail around in excited bursts of movement that reminded Amy of a symphony con-ductor. One hand would point out the window, and the other arm would rocket straight up into the air. Then his hands would fall to his sides until he repeated the arm gestures again and again. Watching that cute little boy had made Amy want a child so desperately, she considered tossing aside the idea of waiting until the wedding and destroying her birth control pills in a gigantic bonfire. She knew that she and Eric would create the most precious, adorable babies, and she couldn't wait to see exactly what they would look like.

Amy, Caitlyn, and Leah walked to the perimeter of the pool

where other guests were gathered, waiting for the guided hikes. There were three hikes that left at the same time every day: an easy hour-long one, a medium two-and-a-half-hour option, and a challenging three-hour hike.

"Which one do you want to do?" Leah asked.

"Well, I want to be challenged on this trip," Amy said, "but I don't want to cripple myself on our first day. Why don't we do the medium hike and see how it goes?"

"That's okay with me," Caitlyn said.

"Me, too," Leah said.

Two of the guides were Mexican. One was young and very thin; the other was older with a potbelly and powerful calf muscles. The third guide looked as though he might have an Italian or Greek background. He had dark hair, but his skin and features didn't look Mexican.

Amy asked him which hike was the midlevel hike, and he said he was leading that one, so she waved Leah and Caitlyn over.

Caitlyn took one look at the guide and her jaw dropped— he was that good looking. His thick hair was pulled back into a low ponytail that just grazed his shoulders. He was tall, at least six-feet-three, and he had a smile that gave off enough heat to melt gold. His arms were powerful—he obviously worked out to get that kind of definition. His nails were neat, perfect ovals; his hands were large and strong. Around his neck he wore a black cord with a silver medallion that was etched with a symbol Caitlyn didn't recognize.

"He's gorgeous," Leah whispered to Caitlyn.

"No kidding."

The guests broke into groups depending on which hike they wanted to take. In Amy, Caitlyn, and Leah's group, there were three other women milling around beside them waiting for the hike to begin. They looked to be in their forties. The tallest of them had her sand-colored hair tucked beneath a blue baseball cap and a barrel-shaped body perched on thin stork legs. "Hi." The woman smiled at Caitlyn. "When did you get in?"

"Last night. How about you?"

"This is our last day. We've been here a week. I'm Sarah."

"I'm Caitlyn. This is Amy and Leah."

After they'd introduced themselves and had the where-are-you-from-what-do-you-do conversation (the three women were all teachers from Chicago), Nature Guide God said it was time to get started.

"Hey, everybody," Nature Guide God said. "My name is Jim Maddalena and I'll be your guide. I know some of you, already. And you are?"

"I'm Amy, this is Caitlyn, and this is Leah."

"Well, Amy, Caitlyn, and Leah, it's nice to meet you. Are you ready to get started? Great. Let's go."

The six women followed Jim off the spa grounds to the surrounding tree-lined mountains.

The resort was bordered by long-extinct volcanic mountains and a hot river coming from deep underground. There was an impressive diversity of birds flying through the branches of the dense forest—the motmot with his blue-green body, rust-colored head, and long tail waving behind it like a ribbon in the wind, violet-crowned hummingbirds, and vermilion flycatchers. Trees like the Montezuma pine, tropical palm, and the bougainvillea with its beautiful explosion of red-pink flowers dotted the landscape.

They trudged uphill. At the high ridges, they surveyed the spectacular vistas showing the verdant hills and trees and the rocky deposits of ash flow, pumice, and obsidian.

"Amy, would you please stop taking pictures of just nature? Get a person in the picture in front of the nature," Caitlyn griped. "Plain nature makes for a giant snooze-fest when you're home."

"Okay, you stand over there."

Immediately Caitlyn smiled brightly and posed in a sort of

voila!-look-how-pretty-this-all-is way, with one knee bent and one arm extended with the palm out. The second Amy had snapped the picture, Caitlyn scowled and began marching on.

"Uh!" she grunted. "When you told me we were going to a spa, I thought you were talking about lying around in the sun and eating bonbons, not hiking up freakin' Mt. Everest."

"I told you there would be hiking," Amy said.

"Yeah, but I thought you meant more like going on the occasional leisurely stroll, not actual hiking like, *in nature.*"

"It's a health spa. You're supposed to get healthy and reconnect with nature and all that shit."

"There is only one hot guy for miles, no alcohol, and I'm expected to hike up mountains. What a gyp."

"Caitlyn, that's the point. We're supposed to lose a few pounds, get in shape, cleanse ourselves . . ." Amy's words lacked conviction. When she'd gotten the idea to get together with her friends, she thought a little sun and shedding some weight was all she needed to start feeling better. She had to admit that going to a resort and getting some sun while drinking daiquiris all day without ever lifting a toe off their chaise lounge as the ocean licked the shores didn't sound so bad, but Amy was on a mission for self-improvement. She had a wedding to think about, and she longed to be a few pounds lighter. Was it an ambitious goal? No. It was vain and she should just love herself as she was, but she was a bride, damn it, and she wanted to look good. Plus, she'd always harbored a secret fantasy of having the kind of flat stomach that female rock stars were always showing off with T-shirts that ended above their belly buttons. Logically, she knew that her curvy, voluptuous body would never be thin or sinewy, and it certainly wouldn't become rock hard and fat free in a mere two weeks, but reality did surprisingly little to squelch the fantasy. Unconsciously, Amy quickened her pace.

They walked through a rocky arroyo. In some places colorful flowers decorated the landscape; in other places it felt as though they were walking through a desert. It was like walking through three different seasons, from spring to summer to fall.

"Okay," Caitlyn said to Leah and Amy, "I'm going to make my move." She picked up her pace to catch up with Jim.

"Hi." She smiled brightly.

"Hi."

"What a great job you have."

"Sure is."

"How long have you worked here?"

"About six months."

"Nice work if you can get it."

He smiled.

"So, Jim, where are you from originally?"

"Seattle."

"I've never been there."

"It's beautiful."

"I'm sure. My girlfriend lives just a few hours from there in Portland."

Why wasn't he smiling flirtily with her? It made no sense at all. He was friendly, but he wasn't checking her out. There was no lascivious glint in his eye, nothing. She did not have time for him to play hard to get. She had only two weeks . . . Caitlyn looked up to see Leah standing on the other side of Jim.

"Jim, I wanted to ask you, is it always this dry?"

"No. This is the dry season. The rainy season is from June through September. In those months we wouldn't be walking here. There would be water up to our chins."

"Huh."

They hiked farther along and came to a stretch of fine gray sand that puffed up in light clouds around their feet with each step they took.

"This sand is really interesting. It looks like volcanic ash."
Leah asked.

"That's exactly what it is," Jim said.

"No kidding."

"That's really fascinating," Caitlyn said, attempting to sound
as if she were genuinely interested.

"Leah, you're the one from Portland?"

"Yep, that's me."

"You grow up there?"

"Nope, I'm an Iowa girl."

"Iowa, huh? My grandmother lives in Des Moines."

"My parents still live there, but I have a sister and five
brothers, and every one of us moved out of Iowa as soon as
we graduated high school."

"Seven kids? Wow."

"We're Catholic. After my youngest brother was born my
parents slept in separate bedrooms. It's a rather primitive
form of birth control, but it's quite effective."

He smiled. "I couldn't imagine."

"Tell me about it." Though Leah had been celibate for far
too long, she needed to cling to the belief that she would have
sex again one day.

"Jim is from Seattle," Caitlyn said to Leah. Then, to Jim
she said, "What brought you to Mexico?"

Leah saw his expression just before he spoke. He flinched
slightly; a fissure of pain was clearly visible in his eyes. "I'm a
nutritionist. If you were offered a job in paradise, wouldn't
you take it?"

"So you're the one responsible for feeding us twigs and
berries?"

"Those twigs and berries are very good for you."

"Sure, sure, but a nice juicy steak is chock-full of protein
and iron. It's all about moderation."

"That's true, but people come to a health spa to cleanse

their system of impurities, not have dead cow rotting in their guts."

"I think the food here is very good," Caitlyn said.

"Thanks," Jim said. He gave Leah a teasingly pointed look. "See, somebody appreciates me."

They walked along inhaling the fresh air. "What kind of plant is this?" Leah asked Jim.

"Ahh," Jim said with a smile. "That, my friend, is peyote." He stopped, and the six women gathered around to watch him as he used a stick to dig up the spindly plant bearing just a few anemic leaves, excavating the root from the ground.

"The hallucinogen?" Leah asked.

"Yep. You just chew on the root," he explained. "Do you want it?" He held the root out to her.

"I'll take it," Caitlyn said.

"Oh." Jim looked baffled, looking at Leah to see if she'd mind.

She gestured to Caitlyn. "I'll have a glass of wine or a beer every now and then, but that's as crazy as I get."

"Smart girl." His eyes twinkled.

If Leah hadn't been smiling into Jim's eyes, she would have seen Caitlyn shoot her a glinty look.

"You seem to have a real interest in science," Jim said as they began hiking again.

"I'm a biologist by training and now I write for *Our World*."

"I love that magazine! Although I don't get it anymore, unfortunately. I canceled my subscription when I moved here from the States several months ago. The international shipping costs, you know."

"I'm a writer, too. A poet actually," Caitlyn said, finally getting Jim to look her way, only to instantly lose his attention when Leah said, "That's true. She's won tons of awards and been published in a bunch of prestigious literary magazines."

He turned to Caitlyn. "A poet, huh? You don't strike me as your typical poet."

Leah laughed. "Believe me. She's not."

"Is that a good thing, or a bad thing?" Caitlyn said. There was no possible way he could resist the trademark way she cocked her head and gave just a hint of a smile, but he looked away at the crucial moment.

"It's not good or bad. You just usually think of poets as introverted. Hey." He turned to Leah. "Is your last name Albright?"

Leah nodded.

"You're the one who wrote that article on the kangaroo several months ago?"

"Yeah, that was me. You have quite a memory."

"That article was fascinating. I was just knocked out when I read that mother kangaroos can actually stop the growth of an embryo if there is a draught causing a food shortage, until food is no longer scarce."

Leah smiled. She felt like a minor celebrity. Most people had never heard of the magazine she wrote for, let alone liked it and recognized something she'd published in it.

"I could write articles about Australia from now until the end of time. It has the most amazing array creatures found nowhere else on earth."

"And you're the one who wrote that nutrition article that synthesized the facts and myths of all those fad diets about a year ago?"

"Yep, that was me."

"I made hundreds of copies of that and gave it to all my clients when I was working as a nutritionist in the States. It did a great job of simplifying the truth about incorporating the rules of nutrition into your daily life. I'm probably in violation of about a hundred copyright laws."

"Most definitely, but I won't tell."

"So you're a nutritionist as well as a hiking guide?" Caitlyn asked.

"Everyone here works as a jack-of-all-trades. The other two hiking guides are also gardeners. We all take different shifts driving clients in the van, that sort of thing. Gotta keep busy."

"How very enterprising of you!" Caitlyn said.

They approached a river that was brilliantly green from the algae lining the bottom of it. Steam rose out from the burbling stream, blanketing the air in an ethereal mist.

"Jim, how hot is that water?" Leah asked.

"Hot enough that you could boil eggs in it. I've seen people do it. We're going to be going by one of the sources of the hot water that feeds the spa in just a minute," Jim said.

"It's so great out here," Caitlyn said. "I just love hiking and getting into nature. I can't get enough of it."

Once again Jim smiled at her, then turned his attention to the water.

"Here we go. Here's the source." He used a stick to point to an unremarkable bit of sand that burbled up water from a hole that was no larger than the face of a watch.

"This is the hot water that heats all the water at the spa?" Leah asked.

"There are other sources, but this is the primary one."

"That's remarkable. It's so not impressive looking."

"We'll be going by the other sources on tomorrow's hike."

Leah was already looking forward to it.

They continued hiking through an area where large leaves covered the ground, crackling underfoot. Leah spotted a plant she'd never seen before. It had a deep orange-colored fruit growing on it that was the same shape as a kiwi but smaller in size. "What's this?"

"*Huevo de gato*. Cat's eggs." Jim plucked one of the fruits from the bush and rubbed off the fuzz coating it. "You can eat it."

"Eat the whole thing? Skin and all?"

"Yep."

Leah gave it a try. The insides were goopy with tart seeds. The skin tasted gritty and fibrous.

"Ick. Here, Caitlyn, do you want to try?"

"With that ringing endorsement, how could I not?"

Caitlyn took a bite, and her face twisted in displeasure. "Let's be sure not to get lost in the woods so we don't have to survive on this, okay? Amy, do you want to try?"

"No," she said with a laugh. "Thanks, though."

As they walked the last stretch back to the spa grounds, Caitlyn, Leah, and Amy moved together behind the rest of the group.

"I had so much fun talking to those teachers from Chicago," Amy said. "They are super nice. I can't wait till Eric and I are sending our kids to school. They said—"

"Yeah, yeah, yeah, that's great," Caitlyn interrupted. "Leah, what are you doing? He's mine."

"What do you mean he's yours?"

"Actually, Caitlyn, from my vantage point, if he was interested in anybody, it was Leah."

"Do you really think he was interested?" The faintest trace of a smile appeared at the corner of Leah's lips. "I did notice that he began talking a little louder when he was around me and he complimented me. Both are signs the male is attracted to the female."

"'The male is attracted to the female,'" Amy teased.

"What? Why are you making fun of me?"

"You're just funny, talking about attraction like such a biologist."

"Humans are animals, too, you know. I also noticed that he smiled easily and made eye contact. His pupils were dilated. All signs of attraction."

"Maybe you can plot the progress of his attraction to you on a graph. You'll be able to tell just when he's about to go in for the kill," Caitlyn said.

"I think having that guy flirt with you at the airport gave

you a little extra kick of confidence that makes you even more attractive to males," Amy said.

"Maybe. I have to admit the attention is nice. Caitlyn, I get why you like it so much."

"You know, we didn't come all this way to talk about guys. This is about female bonding," Caitlyn said, marching determinedly forward. "We don't need to think about guys for the next two weeks. In fact, we should swear that we won't spend any more time on guys at all this trip. We'll have facials and manicures and mud wraps . . ."

"Caitlyn, come on," Amy said. "You already are dating three men. Jim and Leah have more in common. Don't worry about it."

"Why do you need every guy on earth falling over himself to get to you?" Leah asked, suddenly annoyed. She distinctly remembered their freshman year in college when the three of them would go to bars and flirtatious Caitlyn and busty blond Amy would get all the attention. Until Leah met David, she'd been more or less invisible to men. A guy actually finding her attractive was so rare her friends should be celebrating it, not begrudging her the attention.

"Girls, girls, girls," Amy said. "Stop fighting. We are at a warm, sunny spa and we're going to have a good time if it kills us!"

Chapter 7

Later that same day

The room where the mud wraps were given was basically a hallway with a small changing room on one side and a shower on the other.

"Hi, I'm here for my mud wrap," Amy said to the short, older Mexican woman who wore a visor, a medical-style white coat, and hot pink leggings over her chunky thighs. "Are you Tia?"

"*Si.*"

The woman gestured at her and said something Amy didn't understand. Amy studied Tia's pantomiming. "Oh! You want me to take off my clothes?"

"*Si.*"

"*All* my clothes?"

"*Si.*"

Amy looked around. Behind her was the unlocked door she'd come in and in front of her was a partly open door that led outside. This woman wanted her to strip naked in a place where absolutely anyone could walk in at any time? Was she crazy? Amy had thought she'd lie on a bed with a modest towel covering her important parts. She'd had no idea this involved total nudity. There was no way in hell she could go through with it. "Um, you know, no, *gracias* anyway. Thanks, though. I'll just go get my friend. She can take my place. I'll be right back."

Tia's face scrunched with confusion, but Amy didn't see the expression because she was too busy bolting from the room back to the cottage where Caitlyn was just finishing tying up the strings of her bikini.

"Caitlyn, take my mud wrap appointment."

"What? Why?"

"Oh, no reason. I just . . . decided I didn't want it."

"It's because you have to get naked, isn't it? Amy, you have a beautiful body."

"It's not that."

"It is that. You think when you gain eight ounces you're overweight."

"You have to admit I'm curvy."

"You're curvy, all right."

"It's just that I've never been one of the 'naked' sort of people. I have no problem being naked in the shower or in bed with Eric."

"Really?"

"Well, I don't strut around naked in front of him, but it's okay for the lights to be on."

"Well, that's impressive."

"Please take my place? I don't want it to go to waste."

Rolling her eyes, Caitlyn agreed.

"Thanks. You're the best."

Caitlyn slipped sandals on and wrapped a sarong around her waist. "See ya soon."

When she got down to the mudroom, she opened the door to see Tia sitting on a chair, waiting. "*Hola!* I, um." Caitlyn pointed out the door and then pointed to herself. "I'm the, um, *chica* who's here to take the other *chica's* place?"

"*Sí. Sí.*" Tia waved her in and gestured for Caitlyn to take her clothes off in the nook in the corner.

Caitlyn went to the nook and quickly stripped out of her clothes, tossing her sarong and towel across the chair. She strutted back to Tia, who gestured for her to stand on a sheet, which she did. Then Tia spread her arms and legs out so Caitlyn was holding a position like Da Vinci's famous sketch of the human figure, *Vitruvian Man*.

Tia scooped what looked like fine dirt—which in fact, was what it was—from a large rubber garbage can and poured it into a copper pot. Then she took hot water and mixed it into the dirt with a trowel. When the concoction was rendered sufficiently mudlike, she took a handful of it and began slathering it on Caitlyn, starting with her breasts.

Caitlyn's nipples were at full mast because it was chilly in the room, which seemed a rather humiliating development. There was no foreplay, no candles, no romantic music—Tia went straight into feeling Caitlyn up, plastering her in mud. Tia moved on to Caitlyn's stomach, to her arms, then the front of her legs. Then Tia said something in Spanish that Caitlyn didn't understand. Tia gestured wildly, and Caitlyn finally understood she meant for Caitlyn to turn around. Tia then covered Caitlyn's butt and legs with mud. Once again Tia said something incomprehensible, but Caitlyn understood that she wanted Caitlyn to follow her outside to a small area that was fenced off and minimally enclosed with a see-through curtain of fabric. There were several lawn chairs covered in white sheets. White sheets seemed a poor color on which to bake in mud, but Caitlyn wasn't the one making the rules around here. There was a woman lying splayed on one of the lawn chairs completely naked except for a washcloth over her crotch.

Caitlyn lay on one of the chairs and used the cloth Tia provided to cover her private bits. Caitlyn shifted uncomfortably. She felt like the Tar Baby. All she needed was to be showered with feathers and her humiliation would be complete. Her skin was the color and consistency of chocolate cake batter.

She tried to relax and let the warmth of the sun calm her. As the mud hardened, she thought about how she damn well better be getting detoxified and beautified, because this was not the slightest bit comfortable. She felt as if she'd been wrapped in shrink wrap that was pulling her skin ever tauter. She watched as the mud went from a rich chocolate brown to an ash gray color.

It was fun to be with Leah and Amy again. Though they talked to each other a few times a month on the phone, the phone was no substitute for seeing each other in person.

In college, they'd seen each other every day. They shared every little event and dissected it in minute detail.

After spending their freshman year in the dorms, they'd spent the next three years of college living together in a little apartment with three small bedrooms and a bathroom that was so tiny they lived with perpetually bruised limbs from turning or moving too quickly to get from the shower to the toilet or the toilet to the sink. Their landlord allegedly paid their utilities, but what that effectively meant was that during the winter their rooms were kept so cold they were forced to wear hats, scarves, and gloves, and their lips were always chapped from inhaling the cold air. They would huddle together on the couch beneath blankets next to a contraband space heater that was strictly forbidden under their rental agreement.

Their living room was so small and narrow and the TV Amy's father had bought her was so big that when they sat on the couch, their knees nearly touched the television. When they exhaled the cold winter air, their breath would fog up the TV screen, and one of them would inevitably yell out the useless admonishment, "Don't breathe so much, you're blocking the view!"

They'd stayed up late many nights talking about school,

Clinton versus Bush versus Perot, Rodney King, the O.J. Simpson trial, and how to strengthen their chipped nails. They discussed boys, their careers, their futures. They watched *Seinfield* and listened to EMF and Concrete Blonde and U2.

One night in Amy and Leah's dorm room late in the second semester of their freshman year, the three of them were buzzed on Everclear and Kool–Aid, and for the first time in all the months that they had been friends, Amy finally opened up and told Leah and Caitlyn the truth about her family life. Caitlyn had always assumed Amy lived a charmed life. Unlike Caitlyn, who had been raised by a single mother in a neighborhood in Chicago that was essentially a ghetto, Amy had lived with her father, who was a well-off lawyer. But that night Amy shed the pretense of living the perfect life and told them the truth. She told them about how her brother, Bill, had always been a troublemaker, getting into fights at school when he was only eight years old. When he was ten he burnt down their garage on purpose. He started using and selling drugs at twelve. He'd started a life of petty crime by the time he was thirteen.

Amy's father believed that Bill should be punished harshly for his crimes; her mom thought loving kindness would solve all. They argued about it so much, it ultimately split them apart. Amy's mother took custody of Bill, and Amy went to live with her father. Because her father worked such long hours, Amy said she felt as though she basically grew up on her own. Her mother focused so much of her attention on Bill that she had no time left over for Amy. Amy tried to get her parents' attention by getting straight A's and never getting into trouble.

On the one hand, Caitlyn had been touched that Amy trusted her and Leah enough to tell them the truth, but on the other hand, she was hurt that it had taken her so long to open up. Then again, Caitlyn knew all about keeping secrets. She had learned that lesson in spades thanks to her mother.

Bridget had never told Caitlyn who her father was. What Caitlyn know was that her mother had been sixteen when she'd gotten pregnant. Everything else was speculation on Caitlyn's part. She suspected she'd been conceived on a one-night stand. Caitlyn knew her mother was Norwegian, but that accounted for only fifty percent of Caitlyn's genetic background. She ached to fill in the missing pieces of who she was and where she came from. Caitlyn had asked her mother a few times, but the questions had set Bridget into such a fury Caitlyn stopped asking. Since Bridget's only brother had died when she was fifteen, and since her parents had been killed three years after Caitlyn was born, there was no one else who'd been around at the time to help Caitlyn solve the mystery.

Two months before Caitlyn was born, Bridget married husband number one. Don was fifteen years older than Bridget. He had white blond hair and a ferocious temper that was too often expressed through his fist. Bridget stuck the marriage out until Caitlyn was almost six. It was Don's name on the birth certificate, but on the night that Bridget left, sneaking Caitlyn out of the house and driving as far as she could before running out of gas, she told Caitlyn that she was glad Don wasn't her real father. He didn't deserve either one of them.

It hadn't been the gentlest way to find out that the man she called Daddy all her life wasn't, in fact, related to her, but it did explain why she didn't look a thing like him.

Caitlyn didn't have any illusions that she would one day find her real father and they'd become the best of friends. She just wanted to know who he was, how her mother knew him, and what the circumstances of her birth were.

Caitlyn wasn't sure how much time had passed when Tia returned and gestured to Caitlyn to follow her inside. Caitlyn tried to stand, but it was as if she'd been cast in armor; she could barely move her limbs. Mud splintered off her, cracking apart like pieces of a broken vase. She finally managed to stand and stagger over to the shower with a Frankenstein-like walk. The only way she could move forward was to swing the entire right side of her body ahead, land on her right foot, and then repeat the swinging stagger on her left side.

The shower wasn't an ordinary shower. It was square, and on the three walls there were faucets facing straight out at about chest height. Caitlyn turned the water on; it came out in feeble drips. She felt as if she was being spat on. It would take weeks to wash the mud off her body at this pace. Caitlyn struggled with the faucet to get more water pressure. Something appeared to be stuck.

"Err! Err!" she grunted as she labored to loosen the faucet. At once she broke through whatever had been making it stick, and she was inundated with a deluge of water on all three sides. It was like being in a prison movie where the warden used a fire hose on new inmates to punish and humiliate. It was painful to be attacked by such forceful gales of water, but the spray was so intense that she was pushed against the wall and couldn't reach the faucet to turn it down. Trying to avoid the torrential attack of water while attempting to reach the controls, Caitlyn began dancing around, hopping from foot to foot with her arms flailing extravagantly around her. She couldn't open her eyes, and it was all she could do not to swallow liter after liter of shower water—it was so forceful it nearly pried her clenched mouth open. She felt ridiculous and wondered briefly if there was a secret camera recording her idiotic rain dance. Maybe one of the La Buena Vida staff members sold the video clips on the black market under the Spanish equivalent of the title "Stupidest Home Videos of Rich Gringo Idiots." It could be a lucrative industry.

At last Caitlyn got hold of the controls and managed to turn the water to a reasonable level. The mud softened and melted away, gathering up at her feet until she was in an ankle-high mud puddle. Eventually the mud washed down the drain, and she turned the water off and struggled to catch her breath. Trying to get beautiful took so much damn work.

While Caitlyn was suffering her mudwrap, Leah was sitting poolside getting her first ever manicure and pedicure. Leah was kept her nails and toenails cut short, and it usually took her all of five minutes to cut her nails and file them into ovals. She marveled at just how long it took the young, plump Mexican woman to file and buff each of her nails and toenail and remove all her cuticles.

Leah chose a metallic plum shade of nail polish. It was fun being pampered in this way, sitting in the warm air as a gentle breeze caressed her skin. She liked the results, too. The shimmery brightness of her nails and toenails was a fun change from her nature girl look. She knew she would never be a glamour girl, but it was fun to try the persona on for at least a little while.

Leah had never been big on make-up or dressing up, even as a little girl. It had always driven her mother crazy that Leah preferred muddy overalls to dresses, but overalls were better for hiking and fishing. With seven kids in the family, her parents had been too busy to notice when Leah would wander off for hours at a time to sit in a field and watch, transfixed, as a cricket went about its day. She could relax in front of a tree and observe a squirrel scampering up and down and around it for hours, contemplating the beauty and magic of sharing her world with such a creature as it calmly went about the ordinary business of living. She'd also been an avid bird watcher. Of course, in the bird world, unlike the human world, it was the males who had brightly colored feathers to attract females. Leah wriggled her bright fingers and smiled. Would her colorful nails get Jim's attention?

She shook her head, trying to banish the thought from her mind. Even if Jim did find her attractive, what was the point? She was leaving in two weeks.

Although maybe a little illicit tryst wouldn't be so bad. How long it been since she'd made love to someone?

Leah hadn't realized what a rut she'd fallen into at home until she'd broken her routine on this trip. Seeing David the lookalike and then meeting Jim had awakened a part of her that had been asleep for a long time.

She would have to be more proactive about her dating life when she got back home. Maybe she would give that Russ Evans, recruiter, a call. Maybe she would finally agree to go on a blind date with that guy her friend Lindsey had been trying to set her up with for months.

Leah had no expectations that she would fall madly in love with the man of her dreams and they'd be so hot for each other they'd have sex five times a day and never be able to keep their hands off each other for the next fifty years until one or both of them were in their graves. Leah thought the expectations for love were too high. Books and movies and TV shows made it seem as though for every woman, there was only one man in the world fated to be with her. In fact, marriage had little to do with love and much more to do with a financial business arrangement. When a couple got divorced, it was all about assets and money and who owed whom what. Arranged marriages were made so husbands had wives to bear their children and take care of their houses. All Leah needed to do was look at her own parents. They somehow managed to have seven kids, though Leah had never once seen them exchange a hug or a love glance. Why should she be surprised? In the animal kingdom, sex was about procreation and survival of the fittest. What else were people except human animals? All that blather about true love and destiny was a marketing gimmick to sell books and movies and false hopes, to sell diamond engagement rings and expensive weddings and romantic weekends in the tropics. Leah was above all that.

But that didn't mean the occasional romp in the sheets wasn't welcome . . .

As Leah's nails dried, Amy sat on the other side of the pool, people watching. The middle-aged women who made up the bulk of the guests seemed fit for their age, but even the thinnest women's flesh jiggled in cascading ripples like paint on a painting that had been hung before it was dry. It was only a matter of time, Amy thought, until her body looked like that. She was body conscious enough. She'd spent years trying to find baggy sweaters that would somehow stop boys from staring at her voluptuous figure and soon she would have to find baggy clothes that would conceal her wobbly flesh and rippling stretch marks. She knew that as a smart, talented woman, Amy was supposed to love her body just the way it was, but she couldn't stop secretly fantasizing about being more fit and toned.

Leah stood and padded across the stone-tiled pool area to Amy. "Look." She twinkled her nails and toes. "A professional manicure and pedicure. Will you take a picture?"

"But of course." Amy pulled the camera from the tote bag she'd brought, and Leah posed campily in front of a backdrop of bright begonias as Amy snapped off a couple of shots.

"Hey, you."

Amy pulled the camera from her eyes and saw Caitlyn standing over her.

"Hey. How was your mud wrap?"

Caitlyn sat on the lounge chair next to Amy. "She slathered my entire body in mud, and then I had to lie in the sun until it hardened. I was human pottery baked in a kiln. Do I look any different?"

"What is the mud wrap supposed to do?"

"Remove your dead skin to make your skin softer."

"Let me feel."

Caitlyn extended her arm.

"Baby soft," Amy declared.

"The rough patches of my arms do feel a little softer, but I'm not sure it was worth it just for that."

"Did you think the mud wrap was going to turn you into Heidi Klum?"

"I guess not. But a girl can dream. Maybe it's just a big joke they play on us. Maybe it doesn't do anything and it's the tsunami-force gales of water in the shower that peel all the dead skin off."

They lay in comfortable silence for a few minutes with the warm sun on their skin.

"Is it lunchtime yet?" Leah asked.

Amy consulted her watch. "As soon as we throw some clothes on and walk over to the dining room, it will be."

Lunch consisted of lentil loaf, a shredded carrot salad with nuts and cinnamon, and slices of tomatoes topped with scoops of cottage cheese. Maybe it was just because they were ravenous from their hike, but the food was actually delicious. It was no Big Mac and fries, but for health food it wasn't bad.

After they'd eaten, they returned to the pool. Leah sat beneath the shaded awning while Amy and Caitlyn worked on their tans in the sun. Foliage in a pleasant mix of heights, hues, and textures wrapped around the pool. She saw the soft sage green of the Montezuma pine trees, the low yellow-green bushes, the rubbery-prickly look of the tall, light green palm trees.

Leah opened a folder of xeroxed articles she'd printed about influenza, Amy opened a novel, and Caitlyn lay languidly with her eyes closed.

As Leah furiously took notes in her notebook, Amy cast her a sidelong glance. "You're not working, are you?"

"I'm doing what I love, so it doesn't qualify as work."

Amy raised her eyebrows but said nothing. Caitlyn had brought a book of poetry, but she wasn't in the mood for it right now. She daydreamed instead about the guys she was dating. Sean was only okay looking, but he was utterly amazing in bed. He was the best lover she'd ever had. The only problem was when they finished having sex, trying to come up with something to talk about wasn't easy. He was a smart guy; they just had nothing in common. Caitlyn loved to go to plays, book signings, and poetry readings. He liked going to hockey games, NASCAR races, and really bad movies. Caitlyn loved going dancing at clubs; he liked dark pubs. She loved cooking gourmet meals; he was a junk food junkie.

Kyle was the guy she went to when she wanted intellectual discussions. He had worked in Europe for several years and had traveled to five of the seven continents. He could speak intelligently on art, politics, and literature. The problem with Kyle was that he was only 5'8". That was only an inch taller than Caitlyn, but since she normally wore shoes or boots with at least some sort of heel, she towered over him. She slept with him occasionally, but it was so lackluster there wasn't much point in bothering.

Reg worked on the stock market and made a killing. He was always taking her out to nice dinners and buying her presents. He was fun to be with and the sex was good, but as with Sean, they didn't actually have that much in common. Caitlyn could always make him laugh with her little anecdotes, but he didn't make her laugh. She really wanted to find a guy who could make her laugh.

"Guys, I'm going to check my e-mail. I'll be right back."

Caitlyn slipped a see-through cover-up over her suit and slid her sandals on. She went to the activities lodge where the computer with internet access was. She waited half a millennia for the computer to connect with the Internet; then she logged onto her email account and smiled. She loved seeing the guys she was dating in her inbox.

To: chameleon0306@hotmail.com
From: r.davis@msn.com
　I hope you're having fun in the sun, beautiful! It's no fair you leaving me up here in chilly Chicago without you to keep me warm. Don't go finding yourself any slutty cabana boys while you're down there, hear me?
Thinking of you,
Reg

To: r.davis@msn.com
From: chameleon0306@hotmail.com
　I'm having fun and don't you worry, there are only old women here. It's this New Agey–type healing place. Apparently the hot springs attract this type of crowd. I'm having fun with the girls, although they are making me hike up mountains and eat these disgustingly healthy foods. Blech. I can't wait to come home and grab a cheeseburger with you.
Smooches,
C

To: chameleon0306@hotmail.com
From: sean_cobier0225@netscape.com
　Hey babe, how ya doing? Fending off lots of guys, I imagine. Me? I'm just freezing my ass off. You picked a great couple weeks to take off. We've got record colds. Brr!
　Can't wait till you're back. I miss you in my bed. You know who misses you, too,
　Sean

To: sean_cobier0225@netscape.com
From: chameleon0306@hotmail.com

I'm having fun and don't you worry, there are only old women here. It's this New Agey–type healing place. Apparently the hot springs attract this type of crowd. I'm having fun with the girls, although they are making me hike up mountains and eat these disgustingly healthy foods. Blech. I can't wait to come home and grab a cheeseburger with you.
Smooches,
C

To: chameleon0306@hotmail.com
From: Donovan_Kyle@yahoo.com

Good evening, my angel. (At least, it's evening here, who knows when you'll be able to tear yourself away from your well-deserved fiesta to read this, if you even do. I wouldn't!)

Things are bleak here without you. Mainly I've been trying to stay warm. I've rented a number of videos. Are you familiar with the works of Lars von Trier? Krzysztof Kieslowski? Alejandro Gonzalez Inarrtiu? They're wonderful.

I'd hoped to see the opening at the art museum, but I'm afraid I just wasn't up for braving the cold. I've lived in Chicago all my life and I'll never get used to winds this biting and bitter, as though they have a vendetta against you.

I hope you are well and enjoying yourself.
—K

Caitlyn smiled. Kyle deserved a personalized message. He was one of a kind. If only he were a little cuter, a little richer, a little more wild in bed, he'd be perfect.

To: Donovan_Kyle@yahoo.com
From: chameleon0306@hotmail.com
   Hey, sweetie,
   I'm having fun getting back in touch with nature and hanging with the girls. I've written a little, though not as much as I'd hoped. Amy and Leah make me hike up mountains all morning—I feel like I need all afternoon to recover!
Missing you,
C

Caitlyn returned to the pool and lay on a lounge chair beside Amy. With a sigh, she opened the spa's pamphlet that detailed the activities for the next few weeks.

"So, you guys," Caitlyn said, "tonight there is a seminar on improving your psychic abilities, and the night after that there is a seminar on healing your chakras. And after that there is a seminar on reversing the aging process."

"Said by a woman who is sitting in the cell-destroying sunlight," Leah said. "Here's a tip; if you want to *slow* the aging process—because, let me just point out that aging is inevitable and can't be *reversed*—GET OUT OF THE SUN."

But before Leah could answer, Amy chimed in with a question of her own. "What is a chakra anyway?"

"Everyone has seven chakras," Caitlyn explained. "They are energy centers in your body. They control different things like psychic abilities and communication skills."

Leah laughed. Then, when she saw that Caitlyn wasn't amused, she said, "You're not actually proposing that we go to such a ridiculous thing, are you?"

"Yes! I want to go."

"Well, you can't expect me to go with you," Leah said.

"Come on! You can write about the experience," Caitlyn said.

"Do you think I write science fiction? Hello, I'm a science writer. I write about *facts.*"

"Actually, Leah, Caitlyn might be right," Amy said. "You could write an article about why people believe in such things."

Leah paused a moment and mulled the idea over. "That's actually kind of a good idea. Maybe I will. But if I go, you have to go, too, Amy."

"Me? Why would I go to something like that?"

"Amy, what else are you going to do with yourself?" Caitlyn said. "There isn't a TV or anything."

"I could read. Hell, I could stare at the ceiling—that would be more constructive than 'improving my psychic abilities.'"

"Come on, Amy, come with us," Leah said with an amused smile.

"Oh, fine. Honestly. The sacrifices I make for my friends."

Amy lay back and relaxed in the warmth of the sun. She was feeling a little better. Exercise and sunshine were much more helpful for fighting unhappiness than cold weather, gray skies, and long hours at the office, but Amy didn't understand why she couldn't stop thinking about Brent. She simply couldn't change the channel of her thoughts—it was like getting stuck with a presidential speech on every single station of her brainwaves. It was all Brent all the time.

"Hey, the water aerobics class is starting," Caitlyn said. "Want to join me?"

"Why not?" Amy said, taking her prescription sunglasses off.

Amy, Caitlyn, and Leah followed the other women, who were grabbing weights from the rows of equipment on the wall. From a distance, they looked like real weights, but up close Amy saw they were made of Styrofoam.

"These don't even weigh a single ounce. How are these supposed to work our arms?" Amy asked.

"Water will create plenty of resistance, don't worry," Leah said.

They got in the water with the others. The instructor was a middle-aged woman. An ethereal blonde, she was thin, with skin as opalescent and pale as skim milk. Her thin, straight hair was nearly white it was so light. Her figure was enviably fit.

"Hello," she said in a feathery light tone, as a serene smile spread across her face. "My name is Kiera. Let's start by jogging in place."

Amy tried to do as she'd been told but found it nearly impossible to jog underwater. She felt as if she were walking on the moon.

Kiera asked them to add underwater bicep curls while they jogged. Leah had been right; Amy could feel her arms working in no time at all.

Kiera then told them to put the "weights" under their armpits and curl their knees up to their chests so they were on their backs just below the surface of the water. "Then extend your legs out and pull them back. This is a great exercise for your stomach."

Amy did as she was told, but even using the weights as flotation devices, she couldn't seem to keep her head out of the water. Each time she extended her legs, her head dropped down and she spit and snorted large gulps of water, coughing and hacking, blinded by the waves caused by her thrashing body. She was far too busy trying to avoid drowning to actually get much of a workout. They finally moved on to more jumping and arm exercises. While these were strenuous, at least Amy wasn't facing any immediate threats of death. The class lasted forty-five minutes, and when it was over, Amy's arms felt as though they were ready to fall off.

"I'd better look god damn beautiful at the end of these two weeks," Caitlyn said as they dripped their way over to their towels.

After they showered and dressed, Amy, Caitlyn, and Leah combed and dried their hair and headed to the cafeteria for dinner.

"Broccoli soup and lettuce? What bullshit is this?" Caitlyn demanded. "The price of health is too high, I'm telling you. Let's just die young of cancer. I mean really."

"Look at the bright side; at least we're not at work," Amy said.

"I know, I'm having withdrawal symptoms." Leah cast a casual glance across the dining room to see if a certain guide-slash-nutritionist was around.

"But you worked two hours by the pool."

"I know, but it's like a three-pack-a-day smoker going down to ten cigarettes. I'm having withdrawal symptoms."

After dinner they went to the activities building, a round structure with a thatch roof that was the size of a large living room with approximately twenty folding chairs lined up in rows. Leah and Amy pretended not to notice the pamphlets laid out on the table that everyone had to walk past to sit down, but Caitlyn took one for each of them. Since Leah didn't have anything else to do, she opened the pamphlet and read the biography of Aisling Sullivan, who billed herself as "an exceptionally gifted healer and psychic." Next to her biography, Aisling had a glamour photo shot of herself in which she wore a great deal of make-up and a two-piece dress in a long, flowing fabric over her plump figure.

"Welcome, everyone," Aisling said in a high-pitched, girlish voice. "I'm Aisling Sullivan. I come from a long line of psychics and healers. Tonight, we're going to work on developing our psychic abilities. We all have them, but some of us let our doubts about our abilities get in our way of being able to achieve our full potential. To get our bodies and minds ready, let's begin by clearing any negative thoughts. Close your eyes. Imagine there is a bubble floating in front of you.

Let anything that might distract you go into that bubble. When your bubble is full, push the bubble out of the room outside.

"Imagine golden light filling your throat, your chest, your stomach, your legs, your feet. Imagine that every cell in your body is flooded in golden light. Just let it pour in."

Amy suddenly realized that she desperately needed to use the bathroom. As Aisling went on and on about golden light flooding their every cell, Amy crossed her legs tighter and rued the fact she'd let Caitlyn and Leah talk her into this.

They spent a great deal of time filling their bodies with golden light until at last Aisling told them to open their eyes and choose a partner.

Amy, Caitlyn, and Leah opened their eyes and looked at each other. Caitlyn did not want to partner with a stranger, so she said, "Leah, you and I will be partners," because Leah was sitting closest to her.

Amy scowled at Caitlyn and then looked for someone who wasn't partnered up yet. Her gaze first fell upon a woman with dyed black hair and oversized glasses.

"Do you have a partner?" the woman asked.

"Not unless you'd like to be mine."

"I'd love to. I'm Devin."

"Nice to meet you. I'm Amy."

With the partners now chosen, Aisling said for each pair to pick which partner was going to go first.

"You go first," Caitlyn said.

"Okay," Leah said.

"What I want you to do for this first exercise," Aisling said, "is to have partner number two think of a number between one and ten. Don't let any stray thoughts cloud up your mind, just concentrate on that number. Then, partner number one, focus on reading your partner's mind."

Devin raised her hand. "In a room this small, isn't it possible that we might read the numbers from one of our neighbors' minds instead of our partner's?"

Leah jammed her thumbnails into her palms as hard as she could to keep from falling on the floor with laughter.

"That's an excellent point," Aisling said. "To avoid that, partners, imagine there is a bubble around you and your partner, protecting you. Okay, partner two, when you have your number, give partner one a nod," Aisling said.

Caitlyn nodded. Leah closed her eyes and tried to clear her mind.

"Seven?" she said.

"No."

"Three?"

"No."

"Five?"

"No. Leah, come on, you're not trying."

"I'm trying! I swear I am."

"All right," Aisling said, "let's switch partners. Partner number one, think of a state in the west."

Leah closed her eyes and concentrated on Oregon. Surely Caitlyn would get that right off, psychic abilities or not, since that was where Leah lived.

"California," Caitlyn said.

"No."

"Colorado."

"No."

"Arizona."

"No."

"Wyoming."

"No."

"Are you lying?"

"It's Oregon! Oregon! Where I live. I think we just have to face it. We don't have any psychic abilities."

Caitlyn frowned, taking this as a personal affront.

"Okay," Aisling said. "Let's switch partners again. This time, partner two, think of a fruit."

When Caitlyn was ready, she nodded.

"Papaya," Leah said.

"No."

"Grapefruit."

"No."

"Apple."

"No."

"Banana."

"Yes! Hey! We're getting better."

Leah rolled her eyes. "Yeah."

They did several more exercises, until at last Aisling told them it was time to pop the bubbles encircling the partners. "You need to distance yourself from your partner now because you don't want to be carrying around her energy. Quickly think of five things that differentiate you from your partner, and then imagine that your aura is protected by a strong pink light."

Since Leah hadn't gotten anywhere close to being in Caitlyn's mind, she suspected it would be okay if she skipped the business of detangling herself from Caitlyn's "energy" and "protecting" her "aura" with pink light.

When the seminar was over, the three friends walked across the grounds to their room. "That was fun, wasn't it?" Caitlyn said.

"I've had more fun clipping my toenails," Leah said.

"My partner was really into it. She was breathing all deep; it was kind of creepy," Amy said.

"I should interview her and ask her why she believes in that shit," Leah said.

"Leah, *I* believe in this shit. I think we do all have some psychic abilities. I might sign up to get a reading done." Caitlyn said. She waited a beat and then said, "Okay, tell me it's a waste of money."

"It's a waste of money," Amy said.

"Amy! I would have expected that from Leah, but from you!"

"Come on, Caitlyn, it's crap," Amy said.

"Actually, even though I don't believe in it, I don't think there is anything wrong with it. What I think," Leah said, "is that going to a psychic is like going to a therapist. I think psychics throw out some general stuff, and then they read your reaction to what they say and keep going based on your facial expressions. Like if your eyes get a little bigger and you lean in just a centimeter, she knows you're interested in what she's saying. Then if she says something that's off, you'll frown just a little bit without even knowing you're doing it. Psychics are extremely adept at reading people's emotions. I think that deep inside you, you know if you need to break up with your boyfriend or get a new job or fix whatever is wrong with your life, but you're scared of making the wrong decision. So you go to a psychic or a therapist and they act as a sounding board, but ultimately you're figuring out for yourself what changes you need to make."

Amy wished she believed in psychics. She would love to have someone tell her what to do about Eric and the wedding and her life.

In the cottage, Amy, Caitlyn, and Leah got ready for bed, orbiting each other in the bathroom as they brushed their teeth and washed their faces just as they did when they'd been in college.

Amy climbed into bed. Leah sat on the edge of her own bed, appraising her friend.

"Amy, are you stressed out about wedding plans or something? You're not acting like yourself."

"No, of course not. What could be wrong? I'm in Mexico with my two best friends."

"Amy," Caitlyn said. "We're your best friends. We've known

you for fourteen years. Don't pull that everything's-perfect shit with us."

"Just give me a few more days to relax and unwind. I'll be fine."

Amy knew that Caitlyn and Leah didn't believe her, but they let the matter drop, at least for now.

Chapter 8

Day Three

Amy woke first as usual, and this morning, thanks to having the forethought to leave the bathroom light on, she managed not to topple over any furniture and batter her nose into any walls as she moved around the room getting her clothes and going to the bathroom to change. When she was dressed, she carefully folded her pajamas and put them back into her suitcase.

When Caitlyn awoke, she jumped out of bed with uncharacteristic enthusiasm. "I have major news!" she said in a whisper to avoid waking Leah.

"I'm listening."

"Four cute guys came in last night! They're on some major league soccer team and—Oh. My. God—they have the *best* bodies. You wouldn't believe it."

"How do you know they're here? You just woke up."

"I couldn't sleep last night, so I went to go swim and there they were! Geoff is the one I want. He is *so* sexy. They play for some team in Arizona."

Caitlyn's excited whispers roused Leah, who flicked the light on, illuminating the room much better than the faded light from the bathroom. Now that the room was lit up, Amy could see that it looked as if it had been hit by a tropical storm during the night—Hurricane Caitlyn.

"Caitlyn, how did you manage to turn the room into such a complete and utter disaster in a single day?"

"I had to find something that turned out to be on the bottom of my suitcase."

"Okay, but you couldn't put your other stuff back?"

"Amy," Caitlyn whined, "come on. We're on vacation. You were the one who said we should just enjoy ourselves. Don't you want to hear about the guys?"

"What guys?" Leah asked groggily.

"Of course I do," Amy said. "Let's talk about it over breakfast."

As Caitlyn chatted happily away about her swim with the soccer players, Leah kept glancing at her sports watch, counting off the minutes until it was time to meet at the edge of the spa grounds and head out for a hike.

"They are only here for a few days," Caitlyn said, looking around the dining room. "So I have to act fast. I don't see them. I doubt they are going on the hike this morning. One of them hurt his knee or something. They're just here to relax."

At last it was time for Amy, Caitlyn, and Leah to meet Jim, who was standing with two older female guests. One of the women had curly steel grey hair like an S.O.S pad; the other had long white hair parted down the middle.

At the sight of Jim, Leah's pulse raced. It had been a long time since Leah had been so attracted to a man that the sight of him made her bodily functions go haywire.

At nine-thirty, Jim got the hike under way. As Leah inhaled the fresh air and admired the beauty of the mountains, the trees, and the grass swaying in the fields, she realized that even though she loved to go hiking, she never got out and did it anymore. She'd spent hours and hours outside as a child, but these days she never strayed very far from her computer or her desk.

The farther they walked, the more dense the forest became. It was so thick almost no sunlight could get through.

"How on earth do you know where you're going?" Leah asked Jim. "How is it that you manage not to get lost?"

"See those little green marks?" He pointed to a rock ahead of them that had a neon green stripe of paint on it.

"I do now. You'd have to be walking on top of it to see it."

"Yeah, well, you get to know your way around after a while."

As they walked, Leah strained to make out the green marks. Sometimes they were shaped like an arrow, and other times they seemed more like generalized slashes that merely let hikers know they were going the right way.

"How's your trip been so far?" he asked.

"It's been fun. Different. Last night we went to this seminar on how to improve your psychic abilities." She told him about the guessing game she and Caitlyn had played the night before. "I don't think I can quit my day job to become a psychic anytime soon.

He chuckled.

At that moment, Caitlyn charged up beside them. "Good morning!"

Without breaking his stride, Jim turned and looked at her with a smile. "Good morning, Caitlyn."

"So I was wondering, does the spa have any kind of policy against staff dating guests?"

He laughed. "Why? Are you looking for some guy to turn into your own personal cabana boy for a couple of weeks of meaningless sex?"

"Not some guy. You. And it would only *start out* as meaningless sex."

He smiled. "Sounds like fun but I don't do meaningless. I'm a serious kind of guy."

"You can't blame a girl for trying." Caitlyn smiled, but a flush of humiliation washed through her.

Gay. He was so gay. Normally she was better at figuring these things out. He was a tricky one.

Well, gay or not, it didn't mean she didn't rejoice when they hit a steep patch and she got to watch his ass climb the mountain in front of her, his muscular calves flexing with every step. "It's okay," Caitlyn continued. "There are some soccer players here. Leah and I can have some fun with them." Leah flashed her a look.

"I have something good to show you all today," Jim said, addressing the entire group.

"What?" Leah asked.

"It's a surprise."

They walked for about ten more minutes before the trees cleared and they could see what Jim had been talking about: a waterfall. Steam billowed above it like floating lace from the underground hot spring beneath it.

"Wow. I definitely need to get a picture of this," Amy said, rooting through her day bag for her camera.

"Be sure a human is in it, Amy, I'm serious," Caitlyn said.

"Fine, fine. Take one of me."

Amy handed the camera to Caitlyn and stood in front of the waterfall smiling, her hands on the waist of her Eddie Bauer twill walking shorts.

"I'll get a group shot," Jim said. Leah, Amy, and Caitlyn posed as Jim snapped a few pictures. After they spent a few minutes taking pictures and marveling at the beautiful vistas, they followed Jim through the last stretch of woods to the spa. Just before everyone went their separate ways, Leah turned to say goodbye to Jim and found herself inexplicably nervous.

"Thanks, Jim," she managed.

"Have a great day. See you tomorrow."

She smiled. Watching him go, she felt like a popped balloon—everything that hadd been keeping her floating on air disappeared into the ether.

Caitlyn flung herself across her bed. "I'm *famished.*"

Amy sat on the edge of her bed and took her hiking boots off. "Me, too."

"Sorry, guys, but lunch doesn't start for another hour."

"We should hit a yoga class," Amy said.

"*More* exercise?" Caitlyn said.

"It'll get our minds off food."

Leah shrugged.

With a groan to let Amy know she wasn't happy about it, Caitlyn grudgingly agreed to join them, and they changed into tank tops and yoga pants and made their way to the building where the yoga classes were held.

They slipped their shoes off as a handwritten sign asked them to before entering the building. Inside, they grabbed mats from the corner and rolled them out, each finding a space on the wood floor. The room had lots of windows, and the open door let in a gentle breeze.

Their instructor was the same woman who taught the water aerobics class. "I see some new faces here today. Has everyone done some yoga before?"

Everyone nodded.

"All right. Let's begin by doing some breathing exercises. Lie on your back." Kiera lay down and her students did the same. "Inhale deeply. Exhale until your lungs are completely empty. Inhale, exhale, inhale, exhale. Wonderful. Now spread your legs and reveal your genitals to the world."

Amy gulped in surprise. The sound, along with the unusual instruction, made Leah start laughing. Leah's laughter infected Amy, and the two of them struggled not to laugh out loud; fighting to keep it in made them vibrate with restrained giggles.

"Relax your body and your mind. Just concentrate on breathing in and breathing out," Kiera said. "Block out all thoughts of past regrets and future worries. Don't think about how things are going back at the office. Don't worry about bills you have to pay. Just think about today, about right now. When you worry about things you can't control, like the past or the future, you stress yourself out for no reason. Buddhists call it our monkey mind. Internal chaos. You can control anxiety and worry. It doesn't control you. You need to let go of the worries and focus on living in the moment. When you eat, be sure to savor every bite. When you do your laundry, do the laundry the best that you can. When you make love, really be present in body and mind; don't be worrying about getting the kids to bed or what your stomach looks like or whose turn it is to do the dishes. Right now, feel that gentle breeze. Inhale the fresh air. And exhale. Inhale. Exhale . . ."

Surely, Amy thought, they'd done enough breathing. When did they get to the good stuff, the stuff that would make her lean and strong and stretchy?

"Yoga comes from the Sanskrit word *yug* which means 'to yoke or bind,'" Kiera continued. "It's the experience of connection and reconnection. It's the union of mind and body. In our daily lives we are pulled in many directions at once. When we're talking to friends, we're really thinking about what we're going to make for dinner, and when we're making dinner we're thinking about what we have to get done at work the next day. When we're at work, we're wondering how our friends are doing. We live our lives only partially there, only somewhat present. Yoga makes us sensitive to the feelings that arise within us, both physical and emotional."

"So if we practice yoga, we'll no longer get stressed out and sad? We'll be miraculously cured of all our problems?" Amy said.

"You will never be 'cured.' You will still have days when your body is sore and tired. You will still have days when you feel irritable and sad. Life is a journey, a process. The goals you seek of patience, health, and happiness are moving targets. You can't focus on attaining happiness but on being happy with the process of working toward happiness.

"Yoga is a way of life. It teaches that joy is within you; you just need to look for it. I don't mean that you should expect yourself to feel good and happy all the time, but happiness isn't something that comes to you externally, not true happiness."

"True happiness? Is that like nirvana or something?"

"There are different kinds of happiness. *Sukha* is fleeting pleasure. It's the happiness we feel when we're in our comfort zone. That happiness disappears when things don't go our way. The thing about fleeting happiness is that it depends on external forces, and therefore its corollary—pain and unhappiness—is inevitable."

Amy thought about how intensely, insanely happy she'd been when she and Eric first met. Maybe the lows she was feeling now were unavoidable—there was no way she could sustain the happiness of first meeting and falling in love with him forever. She had been high on love and excitement and infatuation, and now she was crashing.

"The next stage is *santasha*, contentment," Kiera continued. "It's about being okay with what you have and not always striving for what's out of reach."

Amy could understand not always thinking about getting a bigger house or nicer car, but when it came to work, Amy simply couldn't imagine not always striving for the next promotion or the next raise or the next big deal.

"*Midata* is spiritual happiness. It comes from deep within us and gives us the ability to see beauty all around us, to feel grateful for the smallest bounty. When you can feel grateful for the small things in life, happiness will be yours. All right, class, roll to your sides."

Good. Action. They were finally getting somewhere.

They began a set of Sun Salutations, a series of moves that brought their arms overhead, then their hands to the floor with heads to their knees, then into a lunge, then into cobra, then to downward dog, back to a lunge and back to a straight-leg stretch before finishing with their hands in a prayer position in front of their hearts.

At the end of the hour, Kiera asked everyone to sit in lotus position. "Let's just clear our minds and focus on our breathing."

Amy closed her eyes. She exhaled and tried to push all thoughts out of her head. *I wonder how long we're going to do this for. It's really kind of boring. Clear head, clear head, don't think. I wonder what's for lunch. I'm starving. Oh, God, I think I brought my sports watch in my bag. What if the alarm goes off while we're all meditating and I ruin everyone's Zen moment. Clear head, don't worry about this right now. Why is it so difficult to stop the endless chatter in my . . . oh, my goodness, did I send off my credit card bill? I don't think I did. Shit! They're going to charge me that exorbitant late fee, those bastards. When is this stinking class going to end?*

"Breathe in love and breathe out selfishness and worry. Be grateful for what you have and don't worry about what you don't have. *Namaste,*" Kiera said, using the Sanskrit word that meant *I bow to the divine within you* as she bowed with her palms touching in front of her heart.

Caitlyn, Amy, and Leah rolled up their mats and walked to lunch. "You know, I don't really see the point of meditation," Amy said. "It's not like it helps you relax or anything. In fact, it's a very stressful thing to do."

In the dining room, Caitlyn looked around for Geoff and the other soccer players, but she didn't see them. She was beginning to wonder if her night-time, pool-side conversation with them had been a mirage—she'd been so ravenous for male attention her sex-starved mind conjured them.

As Caitlyn scoped for men, Amy tried to do as Kiera had instructed and breathe in love and breathe out her own selfishness and worries. She let people cut in front of her in line. She smiled at everyone. And she did feel better. If this was the secret to being a happy human being, it was going to be a snap.

Then an older woman she'd let cut in line in front of her

stopped to ask the server a question. Amy exhaled. She was starving.

"What's this made of?" the woman asked. "There's no dairy in this, is there? I'm lactose intolerant. You wouldn't believe what dairy does to me."

The server was Mexican and didn't speak much English, so their conversation took much longer than it otherwise would have. With every second that passed, Amy grew more irritated. What had she been thinking letting this lady cut in front of her?

Ooh, shut up, shut up, shut up. I just want to kick you! My God, woman, eat it or don't eat it! I'm starving!

As soon as the woman finally moved along, the intense feeling of irritation passed. Amy exhaled, and once again she attempted to work on achieving inner harmony and peace with the universe.

Today's menu featured marinated tofu. Amy wasn't a fan of tofu, but if she didn't get some protein into her, she was going to pass out, so she not only took a serving, she asked for extra. She also had cucumber salad and a vegetable medley of zucchini and peppers and kidney beans.

"This is pretty good," Leah said as she took a bite of tofu. "I wish I had somebody else cooking me healthy meals all the time. I don't mind eating well; it just takes so much more time to prepare than junk food."

"Wouldn't that be great if we could all have our own private chef? I could be a rich person really easily," Caitlyn said.

"Ooh, me, too," Leah said. "Speaking of guys with money, how's your dad?"

"He's good," Amy took off her prescription sunglasses and exchanged them with her regular glasses.

"Has he settled down yet?"

"Yeah right."

"Still a new blonde every week?"

Amy nodded. Ever since he and her mother had divorced, Amy's father had gone through one woman after the other.

They never lasted in his life for more than a few months. Each woman he brought into their lives looked as though she would have been comfortable flitting about Hugh Hefner. They were all technically sexy and pretty, but they were so similar it was hard to tell them apart. It was like the difference between eating at McDonald's and a gourmet restaurant—at McDonald's you could get the exact same thing every time, but the meal was rarely memorable.

Occasionally her father would introduce his girlfriends to Amy, but she had quickly learned not to bother remembering their names. She could see how hopeful these women were. Part of her wanted to warn them that their expiration date was coming up soon, but the other part of her hated them just a little for being so willing to be unremarkable and unoriginal. They were all stereotypes without personality, as interchangeable as new batteries replacing the old. If these women dressed and acted like bimbos, how could they expect to be treated like anything else?

Caitlyn looked at her watch and announced, "Well, ladies, it's time for my facial. And then, boys, watch out!"

"We'll meet you by the pool," Amy said.

Caitlyn wandered down the path to the building where the massages and facials were given. The young woman who gave the facials was tall and thin and wore a white lab coat. Her hair was short and slicked back like Trinity from *The Matrix*.

"Hello, my name is Manuela," the woman said.

"I'm Caitlyn."

"What treatment can I give you today?"

"I'd like the deep pore facial."

"Ah, yes," Manuela said, examining Caitlyn's skin closely, with a *tsk-tsk* sort of facial expression.

Manuela began by having Caitlyn take off her shirt and wrap a towel around her chest so that her bra was covered but her arms and shoulders were completely bare. She gestured for Caitlyn to sit in what looked like a dentist's chair.

While Manuela prepared some things in the sink, Caitlyn looked around the room. The exposed brick wall held an enormous wood-framed mirror, and there were two wood dressers with hand-carved flowers decorating them.

Manuela began by washing Caitlyn's face. Next she scrubbed it clean with a sandy-textured facial scrub. Caitlyn smiled, eased a little deeper into her chair, and relaxed. To think that here she was in balmy, sunny Mexico—"Oww!" Caitlyn's eyes snapped open. "Oww!" she cried again as Manuela jabbed at her skin to force the blackheads and oils out.

So much for relaxing. Caitlyn gritted her teeth and endured the pain in the name of beauty. After Manuela attacked Caitlyn's nose, she showed Caitlyn the tissue full of nose grease. It was disgusting, no doubt, but did her facial expert need to shame her in this manner? Caitlyn already knew she had cavernous pores. She washed her face twice a day, she swore she did! She had oily skin—it wasn't her fault!

When the torturous part of the facial was over, Manuela applied a mask over Caitlyn's face and massaged her scalp, neck, and shoulders. This was more like it. Caitlyn fell into a relaxation so deep and pleasurable she felt hypnotized.

After Manuela washed off the face mask, she rubbed some sort of goopy stuff softly into Caitlyn's skin and told her she was done.

Caitlyn went to the pool to find Amy reading her novel.

"Where's Leah?" Caitlyn asked.

"She's doing some research on the Internet," Amy said.

Caitlyn laid her towel down next to Amy and opened her notebook. The blank page stared tauntingly up at her. She looked around pensively. She often thought the biggest part of the writing process involved staring out the window dreamily or puttering around the house in a thoughtful daze. She tried to brainstorm and free-write, shutting off her internal editor, but every word and phrase that came out of her was complete crap.

She couldn't say she wasn't grateful when she saw Leah

walking down the path toward them, giving her an excuse to put away her pathetic metaphors and random ideas. When Leah got closer Caitlyn could see the haggard expression on her face.

"What's wrong?" Amy asked.

Leah collapsed on the chaise lounge on the other side of Amy and covered her eyes with her arm. "Dial-up Internet access makes me want to kill myself. *If* you can even get on-line—and that's a big if—it times out on you half-way through whatever e-mail to your boss you are trying to compose, so you have to play Internet roulette and see if you can get back on and do the whole thing all over again. It was so frustrating I didn't even bother doing any research. I miss my lovely cable access modem."

"You shouldn't be working anyway," Amy said.

Leah didn't want to admit that she had an ulterior motive for working—it helped her keep her mind off Jim. If Amy and Caitlyn—*especially* Caitlyn—knew just how attracted she was to him, they would badger her to put the moves on him. He would reject her and she would be devastated. Possibly, she'd never recover and she'd die a spinster. Or maybe by some miracle, he wouldn't reject her and they'd have two weeks of fabulous sex. Then she'd go home and no guy she would ever meet would compare to Jim, and she would die a spinster. There was no possible way things could work out, so it was best just to quietly admire him from afar.

"I know something that might cheer you up," Amy said.

"I doubt it. What?"

"It's time for dinner."

Leah dropped her arm from over her eyes. "Actually, that does make me feel a little better."

They walked up the path that led to the dining hall. All the paths had been paved with rocks that looked pretty but were uneven, thereby assuring the maximum threat for constant tripping and perpetual injury.

"Ugh. Soup again. I feel like a refugee." Amy ladled herself some of the black bean soup and served herself yet another salad that tasted like hay.

They sat at a table in the corner, and Amy poked at the green leafy lettuce leaves on her plate. "I'm craving chocolate like crazy. It doesn't make any sense. I never eat chocolate or any kind of sweets when I'm at home. I never crave chocolate, and now I'm having elaborate fantasies about it. There is something about the deprivation of eating light meals of lentil loaf that's driving me to it. Wouldn't a slice of chocolate cake be nice right now? Moist and light with rich, creamy frosting . . ."

"Stop it. I haven't had any cravings this week, and normally M&Ms make up about fifty percent of my diet," Caitlyn said. "They're peanut M&Ms," Caitlyn added hastily, as if that made them as nutritious as broccoli.

"You know what else I would kill for right now? A margarita. Wouldn't a margarita on the rocks with salt be a slice of heaven?" Amy said. "With chips and salsa." Amy nearly licked her lips at the thought of it.

"You know," Caitlyn said, "it's really too bad that Jim is gay."

Leah skewered her eyebrows. "Jim is not gay."

"He *so* is."

"You think any guy who doesn't fall for you has to be gay?" Leah said.

Caitlyn's eyes grew wide. "Oh, my God, you have a crush on him, don't you?"

"Don't be ridiculous."

"You do."

"I don't. I'm serious. I just know he's not gay. You're only trying to convince yourself that he's gay to assuage your bruised ego. Why is it so important to you that every guy on the planet finds you attractive?"

Amy watched Caitlyn and Leah bickering as she ate the

last bite of her dinner. She pretended she was eating nachos dripping with melted cheese and covered in sour cream, washing it all down with a margarita on the rocks.

It wasn't that she was hungry. Though she wasn't eating lots of calories, what she was eating was so packed with fiber, protein, and nutrients that her light meals were miraculously satisfying. She craved something else, something to fill a need that went beyond physical hunger.

Eric was like the meals here at the spa—good for her, even tasty at times, but a little too wholesome. Brent on the other hand, was homemade ice cream, deep dish pizza, and filet mignon. He would be terrible for her, but oh so delicious . . .

Amy was thirty-two years old, and she'd spent her whole life being the good girl, eating carrots and celery and skinless chicken. She wanted to start living a life full of steak and ribs and potatoes au gratin.

Amy smiled to herself. She clearly needed to start eating regular food again soon. She could no longer think of anything without using food metaphors. She'd become a woman obsessed.

She'd always watched her weight. Amy had never been fat, but she'd never been thin, either. Her breasts had started developing the summer before fourth grade before any of the other girls in her class. To hide them, she'd worn clothes that were several sizes too big for her. In junior high and high school, she'd wanted to go unnoticed. The girls who were jealous of her would taunt her about being a slut; the last thing she needed was to call attention to her curves and add fuel to the fire. Already, her brother was getting in the news for his petty thievery. It was important to Amy that no one thought she was anything like him. She wanted people to know she was a good girl. It was humiliating having to go through school always hearing the rumors and whispers about her family. Amy did her best to prove people wrong about her.

She'd finally started wearing clothes that actually fit her

when she got to college and Caitlyn declared her wardrobe a hazardous waste site. In Iowa City, no one knew anything about Amy or her family. She was free to let her guard down, at least a little. Caitlyn insisted that Amy had a gorgeous figure and it was time she started loving her body as it was. Amy did manage to become more comfortable with her body, but whenever she put on weight—something she did with distressing ease—she wasn't thrilled about it. The fact of the matter was that Amy liked being in control, and when she gained weight, she didn't feel like she was in control. When she put on weight, the extra pounds were out there for anyone to see. Anyone could see that Amy wasn't perfect.

Amy Harrington had to be perfect.

Chapter 9

Day Four

On the hike the next day, Amy found herself trailing behind the rest of the group. She looked at the gorgeous sapphire ring on her left hand. She was suddenly struck by exactly what it meant. Most of the time, if she caught its reflection in the mirror when she was doing her hair or putting on make-up, she would smile at what a beautiful piece of jewelry it was. But for some reason this morning as she walked, the weight of its symbolism hit her like a bat to the gut. It felt like the time she'd gone to Jamaica—most of the time, Amy didn't give much thought to her skin color, but when she found herself a pale minority on an island of dark-skinned people, she'd suddenly become acutely aware of just how white her skin was. Or like that time she'd found herself staring in the mirror for so long that her features no longer made any sense to her. Unlike those Magic Eye pictures in which an image becomes clear the more you stare at it, everything became more surreal and unfocused the longer she looked at her image. That was how she felt today. She was getting married. She was getting *married*. She'd longed to get married for years. All those lonely weekend nights she'd spent in high school, she'd dreamed about getting away from her trouble-making brother, distant mother, and workaholic father and starting her own family. She would find a loving, attentive husband (which, in Eric, she had), she would be a wonderful, loving mother (at least, she was going to try her best), and, if all went according to plan, she'd have one or two or three happy, healthy kids. The future she'd fantasized about for so long could disappear before her very eyes, and all because she'd rather go to the dentist or clean the grout in her shower than have sex with her fiancé. She had to find a way to get excited about Eric again.

Amy hadn't called Eric since she'd arrived, except for a quick call to let him know she'd gotten there safely. Cell phones didn't work where they were staying, and the international calling cards were a pain to use, but that wasn't the reason she hadn't called. She hadn't called because she felt too guilty about how much she thought about Brent and the things she thought about when she thought of him.

Amy considered talking to Caitlyn and Leah about her feelings. Well, Leah anyway. Amy was pretty sure Caitlyn had never experienced a drop in her sex drive. Leah, on the other hand, might be able to assure her that it was normal. But what if it wasn't normal at all? Then where would she be?

Amy continued marching forward. Her legs were slightly sore from the day before, but it felt good. The hikes were the perfect workout for her leg muscles, but because the majority of the guests were older, the pace wasn't as rigorous as it could have been.

Her roving thoughts brought her back to Brent, but Amy didn't want to be attracted to other men. She wanted to be in love with Eric again. She just needed to change her thinking—attitude was the secret to success.

When Amy had been a little girl, her father taught her that if she was anxious or upset, she should think back to a happy memory. She stared into the distance and did that now, thinking back to when she and Eric had first fallen in love.

They'd met up at the gym when she inadvertently whacked him in the gut with her gym bag. It was perhaps not the most romantic way to meet, but at least it broke the ice. She'd been at the front desk looking for her pass. Weighed down by her enormous gym bag on one shoulder and her large purse on the other, she was flustered as she searched for her wallet. She cleaned her purse out on a regular basis, but somehow on that day her wallet, which contained her membership pass, was not where it was supposed to be. When she finally found it, she flashed her pass, carefully replaced her wallet, and turned abruptly. She hadn't realized there was someone so close behind her in line, and when she turned, her gym bag walloped Eric so hard in the stomach he literally doubled over.

"Oh, my gosh, I'm so sorry," Amy had said. "I'm mortified."

He smiled good-naturedly. "Don't worry about it. I'll be fine."

"You're sure?"

"I'm sure."

Half an hour later they ran into each other when Amy was lying on a bench working with free weights.

"I'll stand over here so in case you drop one of those weights, you won't break my toes," Eric said.

Amy smiled. "Don't make me laugh or I really will drop these."

"Careful, now, that you don't let go of those over your head. You could become the kind of person who spends her day creating art by gluing noodles to construction paper."

Amy chuckled, and she found it impossible to do butterfly presses while laughing, so she set her weights down.

"I really am sorry about knocking into you."

"Don't think anything of it. I'm Eric."

"Amy."

"So what do you do for a living? Are you a street fighter? A boxer of some kind? A bodyguard perhaps?"

"Nothing that exciting, I'm afraid. I'm a financial consultant. Sounds riveting, doesn't it?"

"Don't worry. I know all about boring jobs. I'm a tax attorney."

"Oh, that is even more dull than my job."

"The world needs ditch diggers and tax attorneys as much as it needs stunt men and deep sea divers, right?"

"Absolutely. Well, Eric, it was very nice meeting you, but I've got to get back to work. I have budgets to balance."

"It was nice meeting you, too. Maybe I'll see you around."

Suddenly Amy was always careful to touch up her make-up before she worked out. She didn't see him every time she came to the gym, but over the next few weeks she bumped into him several times. She hadn't been attracted to a man with such ferocious intensity in a long time. It wasn't that he was dashingly handsome. Eric wasn't the kind of guy you'd find posing without his shirt on the cover of a romance novel. He had a trim build and a largish nose and dark hair that was thinning on top. It was his dark eyes and his magnetic smile that pulled her in.

Every time they ran into each other, they would joke around and get to know each other a little better. Amy was trying to work up the courage to ask him out when he asked her first.

For their first date, he drove her up to a pricey restaurant in the mountains. The meal was delicious. The view was spectacular. The conversation clipped along with easy banter and teasing smiles.

First dates were usually harrowing: the "Will he like me? Will he find me attractive?" questions loomed like mushroom clouds. But that wasn't the way Amy felt with Eric. Their connection was immediate. She never felt as though she had to *make* conversation as if conversation were a complex gourmet meal that needed lots of work and careful attention. She never had to pull out lines like "So, seen any good movies lately?" to keep the discussion rolling along.

The next day he sent her an e-mail that said, *I had a great time last night. I still have a smile on my face. When can I see you again?*

She had immediately replied that she'd had a great time, too, and she couldn't wait to see him again.

Their second date was when her suspicions were confirmed: this guy was something special.

He took her gambling in Cripple Creek, an old mining town nestled in the mountains. "My parents are pretty regular visitors up there," Eric explained. "They got this pass for a free stay at a hotel, a free dinner, the works. They can't use it, so they gave it to me."

"I've never gambled before," she told him.

"You can't be serious."

"I am serious. I've never even played poker. I think when I was young I might have played Go Fish for pretzels, but those are the highest stakes I've ever played."

"Well, don't you worry. I'll take care of you."

At first Amy was too scared to play blackjack, which was Eric's game of choice. He gave her all the tips he had on when to hit, when to stand, when to double down. In no time at all, Eric turned his twenty dollars into a hundred and twenty dollars.

"Are you ready to play?" he asked her.

"I'll just lose the money."

"Take some of the money I won. It's free money. Easy come, easy go."

"I'll play, I promise. Just not yet."

After Eric and Amy had a few drinks in them—courtesy of the casino—Amy was finally ready to play. She sat beside Eric, and he gently touched her back just below her neck, sending an erotic charge through her body.

She played at the low-stakes tables, but even so she couldn't believe the terrifying thrill of it. She managed to win twenty bucks, and as far as she was concerned, she'd won the lottery. Twenty dollars or twenty million, it was free money and it was awesome! She was on fire that night. During the week she wore conservative business suits and conservative shoes.

She had a sensible haircut and a sensible job. That night, though, that night she was a risk taker. A daredevil. A woman who was sexier and more daring than her nine-to-five alter ego.

Amy and Eric enjoyed their free meal, which was somehow especially delicious since it was free, along with more free drinks. Afterward, they left the casino and walked along the street outside, which was designed to look as if they were in the Old West. Amy took his hand in hers and impulsively kissed him. After that first kiss, they couldn't keep their hands off each other. They ducked into alleys and behind buildings to make out. Eventually they managed to unglue their lips and wander into another casino, but they found they simply couldn't sit still at the blackjack tables or the slot machines. Their lips and bodies ached for each other.

"Let's find someplace private," Amy whispered in his ear.

Laughing like school kids, they tried to find someplace away from the garish noises and blinking lights and *dingding-ding* chorus of the slot machines and discovered a darkened room meant for private meetings and receptions. Eric lifted her up and set her gently down on a table, then nearly knocked her flat with the force of his kisses. He pushed his way between her legs with his body. Their hands groped urgently, moaning with desire and unmet needs.

Then, abruptly, Amy thought she'd heard a noise and pushed him off her. "What was that?" she asked breathlessly. She felt woozy with lust and longing.

"Nothing. I don't hear anything." He moved his lips to her to kiss her again, but she stopped him.

"Let's go back to the room."

"Yes. Great idea. Let's."

They nearly sprinted back to their hotel room and tore off their clothes and continued their make-out and groping session naked.

Amy hadn't had sex like that since college. She knew that the common denominator wasn't simply the skill of her lovers—though there was that, too—but that she felt utterly and completely comfortable, totally able to just let herself go with Eric.

Everything was like that with him. Everything just worked. She liked his friends and he liked hers. She was comfortable with his family, as he was with hers. They had common interests and got along well . . .

Had she imagined all that lust and love and happiness? Had she conjured her feelings for Eric because she thought it was time to be married and start having kids? Was the romance she'd felt with him as fragile as gossamer—something thin and insubstantial upon closer examination?

Amy had always followed the rules. She went to college right after high school, just like she was supposed to. She didn't take a year or two off to "find herself" or travel the world or be a groupie following a rock band around on tour. She got a good job right out of school, worked on her career through her twenties, and now, right on time, she was getting married. Now it was time to start popping out kids. She'd see them grow up, go to school, and have kids of their own. She'd retire. Then she'd die. And that would be it. Her dull, predictable life.

Several feet in front of Amy, Leah and Jim were walking side by side. "Did you see the moon last night?" he asked.

She nodded. "It was beautiful, all fat and full. I love how you can see so many more stars down here without all the city lights."

"Be careful. Crazy things have been known to happen when there's a full moon."

Leah smiled indulgently at him. "Yeah right, and soon you'll be telling me that Aisling Sullivan really does have psychic powers and that the Easter bunny really exists."

"What, you don't believe that full moons stir up passions? What about all those stories about how there are more emergency room visits due to people doing crazy things when there's a full moon? Also, the moon inspires romance."

"Actually, studies have shown that there are actually fewer hospital admissions on nights when there is a full moon. That myth gets perpetuated by journalists looking for a sensationalistic angle. And the romance thing, well, it's like aphrodisiacs. Any food can have aphrodisiacal effects if you believe it does. It's the placebo effect."

"Wow, you're not a romantic, are you?"

Leah laughed. "Guess not. I'm a pragmatist. All that science training."

"Being a scientist doesn't mean you have to stop believing in magic."

"You believe in magic?" Leah asked, incredulous.

"Of course. How else can you explain this beauty?" Jim gestured to the view of the mountains and forest around them. "All the beautiful, colorful birds. The incredible variety of trees. The steam rising out of the waterfall . . ."

"Actually, that can all very easily be explained by evolution."

"Evolution or not, all this is pretty incredible. How can you explain love? Romantic love, the love of a parent for a child?"

"That actually has an evolutionary basis as well. The thing is—"

"No! Stop. I don't want you to ruin the magic for me. You never believed in Santa Claus as a little a little kid, did you?"

Leah laughed again. "For a few years I did. When I was about four or five, I kept asking my parents and older siblings all these questions. I found the logistics of Santa getting around the world in a single night, arranging all those presents under all those trees, eating all those cookies, really hard to figure out. People would give me different, contradictory answers to my questions. I found it all very suspicious, and my father finally cracked under the pressure and told me the truth but said he'd beat me senseless if I ever spilled the beans to my little brothers."

"You don't believe in fate? Karma? Destiny?"

"No, no, and no."

"Leah, Leah, Leah, what are we going to do with you?"

She shrugged. With every step they took, the closer they came to the spa. Leah didn't want the walk to end. When they got to the spa grounds, Jim said, "I guess I'll see you tonight. There's going to be a campfire. We'll roast soy hot dogs over the fire."

"I wish we were grilling up some steaks, but at least it's a break from soup and salad. I'll see you later."

After lunch, Leah, Caitlyn, and Amy sat outside by the pool. Leah was carefully shielded from the sun in her spot in the shade.

She spent the afternoon furiously writing a draft of her influenza A article in longhand. Whenever thoughts of Jim flickered through her mind, she determinedly pushed them away and tried to focus that much harder. But she couldn't concentrate. She kept thinking about how she'd spent the last few years of her life living like a robot, going through the same routine day after day. She worked and worked and worked. She rarely got out of the house to enjoy nature. She rarely ate anything that didn't get nuked in the microwave first. She consumed the same foods week after week. She did the same workout day after day, riding her treadmill, going in circles like a gerbil trapped in a cage. She needed to make a change. She would definitely agree to go out with that guy Lindsey wanted to set her up with. She would call Russ Evans, recruiter. She was going to join a book club, start going on hikes, and maybe even join some sort of softball league or volleyball team. She would start wearing make-up and get manicures from time to time . . . Leah laughed. Okay, manicures were pushing it. The volleyball team she could handle. Hey, it was a start.

The air was balmy for campfire night at La Bueno Vida. Along with the other guests, Leah, Caitlyn, and Amy sat beside the crackling fire.

Everyone was given soy hot dogs, aka Tofu Pups, and long metal skewers to use to roast the hot dogs over the flames. About fifteen guests sat around the campfire. Leah was trying to attach her Tofu Pup to her skewer when she saw Jim approach. She nearly impaled her hand.

Jim sat down next to her and smiled.

As they roasted their Tofu Pups in the crackling fire, Jim told a ghost story. It involved unhappy ghosts and the undead. All eyes were on him as he talked. Leah stared at him so intently that she didn't realize the stick she was holding was no longer hovering over the flames but had fallen into the fire.

She could tell he was coming to the end of his story. She quickly tried to think of something witty to say when he was done, but the words got caught in her throat, and all she could manage was an odd gurgling noise. Embarrassed, she flinched, and the jerking movement launched her flaming Tofu Pup. It went rocketing through the air into Jim's crotch. The Tofu Pup didn't actually make contact with him, falling instead in the dirt in front of him, but it left a sizzling piece of ash in his lap. Leah went diving for it, swatting at his crotch and knocking Jim over in the process. Leah finally stopped attacking his private parts and backed away. Jim looked at Leah in open-mouthed shock.

"I'm sorry! I don't normally go lunging at men's crotches. It's just that my Tofu Pup went flying and I didn't want you to burst into flames."

Jim eyed the projectile Tofu Pup lying innocently in the dirt. It was now nothing more than a blackened, charred, phallic-shaped meat alternative.

"Well, thanks, I appreciate that."

Leah turned around and saw everyone staring at her. She slunk back to her spot, hunched down as if she could will herself invisible, and burned in her own private hell of shame. "Let's get out of here!" she whispered to Amy and Caitlyn fiercely.

"No way. This is my chance to talk to Geoff. You're not going to mess it up for me," Caitlyn whispered back.

Leah looked over to the four soccer players that Caitlyn had set her sights on.

"I'm going to go talk to them," Caitlyn said as she bounded to her feet.

Leah turned to Amy. "Pretend we're talking about something."

"Okay, sure." Amy laughed.

"What are you laughing at?"

"I thought it would help our conversation seem more authentic."

Leah forced a laugh. "Oh, good one, Amy. Man, you're a hoot."

Amy and Leah pretended to talk until Caitlyn came charging back toward them.

"We're all going to play water volleyball with the guys. Come on, we have to go change into our suits."

"No way Caitlyn, you know how unathletic I am. I hate making an ass out of myself."

"They're leaving tomorrow; you'll never have to see them again."

"I don't think so."

"Come on, Amy, don't be so repressed. Live a little."

The comment stung—because it was true. Maybe Amy's problem was that she was too prim and proper. If she wanted things with Eric to work, she needed to get a little crazy, a little spontaneous. When she was with Brent, she felt crazy and daring. She just needed to bring these feelings home. A game of water volleyball, while terrifying, was a small step in the right direction. Who knew, soon she might be changing her career and becoming a hired assassin or an international spy who raced cars for fun and relaxed by traveling through war zones.

"Fine."

"Yes!"

They returned to their room and changed into their suits. Amy's was navy, and it had two straps that tied around her neck. It supported her large breasts well and revealed no cleavage. It still showed off more of her figure than she wished it did, but unless she dressed head to toe in a body suit, that couldn't be helped. Leah wore a fire red Speedo, and Caitlyn wore a hot pink bikini with a string-bikini top and bottoms the size of a comma. While not as big as Amy's, Caitlyn's breasts were beautiful and she knew it.

By the time the got out to the well-lit pool, the guys were already stringing up the net.

"What's that one guy holding up?" Amy said. Without her glasses on, Amy had to squint.

"That, Amy, is a bottle of tequila," Caitlyn said.

"Are we twenty-three? Shots of tequila? Are you serious?" Amy said.

Caitlyn nodded.

"Amy, Leah, this is Geoff, Lionel, Alan, and Charlie. Guys, this is Amy and Leah. Who's got the volleyball?"

Geoff's thick dark eyebrows accented denim-blue eyes.

Charlie's purposely tousled blond hair was as playful and boyish as his smile. "Lionel here busted his knee a while back, and we were told the natural hot springs would help him get back on the field again, so here we are. You girls ready to play?" Charlie's smile was wildly uninhibited. It was carnal and sexy, and he had I HAVE AN STD written all over him.

Alan's voice was as rich and deep as the dark chocolate color of his skin as he suggested teams. They divided up with Caitlyn, Geoff, and Alan on one team, and the rest of them on the other. Amy hadn't played volleyball in years. "Wait, wait, wait, I don't want to serve first."

"Sorry, girl," Lionel said. His skin was caramel colored, and his lithe frame showed off an enviable six-pack.

How did this happen? Amy swallowed, took a moment to compose herself, then lofted the ball in the air and batted at it with the base of her palm with everything she had. After hitting the net, the ball sprang right back to her.

"You have to do a shot." Charlie raised his arms out, palms up, and gave a shrug. It was an expression that said, *Sorry, I don't make the rules, but watcha gonna do*?

"I was just warming up."

"Sorry, sweetie, you need to do a shot. It you miss, you need to do a shot."

"I'm going to drown by the end of the first game if we play that way."

"Those are the rules, sistah."

With an extravagant role of her eyes, Amy swam to the edge of the pool where Charlie was kind enough to pour her a shot into a plastic cup.

"It's been years since I've done tequila shots," Amy protested, holding the cup near her mouth and smelling that old familiar odor.

Charlie smiled with unconvincing sympathy.

"The last time I did a tequila shot I was with you!" she yelled to Caitlyn, stalling for time.

"You need to live a little, don't ya, then! You shouldn't wait for ten-year reunions to do tequila," Caitlyn shouted back.

Amy downed the drink. "I'm sure *that* will improve my game."

"I'm sure it will."

Amy returned and tried her shot again. It was a pitiful serve but it got the game in action.

After several volleys, Leah spiked the ball hard. Caitlyn dove for it, missed it utterly—it landed on her head—and went headfirst into the water. She came up laughing, raking her hair back with her fingers.

"Good shot." Lionel patted Leah on the back.

"Shot!" Geoff yelled.

Caitlyn had none of the hesitancy Amy had exhibited over being made to take a drink. She just smiled and went to the edge of the pool. Caitlyn paused a moment to make sure that all eyes were on her and then downed the shot to a chorus of claps and whoops.

Geoff threw the ball over the net. It was Charlie's turn to serve.

"I'm serving this thing, so get ready," Charlie said.

Alan sent the ball back easily. It was coming Amy's way, but she just looked at it as if it were a nuclear bomb and stood immobile. She'd read once that if you encountered a bear in the woods, you should just stand still. (Yeah right.) But now with something equally as intimidating coming at her with menacing determination, she took that advice.

Seeing that she wasn't going to go for it, Lionel made a play for it, but it was too late, and the ball hit the water with a splash.

"Loser!" Alan called. "Do a shot."

At first Amy thought they meant her since it was obviously hers to return. Then Geoff called, "Lionel, you wussy man, that was the easiest shot *ever.*"

Lionel took a shot and the game recommenced. Fortunately for Amy, so much time was taken up distributing tequila, there weren't all that many opportunities for her to screw up.

Over the course of the next hour, they'd each done a number of tequila shots, though Amy and Caitlyn had taken the brunt of them because they were shorter than the other players and not as athletic. But even the haze of alcohol couldn't diminish Amy's embarrassment each time she missed a play.

"The important thing is that I'm trying, right?" Amy said hopefully after her latest error.

Amy tried to stay out of the way as much as possible. Even so as the score remained close the entire time, she felt herself filled with hope that her team would win. Sure, she hadn't done anything to help, but it was her team and she wanted victory.

The score crept up so Amy's team had twelve and the other

group had eleven. Then the other team scored, tying the score twelve-twelve.

Geoff lobbed the ball over the net. Lionel sent it over to Leah for a flawless assist, and she spiked it down easily

The score continued to climb steadily. Just when it looked as though one team had the advantage, the other team turned the tide until the score was tied fourteen-fourteen.

Game point.

Amy was at the right front of the net. She knew that Geoff was going to serve it her way since she was the weakest player, and sure enough, she watched the ball come directly her way. For a moment, the world seemed to go into slow motion as she realized it was the perfect height to spike it. But she'd never spiked a ball. She was too short. Some instinct in her took over, and she jumped for it. Using all her strength, she battered the ball down . . . over the net and into the water.

Shouts and cheers went up from Amy's team. She couldn't believe it. She'd actually made a shot!

"Whoo!"

"Awesome!"

"Good shot!"

She jumped and bounced in the water, screaming along with the rest of her team.

Then, abruptly, the cheers stopped, and silence filled the air. It took Amy a few more jumps and screams to notice that every eye was on her chest. She looked down to discover that the tie that kept her bathing suit fastened around her neck had come undone—she'd been bouncing around in the water with her breasts exposed for the world to see. They looked like headlights—their neon whiteness against the tan she'd gotten, her pink nipples erect in the air and her pink-brown aureoles like bull's-eyes on targets.

She quickly attempted to retie her suit, and she shimmied out of the water with her face ducked down like a prisoner hiding from news cameras as he was being taken into custody. She raced back to the cottage, her bare feet tripping through the ticklish grass.

"Amy! Amy!" Leah called, rushing out of the water after her.

Amy didn't respond. Instead she ran to the door of the cottage, where she realized she didn't have the keys. This new obstacle seemed too overwhelming to bear.

Leah caught up to her then, slightly breathless.

"Fuck! Leah, I forgot the keys. Please go back and get them for me. *Please.*"

"I will. Are you okay?"

"No. I'm very busy dying of humiliation and trying to think of a way to kill myself, thank you for asking."

"Amy, it's no big deal. It's dark out, we've been drinking . . . Anyway, they're just breasts."

Amy's eyes filled with tears. "No, Leah, they're not just breasts. They're *my* breasts, and I just exposed them to four strange men and my two best friends."

Just then Caitlyn caught up to them, slightly out of breath from running to catch up.

"Please tell me you have the keys."

Caitlyn nodded and started unlocking the door. "Amy, are you okay?"

"No! Of course I'm not okay. I'm a laughingstock."

"No one is laughing at you."

"I distinctly heard laughter!"

"Well, but . . . it wasn't *at* you. You know how people laugh in an awkward situation."

Caitlyn got the door unlocked, and Amy rushed in, pulling the covers from her bed and diving under them, hiding her entire body including her head. "I'm not leaving here until they leave. Maybe not even then. Maybe never!"

Caitlyn and Leah tried to console her, but Amy just moaned. "And then I had to run off crying. They must think I'm the biggest geek in the world. I hate to think of what they're saying about me."

"The only thing anyone said was that you have beautiful breasts," Caitlyn said. "Well, actually, the exact phrasing was more like, 'Damn, that girl has got some awesome titties on her.' That was Alan, I think, and Charlie said they were real beauts and asked if they were real."

Amy pulled the covers down and looked skeptically at Caitlyn for a long moment, her eyebrows furrowed. "They said that?"

Caitlyn nodded.

"He thought they looked good enough to be fake?"

Caitlyn nodded again.

Amy looked at the ceiling and considered this. "Huh." She thought another moment. "I mean, Eric has always told me they were the most beautiful he's ever seen, but he has to say that because he's going to be my husband."

"Well, we saw them, too," Leah said. "They're really nice."

"Flawless."

Amy again said nothing. "I can't believe I just performed a topless water ballet! Fuck!" She took her pillow and put it over her head.

"Seriously, Amy, are you going to be okay?" Leah asked, trying to suppress a laugh.

"I might be. But I'm going to need to get a lot more drunk."

Caitlyn pulled what remained of the bottle of tequila out from behind her back. "You, my friend, are in luck."

"Caitlyn to the rescue," Amy said, sitting up. She took the bottle from Caitlyn and drank a long gulp straight from the bottle. After a few more shots of tequila, the night's events did seem rather amusing. The three of them roared with laughter until at last Amy stopped flinching every time she thought about flashing perfect strangers and gratefully passed out across her bed.

It felt just like college again.

Chapter 10

Day Four—later that night

When Amy and Leah were finally asleep, Caitlyn slipped out of bed and quietly dressed. She'd promised Geoff she would meet him.

She'd never needed as much sleep as Leah or Amy. What she needed was stimulus. Maybe it was from being moved around so much as a kid from house to house, stepfather to stepfather. Always living on the edge got Caitlyn addicted to change and excitement.

It was no easy task to scurry across the cobblestone paths in heels and a flouncy skirt, but it had taken longer for Leah and Amy to fall asleep than she had anticipated. It was a particularly dangerous feat after several shots of tequila.

"Ah! Shit!" Caitlyn picked herself up off the stone walk and inspected the knee she'd fallen on. She'd scraped it pretty badly. "Ouch. Damn." She took off her shoes and walked more carefully the rest of the way.

She rapped lightly on Geoff's door.

He opened the door looking amused. "What took you so long?"

"Sorry. They took forever to fall asleep."

"Your friend okay?"

"She'll be fine. She's kind of shy."

"Guess so. You look gorgeous." His eyes scanned her body.

"Hey, you." Charlie came up from behind Geoff, carrying another bottle of tequila.

"Hey, Charlie."

"We'll grab Alan and Lionel and take off." Geoff took her hand, and they went to the cottage next door where Alan and Lionel were staying.

"Man, I thought you two had forgotten about us." Lionel had changed into jeans and a loose white cotton shirt that looked great against his dark skin.

Caitlyn tripped again on the cobblestones and careened into Geoff. "Sorry. My fault."

"You okay?" Geoff asked.

"No. Some guys I know poured too many shots of tequila down my throat tonight. I'm a little tipsy."

"That's a shame. We'll fix that," Charlie said, holding up the tequila.

"Oh, yeah? How're you gonna do that?"

"We'll get you *wasted.*"

The soccer players had rented a car for the few days they were in Mexico, and Caitlyn squeezed into the front seat next to Geoff and Charlie, who was driving.

"Here. Do a shot. Pass it around." Charlie handed Caitlyn the bottle.

"I'm good. Here, Geoff."

"No, no. House rules. You have to do a shot," Charlie said.

"Absolutely. No sober people allowed," Alan agreed.

"As long as you boys promise to hold my hair back when I puke."

"Of course," Geoff promised.

Caitlyn took a slug from the bottle. It burned going down her throat. Her expression tightened; she exhaled. When she recovered, she passed the bottle to Geoff. "Okay, your turn."

"None of your friends wanted to come?" Charlie asked.

"Amy's engaged, and Leah has the hots for this guy. Sorry,

boys. Hey, couldn't we get thrown into a Mexican prison for the next thirty years for drinking and driving?" Caitlyn asked.

"Probably. I don't know the laws," Geoff said.

"Very reassuring. Thanks."

By the time they got to the bar, Caitlyn was officially drunk. Only certain facts could make their way through the hazy barrier of tequila. The first detail was that the bar was nearly empty, and the people who were there were all Mexican and all male. The second detail to penetrate her brain was that the room seemed particularly run-down—it made the "dive" bars back home look like hip clubs. The place had dubious hygienic standards—the wood floors that looked as if they hadn't been washed in years, and chairs that appeared to have been found in salvage yards and then beaten with a bat. The third fact was that she was being handed a Dos Equis with a lime in it, which she took automatically, though in the back of her tequila-soaked mind she was thinking, *This may not be such a good idea.* The fourth was that Geoff offered her a barstool. She looked at it and wondered if she had enough balance left in her not to fall off. The fifth was that Geoff was squeezing her ass and kissing her neck. They hadn't even kissed yet. Wasn't that supposed to come first?

"I really like you, Caitlyn," he whispered as he nibbled on her ear.

"You barely know me."

"You're fun, you're smart, you're gorgeous. What's not to like?"

Caitlyn felt a little queasy. The world was spinning.

She didn't know how much time had passed, but suddenly she was being urged off the barstool and into another room. She stumbled slightly in her heels, but Geoff had her arm and caught her before she fell.

Pool table. Dilapidated walls. Neon signs advertising beer. Door practically falling off its hinges.

"You sit here, okay?" Geoff guided her onto a chair next

to a small table. She nodded and watched blurrily as the four of them played pool. The five of them had the room to themselves.

Man, she was tired. She'd just rest her eyes for a moment . . .

"Wake up."

"Hmm?" Caitlyn lifted her head from the table where it had been resting on her arm and looked at Geoff.

"How are you doing?"

"I'm fine." Caitlyn felt hazy.

"I asked the guys for a little privacy."

Caitlyn squinted at him. He bent down and gave her a kiss. He put his hands around her. His head was at breast height, and he unbuttoned the top few buttons of her blouse and suckled her breast. Caitlyn couldn't feel much. She was too anesthetized with tequila.

"Come here." Geoff extended his hand. She took it and stood, wobbling for a moment before steadying herself.

Geoff pulled her body into his, and they began swaying to music that didn't exist. Caitlyn looked around the room. They were alone. All the doors were closed.

"Where is everybody?"

"They're guarding the door." He kissed her again. Her arms were wrapped around him more for balance than for romance. Her limbs had a rag-doll limpness to them.

When Geoff tried to pull her shirt off she stopped him.

"What's wrong?"

What was wrong? Wasn't this what she wanted? "Let's just kiss."

Geoff kissed and sucked her neck.

"Not so hard," Caitlyn said. She looked up and saw a neon sign above a door. It was written in both Spanish and English. It took her a moment to focus her eyes on the English.

This is not an exit.

Chapter 11

Day Five

"Amy, there's a phone call for you."

Sleepily, Amy rose from bed. It was still dark out. She had slept in yoga pants and a tank top, so she just slipped on sandals and a sweatshirt and walked up the rocky path to the office where the pay phone was.

"Hello?" Her voice was husky.

"How could you?" Eric's voice cracked with pain.

"How could I what?"

"Did you sleep with him? Did you flirt over drinks? Did you schedule that rain check?"

The e-mails. Eric had found her e-mails from Brent on her computer. What an idiot she'd been. She always synced her BlackBerry with her work computer to her home computer. Of course he'd found them.

"Eric, nothing happened."

"But you wanted it to happen, didn't you?"

"Honey, nothing happened," she repeated stupidly.

"I trusted you. How could you do this? I thought you loved me."

"I do love you. I do."

"I don't believe you. I can't trust you anymore. I can't marry a woman I don't trust."

"No, Eric, you don't understand."

"Goodbye, Amy."

Amy bolted awake, sitting up in the darkened room. Her heart pummeled against her rib cage. As she fought to regain her breath, she picked up her watch from the bedside table. It was seven in the morning. She was in Mexico with her girlfriends. It had just been a dream.

Unless . . . It couldn't have been a premonition, could it?

How could she have forgotten to delete those flirty e-mails with Brent? What exactly had she said in them?

If Eric found them, he'd be devastated. He'd feel betrayed. She didn't want to hurt him. She couldn't bear the thought of losing Eric.

"Amy, you okay? You were talking in your sleep," Leah said in a whisper. She was sitting in the entryway to the bathroom. She'd woken early and was doing research using the bathroom light.

"What? Oh, yeah, I'm fine. It was just a dream."

Caitlyn awakened with a moan. "Whataya guys talking about?"

"Nothing."

Caitlyn got out of bed and went to her suitcase and rooted through her heap of clothes. It was amazing how much more stuff it seemed she had now that they were here in Mexico. It was as if her suitcase had exploded.

As they got dressed, Amy thanked Caitlyn for coming back to the room with her the night before. "I know how much you wanted to hang out with Geoff."

"Oh, don't worry. After you went to bed I went back out there. Geoff and I made out for most of the night. They rented a car so we were able to blow this place and go into town to this dumpy bar. Geoff and I had a beer and then went to the back room and smooched on this pool table."

"You did! And how was it?"

Caitlyn paused a moment to consider. "Well, I think he

was pissed at me for not doing more than kissing, but I was too drunk for sex, which is his own damn fault. I guess he was really kind of an asshole now that I think about it."

Leah looked at her watch. In only half an hour, it would be time to meet Jim for the hike. She didn't want to tell Caitlyn and Amy just how much she'd been thinking about Jim. Of course, her fantasies could all be logically explained—she just didn't want Caitlyn and Amy to read more into them than they should.

"Are you going to see Geoff again today?" Amy asked.

"They left first thing this morning to catch their flight. We said our goodbyes last night."

Amy looked at her watch. "It's time to go meet for the hike."

Leah tried to look as though she wasn't acutely aware of what time it was.

"When are you going to make your move?" Caitlyn said to her.

"What do you mean?"

"I mean, we're only here for so long. If you're going to get into Jim's pants, you have to act fast."

"I have no intention of 'getting into Jim's pants.' Anyway, I thought you thought he was gay."

"He might be. He might just have bad taste. No offense."

Leah threw Caitlyn a look.

"Just in case he *is* straight," Caitlyn said, "you have to go for him."

"What exactly do you propose I do?"

"You need to flirt with him. You can't keep talking to him about boring shit like the weather and the plants."

"Caitlyn, that happens to be the sort of 'shit' that both Jim and I are interested in. It's kind of what got us talking in the first place. Anyway, if things are supposed to happen between us, they'll happen naturally."

"What do you mean 'they'll happen naturally'?"

"The two major relationships of my life both evolved naturally. With both David and Chuck, I had common interests. We got to talking and things went from there."

"I'm not saying it doesn't happen ever, but it can't hurt to help things along."

"Caitlyn, please. Don't do something that's going to embarrass me. I don't need another Lance Woodward incident."

Caitlyn giggled. When she, Leah, and Amy had been college freshmen in the dorms, Leah had made the mistake of admitting to them that there was a guy in her biology class she had a crush on. One night, they'd been sitting in Amy and Leah's dorm room eating pizza and drinking screwdrivers made from vodka Amy had stolen from her father's liquor cabinet. Caitlyn dialed campus information and asked for Lance Woodward's room. Leah had looked up from where she sat and whisper-shouted, "Hey! What are you doing?"

Caitlyn determinedly avoided meeting Leah's gaze. "Yes, please connect me."

Amy just smiled and looked from Caitlyn to Leah, who was looking at Caitlyn with an open mouth and wide eyes.

"Lance. Hi. What are you up to? Me? I'm a friend of a friend. Because she likes you. A lot. She wants to know some things. My name? Uh, call me Melissa. I was calling to ask you a few questions on behalf of my friend. Well, such as, are you dating anyone? No? Why not? Good answer." Caitlyn paused a moment as she considered what her next question should be. "Hang on." Without covering up the mouthpiece, she said, "Leah, what else do you want to know?"

Leah was apoplectic. Caitlyn immediately realized what she'd done. She slammed down the phone and began rolling on the floor, clutching her stomach as she roared with hysterical laughter. Amy thought it was hilarious. Leah, on the other hand, was forced to cower in humiliation for every biology lab for the rest of the semester. There just weren't that many Leahs on campus. If she'd been a Jennifer or maybe Sarah, she might have been okay, but as the only Leah, Lance had to know it was her.

Lance never said a word to her; he didn't have to.

Her little crush on Jim was just that, a silly crush that could easily be explained. She was on vacation, which gave her more time to let her mind wander. There was, of course, simple biology at work. The drive to procreate was even stronger than the drive to eat—neurological studies showed that the human brain thought far more about sex than eating. And biology dictated that women seek out the strongest, healthiest men to impregnate them. Being a human animal meant her intellect and ethical ideals could override her baser instincts and desire, but they couldn't make those baser desires disappear.

Thus, it was perfectly natural that she couldn't stop thinking about Jim's full, soft lips, her muscular arms, his powerful calves, his thick, dark hair pulled back into a ponytail . . .

Amy, Caitlyn, and Leah gathered in front of Jim. Leah glanced at him and quickly looked away. She was afraid that if his eyes met hers, he would know everything she had been thinking.

Amy said to him, "I really like these hikes, but they just aren't tough enough. I want to work my ass off."

"Yeah? Friday I'll take you on our toughest, best hike. It's three hours, and the first hour and a half is straight up hill."

"That sounds great."

"Ready?" he asked.

The women in the group nodded, and he turned and walked toward the mountains.

As they hiked, Amy said, "I feel like I've lost at least a couple of pounds. I feel great. I wish I could live like this all the time. I've heard that people put on an average of at least a couple of pounds every year as they get older. If we came here once a year, we could lose those pounds and never get crazy fat."

"You're not going to get crazy fat." Leah had barely broken a sweat.

"Right," Amy said, "because I'm going to make a point to cleanse myself once a year."

"Hiking isn't just about getting a good workout. It's about enjoying the scenery," Leah said.

"Scenery schmenery. Buy a postcard. I want to lose two more pounds."

After their hike, as they walked to the cafeteria for lunch, Raul from the front desk found Caitlyn and told her he had an urgent message for her.

"What's wrong?" she said.

"It's your mother. She needs you to call her right away."

"Is she okay? How did she sound? Was she upset?"

"She seemed . . ." Raul appeared to be trying to think of the correct word. "Agitated."

"Caitlyn, give me a second. I'll get you my phone card," Amy said.

Amy, Caitlyn, and Leah ran to their room. Amy fished her phone card out of her wallet and handed it to Caitlyn, who raced back to the front office where the pay phone was. Leah and Amy followed right behind her.

Caitlyn attempted to dial her mother's number and then the lengthy list of digits on the phone card, but she was too anxious that something had happened to her mother, and she hit the wrong number. "Fuck!" She slammed the phone down, waited a few seconds, and then picked it up and listened for a dial tone. She started punching in the numbers again, and again she messed it up. "Shit. Amy, help me. My fingers aren't working."

Caitlyn told Amy the numbers to her mother's cell phone. Amy punched those in and then dialed the code for the phone card. "It's ringing," Amy said, handing the phone back to

Caitlyn. It took only four rings, but it seemed forever before her mother answered. She sounded downright cheery.

"Mom? Is everything okay?"

"Everything is better than okay."

"What's going on? Why did you call me all the way to Mexico? I told you only to call me if there was an emergency. I thought something had happened to you."

"This *is* an emergency, and something *has* happened to me. Eddie has proposed! I'm getting married!"

"Eddie? Which one is Eddie?"

"Eddie, for Christ's sake! What do you mean 'Which one is Eddie?' You met him at the dinner party I held."

Caitlyn remembered the dinner party, and she remembered her mother introducing her to her boyfriend at the time, but she couldn't recall what he looked like. She vaguely thought that he was going silver at the temples.

"Oh, right, Eddie. Sorry." Caitlyn knew that her mother had mentioned him a few times, but Bridget was always telling her that she was in love with a great guy. "What does Eddie do again?"

"He's a doctor. A heart surgeon. He has a beautiful condo that overlooks Lake Michigan. He's got a beautiful cottage in Lake Geneva, too. He's got a sailboat. We thought it would be fun if you could come sailing with us this spring. I really want you to get to know him. We'll finally have a chance to be a real family."

Caitlyn's eyebrows furrowed. Her mother had been married four times before, and Caitlyn had never felt as if she'd been part of "a real family." Why would this be such an urgent concern for her mother now that Caitlyn was thirty-two years old?

"I'm really happy for you, Mom. Sailing sounds like fun. When's the date?"

"I'm thinking the end of June."

"The end of June! That's less than three months away!"

"I know, but at our age there's no time to wait."

"Mom, you're only forty-eight."

"You'll be in the wedding of course."

Caitlyn rolled her eyes. She had more bridesmaid's dresses than a bridal catalogue. "Of course. So you're happy?"

"I'm thrilled! I can't wait. Oh! Can you see me living in a spacious condo with a view of the lake? I can't wait to host parties there."

"You love him, right? You think this one is forever?"

"Oh, absolutely. We're going to be together until we die."

"Great. That's great to hear. Ah, how old is he?"

"Sixty."

"Sixty. I definitely want to hear all about him and hear all about the wedding plans, but I'm using Amy's phone card right now, so I should probably get—"

"Oh, of course, dear, I just couldn't hold in the good news any longer. Call me just as soon as you get back. Bye, darling!"

Before Caitlyn could say, "Bye," she heard a dial tone. "My trip's been a lot of fun, thanks for asking. I'm doing great, thanks for asking. Amy and Leah? They're doing great, too." Caitlyn hung up the phone and shook her head.

"So, let me guess, she's getting married?" Amy said.

"I met the guy once a few months ago. I can't even remember what he looks like."

"At least she's not in the hospital. She didn't have a stroke. She doesn't have cancer," Leah said.

"It would be better if she did have a stroke or cancer. Now I have to kill her myself."

Leah and Amy talked over lunch, but Caitlyn didn't have anything to say. She kept thinking about her mother. Caitlyn hoped she would be happy this time, but she didn't have a good track record in the marital arena.

As had quickly become their pattern, Caitlyn, Amy, and Leah spent the afternoon by the pool. Leah, well protected in the shade as usual, tried to take notes on influenza A. She also jotted down her thoughts about people's beliefs in psychics.

After dinner, the friends went to the activities building for another seminar. Tonight, Aisling was wearing a scarlet red shirt and pants in a clingy, unforgiving fabric.

As they had done the night before, they were supposed to purge all negative thoughts into a bubble and send the bubble out of the room. Then they had to fill their bodies with golden light.

Amy imagined a light thick like melted butter filling her up. She tried to think of nothing else but the golden light.

Aisling gave everyone a sheet of paper and asked them to divide it up into three sections and label them "Personal," "Spiritual," and "Professional." She told them to write down all of the things they hoped to achieve in those areas of their lives. Amy had no problem thinking of a million career goals. She started there and wrote *get promoted, get raise, land Turner account . . .* On and on she wrote until she ran out of room on that part of the sheet of paper. Then she went to the "Personal" section. *Eat better, work out more, do yoga three times a week, read more books, slow down and relax more.* Then she paused, her pen posed over the column. She didn't know how to word the most important thing of all: fix whatever was going on with her and Eric. So she didn't write down anything else. The other students were furiously scribbling around her. Amy hoped that Aisling would say it was time to stop, but she didn't. Amy studied her sheet of paper again. She hadn't written anything down under "Spiritual." She glanced at Caitlyn's paper. Caitlyn had filled each of her three sections with an equal number of goals. Amy tried to make out what Caitlyn had written under "Spiritual" so she might get some ideas, but Caitlyn's loopy, lopsided penmanship was too difficult to make out from where Amy sat. Amy looked over on Leah's paper and saw that Leah had left her "Spiritual" section blank, too, so she was no help either.

At last Aisling said, "Okay, excellent. Now we're going to talk through some creative visualization to help you attain these goals. If you don't know what it is you want to achieve, how can you attain what you want? We're going to spend some time thinking about each of these goals and imagining that you've achieved them. Ask your spirit guide to help you. Your spirit guide may come in any form. It might be a color, or a thing, or a person. No matter what form your spirit guide comes in, give your guide a name." Aisling paused to give everyone a chance to become acquainted with her spirit guide. Amy genuinely tried to imagine a force that would be there to help guide her, but absolutely nothing came to mind.

Aisling went on, telling the class to ask their spirit guides to accompany them as they visualized walking through the woods and then into a house. In the house, each room represented a different set of goals—personal, spiritual, or professional—but Amy's thoughts drifted. The two things that she'd been craving since she got to Mexico took up residence in her mind. Brent and chocolate. What she would really like was to pour Hershey's chocolate syrup over Brent's naked body and lick it up, nice and slow, her tongue tracing the muscular contours of his chest, his stomach, his thighs, his . . .

"Okay, everyone," Aisling's soft voice said. "Thank your spirit guides for their help. You may open your eyes."

Amy blinked and looked around guiltily. Normally she didn't even allow her fantasies to get quite so X-rated. She certainly didn't intend to do anything like that in real life. The room came to life as participants stood up, their wood chairs scraping against the wood floors.

Leah, Caitlyn, and Amy exited the building and started home. "That was great, wasn't it?" Caitlyn said.

"Yeah, great," Leah said.

"Mmm," Amy said.

"What did your spirit guide look like?" Caitlyn asked, but she didn't wait for an answer. "Mine was a purple lampshade. I named her Gwen. She was really helpful."

Amy wanted to be supportive of her friend. However, there are times when your friend tells you that her spirit guide is a purple lampshade named Gwen, and it's really a bit of a challenge to muster up any sort of enthusiasm. So Amy decided to go with a time-tested alternative to responding to a statement she didn't want to acknowledge: she changed the subject.

"What did you put in your spirituality column? I'm not even sure that I know how to define spirituality."

"I think spirituality is about your mind-body connection and the connection you feel to nature and the people around you," Caitlyn said. "I went to a seminar once about this, and the speaker said you can gauge your spiritual health by looking at your relationships with your friends and family."

Amy said nothing as she unlocked the door. She and her mother had never been close. She had nothing in common with her brother, who was two years older and had just gotten out of rehab for the second time. She loved her father, but he had always been so busy with work and his girlfriends. They talked once or twice a month and got along well, but their relationship didn't go beyond superficial politeness. Then, of course, there was her relationship with Eric. That clearly wasn't going as well as it could be or she wouldn't be fantasizing about sex with strangers. Evidently her spiritual health needed a spiritual hospital.

Chapter 12

Day Six

Exercising and eating a diet consisting essentially of leaves and twigs made Amy nearly insane with cravings for chocolate, salty foods, and beer.

"We've got to bust out of here. I need a beer. I need chips and salsa," Amy said. She took a bite of soup and tried to pretend it was a steak. She took another bite and pretended it was garlic mashed potatoes.

"I thought you wanted to lose some weight and detoxify," Caitlyn said.

"It's not natural to be this detoxified. I'm an American. I've grown up with McDonald's, Twinkies, and peanut butter fluff. My body is going into shock."

Amy genuinely wanted to lose a couple more pounds, but she had imagined she'd be able to do that in a painless way that didn't involve tofu, brown rice, and sea vegetables. She was really more in the mood for a beer and nachos kind of diet. "You know, honestly, I don't think the occasional chips and chocolate cake are all that bad for you. It's all about balance. It's the same thing with life, right? I say we call a cab and find a bar in the city tonight."

"I'm up for it," Caitlyn said.

"Me, too," Leah said.

"All right!"

After dinner, Amy used a pay phone and called for a cab to pick them up. Minutes before the cab was to arrive, the women scurried out of their room, across the lawn, and over the gate.

"Take us to *la cerveza*. Where ever there is beer, that's where we want to be," Amy said to the driver.

He took them to a bar about half an hour away from the spa. It was a bar with more white faces than brown ones—a tourist trap. The air in the room had an electric energy pulsing through it. Amy ordered two Negra Modelos. A group of thirty-something Americans said something to her. She flashed her engagement ring and sat down with her friends.

Amy looked at her bottle of beer. It was one hundred and forty empty calories. She wanted to look gorgeous in her dress, the dress she didn't have yet, and to her that meant being as thin as possible. She'd waited so long to get her dress because she kept holding on to the hope she would miraculously become a slimmer version of her herself and would then be able to pull off one of those gowns that were created solely to ensure that women hated their bodies and would thus keep eating disorder clinics raking in the bucks.

"What's wrong?" Leah asked.

"Oh, nothing," Amy said. "I just had a sudden flash of guilt about the empty calories after we've been eating so well."

"No, I don't mean just now. I mean you've been weird this whole trip. Don't blame the stress of the wedding. You're always stressed. That's your natural state of being. Something else is going on."

Without pausing, Amy tipped the beer to her lips and nearly swallowed half the bottle in a single swig.

Amy sighed. Sometimes it was a pain having girlfriends who knew her so well. "I'll be fine, I promise."

Leah gave her a look. Amy could see that Leah wasn't going to let this drop. There was a part of Amy that didn't want her to drop it. She was dying to get the weight of her secret off her chest.

Amy addressed the bartender. "Can we get three shots of tequila? And another round of beers. *Gracias.*"

When he set the three shots in front of them, Amy held hers aloft. "To friendship," she said.

"To your final days of freedom," Caitlyn said.

"To never having to eat another bit of tofu or lentil loaf as long as we all shall live," Leah said.

Amy and Caitlyn laughed, and, on cue, the three of them down the shots, chasing them with a long drink of beer.

Thus fortified, Amy said, "Okay, okay. The thing is, I've sort of been having fantasies about having sex with a guy who isn't Eric."

Caitlyn's jaw dropped. *"What?"*

"You are joking, right?" Leah said.

"He's a client of mine. He's been flirting with me, and the thing is, I really like it. I can't stop thinking about him"

"It's just prewedding jitters," Caitlyn said, waving her hand dismissively. "Everybody goes through that."

"How long have you known him?" Leah asked.

"Just a couple of weeks."

"A couple of weeks?"

"I know that doesn't seem like a very long time, but I can't tell you how intense my feelings toward him are. I don't think I've ever had such a carnal reaction to anyone."

"Really?" Caitlyn said. "This is getting interesting."

"How are things going with Eric . . . in the bedroom?" Leah asked.

Amy shrugged. "Oh, you know. OK."

"Amy, this is us." Caitlyn lightly touched Amy's shoulder. "Who was it that bought you your first vibrator and sketched elaborate diagrams of a woman's coochie with explicit user-manual instructions?"

"Coochie, Caitlyn? We're thirty-two," Amy said.

"You're stalling. You're just lucky I didn't use the other 'C' word."

"All right, all right, that was you and Leah. My scientist friend and my sex addict friend who have this ridiculous notion that sex and our bodies are good things."

"Exactly. Now tell us the truth."

Amy took another sip of her beer. "Well," she said at last, "I guess things have gotten a little routine."

"No problem," Caitlyn said. "We can fix this."

"I'm not one hundred percent sure I want to fix this. I think I really want to have an affair with Brent. I'm sick of being the good girl all the time."

"Amy," Leah said, "how long was the sex with Eric really, really hot?"

"I don't know, the first year we were together was amazing."

"Bullshit. I mean the kind of hot that you can't stop thinking about all the next day at work. It's so good it distracts you from getting things done because you can't concentrate on anything else."

"Two, three weeks?"

"Exactly. So no matter how great the sex with . . . What's this guy's name?"

"Brent."

"No matter how great the sex with Brent is, it's going to fade, too. It's the friendship and the laughter that keep a relationship going."

"I know."

"You can be attracted to more than one man at a time," Caitlyn said. "But I can tell you love Eric."

"If I love him, why do I feel so trapped?"

"Getting stuck in a routine is a common challenge with long-term couples," Leah said.

"Has it happened to you?"

Leah didn't say anything for a moment. "When I was with Chuck, he was so busy trying to get tenure, and I was so busy with work, we didn't focus enough time on connecting with each other, and it doomed the relationship. You and Eric are so crushed with work and wedding plans . . . When you're both super busy sex tends to fall to the wayside."

Amy didn't say anything for a moment. "Eric and I only ever do two positions. Missionary or me on top."

"Two positions!" Caitlyn's eyes grew round as baseballs. "This is a sexual code blue!"

"I know. I'm just not sure how to change things."

"Have you tried sex toys?"

"No," Amy admitted.

"Why not?"

"I'd feel stupid."

"Sex is supposed to be fun. It's not like you're going to be graded."

Amy shrugged.

"Do you have lingerie?"

"Yes. But I need to be drunk to wear it."

"That's fine, you can be a little drunk," Caitlyn said. "Amy, this is serious. Sex is an important part of a relationship. You need to try new things. You can't stick to just two positions for the rest of your life."

"I know, but this has been going on so long, I am actually a little scared to try anything new. Isn't that the most ridiculous thing you've ever heard?"

"Amy, that's your pattern. You've always been scared of new things," Caitlyn said.

"But they're not new. They're just not . . . recent. We've just gotten into the same routine."

"Making change is hard," Leah said, "because habits are so easy. Just make little changes at first; you'll realize it's not quite as terrifying as you think. Just because you are the person you are now doesn't mean you can't become someone different."

"I don't even miss him. Isn't that awful?"

"Amy, that's not unusual. Sometimes you need a break. Then you can go back a changed woman," Leah said.

"You were like this in college," Caitlyn said. "You always dated the most nondescript, vanilla, nonsexually threatening guys you could find and then wondered why they didn't turn you on. By dating wussy guys, you felt in control, but they didn't excite you. You've always tried so hard to mask your sexuality with glasses and conservative clothes so that guys would never mistake you for being one of the slutty, disposable women your father dates. It's time you embraced your inner slut. We all have one."

Amy skewered her eyebrows. She didn't like having her shortcomings pointed out to her, mostly because it confirmed her worst suspicions that she was a deeply flawed person. She knew that nobody was perfect, but that didn't mean she didn't hate it when other people were privy to her failings. If she couldn't actually *be* perfect, she wanted to at least be able to fool people into thinking that she was.

"I don't know, you may have a point, but how am I supposed to change?"

"I think Caitlyn's right," Leah said. "A lot of what goes on in the bedroom or what doesn't go on in the bedroom is a psychological thing. For you to truly relax and let go, you have to give up being in control all the time."

"The other solution, of course," Caitlyn added, "is to do what I do and never settle down. That way sex never gets boring."

"Caitlyn, that's not what I want. Yes, there is some fun stuff about dating," Amy said, "but it's tough really connecting with someone. Besides, I want kids, and I want to grow old with someone. I love Eric. At least I thought I loved Eric. It's just that I want Eric and stability and I want Brent and excitement, too."

"It's not wrong of you to want something exciting and new, but you need to work through this with Eric," Leah said. "Hopping from one relationship to the next means you never have to push through the tough stuff. The tough stuff is what helps you change and grow and become a better person."

"Hey!" Caitlyn protested. "Are you saying I'm emotionally stunted just because I don't buy into this crap about settling down and having to have sex with the same person forever and ever?"

"There are some things you give up when you're in a committed relationship," Leah said. "But the rewards of true intimacy are worth it. When you never commit to anyone, it's a really lonely way to live."

"I'm not lonely."

"Americans are addicted to change," Leah said. "I wrote an article about this. As things get tough, we get going as the saying goes. We have too many choices in this country. Other countries don't have eighty brands of toothpaste to choose from. Americans move more often, change jobs more frequently, and divorce their first spouse earlier than any other culture of people. But change creates stress. Think about it. What are some of the most stressful things a person can go through? Moving and getting married or divorced and getting a new job are all right up there at the top."

Leah drained her beer and gestured to the bartender to bring them another round. "In an area of your life, you are going to come to a point where going any farther will be hard and cause pain, either emotionally or physically. Instead of accepting that is simply the way things are and then working through the pain, we choose to do something to distract ourselves. Instead of confronting a difficult time in our marriage, we decide to move to a new house. All the details of packing and forwarding mail and getting the rooms painted the way we like them gives us something to worry about other than our rocky marriage. In this country, too often people don't work through the hard times. They get divorced or get a new job or simply give up. I think you might you might want to consider going to a therapist to deal with some of this stuff, your family issues and your need to be in control."

Amy sighed. Now she needed psychological help to fix what was wrong with her? That sounded much too difficult and complicated. Why couldn't she go back to when she was a nineteen-year-old college student and a vibrator was all she needed to solve her problems?

"You shouldn't get married, because men are untrustworthy scumbags," Caitlyn said. "Look at my mother. Her first husband was physically abusive, her second two husbands were nut jobs, her fourth husband was nice but he left her for another just like Chuck left Leah for a younger woman."

"Eric would never do that," Amy said. "I trust him like I've never trusted anyone."

"If you really want things to work, Caitlyn said, "we're here to help. Fixing stuff in the bedroom will be a snap. You're with me. Who better to help? We'll figure this out. By the time we're done here, you'll be ready to update the *Kama Sutra* with tips of your own."

Chapter 13

Day Seven

The morning air was brisk. Amy was too busy stretching, readying herself for the tough hike Jim had promised. She touched her toes and did stretches with the determined focus of an Olympic athlete readying herself to go for the gold or a marathon runner preparing for a twenty-six-mile race. She'd been looking forward to a really tough workout. She'd lost a little weight and it had gone to her head. She was determined to lose more. She adjusted her glasses, even though they didn't need adjusting, and then went on with her stretches.

Leah looked around, amazed at just how vast the national park surrounding the spa was. Sometimes she couldn't fathom how a forest could be so huge.

Along with Leah, Caitlyn, and Amy were Devin and two forty-something speech pathologists from San Francisco. None of them noticed the frumpy woman asking one of the Mexican guides a question, nor did they notice her joining their group in front of Jim.

"Hey, everybody. I'm Jim Maddalena. I know almost all of you, but you're new. What's your name?"

"I'm Carrie," the new woman said quietly. Carrie had dull brown hair parted down the middle. She wore thick glasses and a smile that gave her the appearance of someone who frequently organized church bake sales. She looked like the kind of person who said things like "Golly!" and "Gosh!"

"Carrie, nice to meet you. I'm Jim. All right, follow me."

Jim walked at the same pace he always did as they crossed the field that led to the mountains.

Amy was walking so briskly she had to stop so everyone else could catch up. "I thought you said we were going to have a tough hike today. Shouldn't we be walking faster?"

"Don't worry, Amy, this hike is straight uphill. You'll get your workout." Jim turned to see that Carrie was lagging behind. "You okay?"

She nodded, but she was sweating, and they'd barely begun.

Next the group had to cross a stream, balancing precariously on rocks. It was a hot spring, so if someone fell, she risked more than getting her shoes wet; she risked being doused in scalding-hot water.

Jim crossed first so he could take each woman's hand and help her cross. Leah made it over without blinking. Caitlyn crossed with a few terrified, theatrical shrieks. Devin and the speech pathologists crossed cautiously but without fanfare.

Amy was next. She stood at the water's edge, watching the steam hovering above it. She looked at the rocks—some were sharply angled to one side, some were more stable than others, some looked barely big enough to support her boot.

"I gotcha, Amy, you'll be okay." Jim reached his arm out and smiled.

She took a deep breath and got her footing on the first rock. Then she let go of terra firma with her other foot and brought it to another rock. That rock wobbled slightly and immediately her arms spread out like a trapeze artist. She took the next step warily and then the next. She grabbed Jim's hand, and he helped her through the remaining few steps. When she triumphantly made the final leap it took to get to firm ground again, her heart was pounding as if she'd just jumped out of an airplane.

Carrie proved to be similarly gun-shy, but eventually she made it over, too, and the group hiked to the base of the mountains.

Amy, Caitlyn, Jim and Leah walked together. "So, Amy," Jim said, "I know Leah is from Portland and Caitlyn is from Chicago. Where are you from?"

"Denver."

"How do you all know each other?"

"We went to college together," Leah explained.

"So this is a little reunion, huh?"

"Actually, Amy is getting married in two months," Caitlyn was sweating and her heart was already beating faster and they had barely been climbing at all. "This is kind of an extended bridal-shower slash bachelorette-party slash get-in-shape-for-the-wedding-photos trip."

"Congratulations, Amy," he said.

"Thanks. It's been good to get away from all the planning craziness."

When they got to the base of the mountain and began climbing the steep terrain, Carrie fell even farther behind. They stopped to wait for her. Then, another ten minutes later they had to stop again. Ten minutes later it was the same thing.

Amy, Caitlyn, Leah, and the speech pathologists huddled in a loose circle to wait for Carrie.

"This is ridiculous," Amy said as she swallowed some water. "I can't give my heart a workout if we're stopping every ten seconds."

"Why did she go on the tough hike if she isn't up for it?" Leah asked.

"I'll talk to her. We may need to turn around," Jim said. "I'll go see if she's up for going on." Jim walked to Carrie. Amy watched impatiently as the two of them talked and walked slowly toward the rest of the group.

When the eight hikers entered the forest, it was so dense almost no sunlight peered through. It was eerie going from the bright day into the gloomy darkness of the forest.

Everyone started walking again and again, Carrie quickly fell behind. "Does she have asthma or something?" Amy asked, cranky about her hike being ruined. "I seriously do not understand how someone without a health problem could be so slow."

"She said she asked Carlos which was the easy hike and she misunderstood. But she doesn't want to turn around," Jim said.

"Do you think it would be okay if I walked ahead, not far or anything, and then doubled-back to meet up with you?" Amy asked.

Jim looked apprehensive.

"Caitlyn and Leah will come with me. Together we won't get lost," Amy said.

"Okay, but don't walk too far ahead. It's easy to get lost in these woods."

Amy charged ahead with Leah and Caitlyn beside her. For a few minutes, they got a good pace going.

"Amy," Leah said. "I've been thinking about you and Eric."

"Uh-oh," Amy said. "That doesn't sound good."

"I'm just trying to figure out where things started going wrong. You said things were great in the beginning. What happened?"

Amy's breathing was labored from their rigorous pace. She exhaled deeply. "I don't know. Things were wonderful at first, like you said. And then . . . and then . . ."

"When did you first think you two might get married?"

Amy thought a moment. "I don't know. When we first started going out, I had just gotten my promotion and I was really stressed about work. I hadn't planned on dating anyone seriously. For the first month or two we were dating, I was just having fun with him. Going out with him and having sex with him was really more about me relaxing and having fun and relieving stress than about building a relationship. Then after we'd been dating several weeks, Eric kept telling me he was crazy about me. I thought he was just really grateful to be getting laid on a regular basis. You know how guys can be. Then one day he said, 'I love you.' I remember it distinctly. We were in bed after making love, and we were joking about something. I made him laugh and then he said it. 'I love you.' I remember thinking, *You love me? But we're screwing around, having tons of sex. You* love *me?* I was caught off guard. I thought a moment, and I knew I really cared deeply about him. For the next month he told me he loved me about twenty times a day. I wasn't totally surprised because he constantly told me I was the sexiest, most beautiful woman in the world. I kept telling him I loved him, too. Then one day, I'm not even sure what happened, I realized that I really *did* love him, and not just as a friend. That's when I knew for sure this was the guy I was going to spend my life with."

"Did things change for the better or for worse after that?" Leah asked.

Amy thought a moment. "Things pretty much stayed the same, I think. Well, I mean we'd been together a little while by then, so of course some of the newness and excitement was wearing off a little. And we were so both so busy at work . . . I don't know."

"I'm just wondering if realizing Eric was more than just a guy to mess around with, if seeing him as your future husband and father of your children, changed things. Or maybe it was more that you realized he saw you as his future wife and mother of his children."

"I don't get it," Caitlyn said.

"Neither do I," Amy said.

"Wives and mothers are role models. They're not like the women your father dates. Maybe you started worrying that if you were too sexually uninhibited, Eric wouldn't take you seriously, just like your father never took the disposable blondes seriously."

"But . . . that's silly. Eric already loved me. Why would he start thinking I was a slut?"

"You know," Caitlyn said. "Sluts get such a bad rap. We

all have an inner slut. We need to embrace our inner sluts."
She shook her head.

Leah ignored Caitlyn. "It might have happened on a sub-
conscious level. You might not even be aware of it. But Eric
loves you. He fell in love with you even when you were a sex-
crazed maniac. He'll love you as a sex-crazed maniac now,
too."

"He'll *really* love you if you're a sex maniac," Caitlyn
agreed.

"You guys, I think we should turn around and meet up
with Jim and everybody," Amy said.

"You're right, that's a good idea," Leah said.

They swung around, caught up to Jim and the others,
waved hellos, and then turned around again and headed out
on their own.

How could Amy not be one hundred percent sure she
wanted to marry Eric? She'd been sure once. What had happened?

She remembered the giggly night a few months into their
relationship when they'd talked about what names they liked
for the kids they would have some day.

"What names do you like for a boy?" he asked.

"I always liked the name Michael."

"Michael. Yuck. Everyone's named Michael. What else?"

"I like Aiden. It's Irish."

"Aiden. I like it."

"What other names do you like?"

"What other names do you like?"

"What do you think about Borden?"

"Borden? That's awful. That's *beyond* awful. Have you
heard of a Miss Lizzie Borden? Anyway, our poor kid would
get teased relentlessly. *Borden* is much too much like *bore-
dom.*"

"What about Braden?"

"Braden isn't hideous, but come on, Braden and Aiden?"

He laughed and then tickled her.

"What about for a girl?" Amy asked, giggling and pushing his tickling fingers away.

"I've always liked the name Hilary."

"No way. There was a Hilary who went to my high school who always used to call me a fat slut, as in, 'Hey, you fat slut, how're you doing?' "

"You were never fat and you were never a slut."

A few weeks later, Eric came home from a business trip with a copy of United Airlines in-flight magazine, *Hemispheres*. Amy had been sitting at the kitchen table writing out a grocery list. Eric lay the magazine in front of her. The page that he'd opened it to had a picture of an array of diamond engagement rings from an upscale jewelry store that had branches across the country, including one in Denver.

"Like any of those?" he'd asked.

She pointed to band she liked. "I've always wanted an engagement ring with a sapphire. They bring out my eyes."

He nodded and smiled. "Any idea what size ring you wear? I'm asking simply out of curiosity, naturally."

"Naturally. Well, this ring"—she held up her hand that had an opal adorning her ring finger—"it's a five and a half, and it happens to fit my left ring finger perfectly."

Months went by before he officially proposed. He even put his house on the market before he formally popped the question with the understanding that she would sell her small house as well and together they would buy the home of their dreams. Every time he took her out for a nice dinner, she wondered if this would be the night he popped the question. When yet another night went by without him asking, she wondered if maybe he'd changed his mind.

Then one night after another nice meal, Eric said he needed to stop by his friend's house to pick something up. When they pulled up to Christine and Adam's house, Amy noticed that there were many more cars parked along the street than there normally were, and she thought maybe someone on the block was having a party. She knew it couldn't be a surprise party for her because her birthday wasn't until November.

When they got inside and she saw all their friends, her coworkers, and her father and his latest girlfriend who'd both flown in from Dubuque, she looked at Eric and said, "What's going on?"

"I'm hoping this will become our engagement party," he said as he got down on one knee and pulled a blue velvet box from his pocket, "Amy Harrington, will you marry me?"

Amy wasn't usually one for public displays of emotion, but she couldn't restrain her tears of joy.

"Yes! Yes, of course I'll marry you." She threw her arms around him and only vaguely heard the people she cared most about in the world clap and cheer. She hadn't felt the tiniest doubt that night. The doubt came later, little by little.

If she did call off the wedding, she'd have to tell hundreds of friends and acquaintances that she and Eric had broken up. Amy never failed at anything. Certainly never on such a grand scale. She wasn't great at everything, of course, but the things she wasn't good at, she didn't do.

If they called the wedding off, they'd lose thousands of dollars on deposits. All that work she'd done . . .

Still, how could she go through with it if she wasn't sure?

"Guys, we should turn around again," Amy said.

They turned around and walked through the dense woods, going back uphill the way they came.

"Which way are we supposed to go?" Leah asked.

"I don't see any green lines," Amy said.

Wordlessly they fanned out, scanning rocks and trees for the green lines that indicated the path to take.

"I think we came from this way," Caitlyn said.

"Are you sure? This doesn't look familiar," Amy said. "But then, I wasn't really paying attention to where I was going."

"I think Caitlyn's right," Leah said.

"Okay, let's try it."

They walked for several minutes without speaking. They were too intent on trying to catch sight of Jim or another hiker or a green line, anything to assure them they were on the right path.

The problem with going uphill was there was always more mountain ahead. They couldn't see what was to come. Each time it appeared that they were about to reach a crest, they ran into more terrain that had been hidden from view. The thickly packed trees were like a dense fog—almost impossible to see through.

The three women plodded along, dodging branches.

"I'm starting to get worried," Amy said.

"Me, too," Leah said. "What should we do? Should we wait here and hope Jim finds us? Should we just try to hike back to the spa?" Leah said.

"Jim!" Caitlyn yelled. "Jim Maddalena! Jim! Jim!"

They walked and called Jim's name, but there was no answer. The forest seemed completely still except for the sound of their feet crunching over dead leaves.

"What are our chances of getting back to the spa without getting hopelessly lost?" Leah asked.

"I think when we reach the other side of the mountain, we'll be able to see it. There aren't any other buildings in the area," Amy said.

"Okay, then I say we go for it. Poor Jim is going to be worried sick, though," Leah said.

"I know. I'm sorry, you guys. I'm sorry I'm so impatient," Amy said.

"Amy, it's not your fault. I wanted to walk faster, too," Leah said.

For a few minutes, they walked in strained silence. Wordlessly, they each scanned the woods for signs of a clearing, of Jim, of a green line.

Amy, who at first had led the way, fell behind, dispirited. She tried to avoid thinking about their predicament. She thought about what Kiera had said about worrying about the future rather than focusing on the present. *Don't worry about what might or might not happen.* Ahead of her, Caitlyn's ponytail swung like a metronome with each step she took.

"So, you guys." Caitlyn's voice was falsely cheerful, taut as a guitar string. "Remember that night when we got busted by the cops? Remember, Amy? We were visiting Leah in Boone?"

Leah adjusted her day pack. Her strides were long and sure. "We started out stealing liquor from my dad's liquor store."

"Amy, you were such a wuss about the whole thing."

"I was afraid we were going to get busted. Which, let me point out, we did."

All three women were breathing heavily. Their sentences came out in stilted bursts as their pounding footsteps negotiated the unsteady terrain.

"Then we went to that party." Caitlyn pushed her bangs out of her face. They were soaked with sweat.

"Which was promptly busted by the cops, so we shimmied down the fire escape and ended up at those two guys' place. What were their names?" Leah said.

Amy tried to tell herself that this was normal. They were talking about old college memories. The good times. The times that made them laugh. The history they shared. But she wanted out of the dark, dense trees. They no longer seemed beautiful and wondrous; they seemed ominous.

"I'm sure I wrote it in my diary," Caitlyn said.

"Then we *had* to go for more beer." Leah shook her head and smiled.

"And we saw the most awful sight underage honors students with a case of beer in the car with them could see," Amy said.

In unison they said, "Police lights!"

The police officer could have busted them for possession. Instead he charged them for not wearing their seat belts and made them pour the case of beer out on the shoulder of the highway, which, to an eighteen-year-old, was a waste roughly equivalent to chucking the Hope Diamond off a boat in the middle of the Pacific Ocean.

"I still have the clipping in my diary from when we made the *Boone News Republic*."

"Isn't that pathetic that my town is so small, three kids getting tickets for seat belts makes it into the paper? That paper was *starving* for news," Leah said.

Amy exhaled, feeling a brief moment of relief. She could see clear sky ahead. She quickened her pace, certain they'd be able to see something once they got out of the trees.

They emerged from the gloom of the forest into sunlight. They were on a plateau, but all they could see were what seemed to be an infinite number of trees and rolling hills.

"That's the volcano," Leah said, pointing. "That should give us some frame of reference."

"It doesn't help me any," Amy said. "If we could find that waterfall, we'd know we weren't that far from the spa."

Leah squinted. "I can't see any water from here. I think we need to stay outside the woods so we can keep an eye on that volcano. The spa should be in this direction-ish." She pointed again. "We'll keep outside the woods, and when we see a good spot to climb down the mountain, we will. Hopefully we'll find the hot springs. If we can find that, we'll know how to get back."

"It's as good a plan as any," Amy said with a shrug.

Amy and Caitlyn followed Leah, who was more anxious than she let on. Who knew how long they might be out here? They were exercising hard beneath the hot sun, and their water supplies were rapidly dwindling. They brought only enough water for a three-hour hike, and they'd been out almost that long already.

Caitlyn continued to attempt to keep the mood light by sharing memories of their days together. They talked about their college antics, straining for normality as they walked, all the while looking for a sign they were going in the right direction.

Eventually, they couldn't keep up the pretense of small talk. Each step became a struggle.

Leah, breathing hard, said, "Hey, you guys, I need to stop for a minute."

Amy wiped the sweat from her forehead and took her water bottle out of her day pack. She looked at the nearly empty bottle with a sinking heart. "If we don't get back to the spa soon, we're going to run out of water." Her voice was strained and tight. She tried, unsuccessfully, to hide the edge of fear in her tone.

Leah nodded. Her expression was grave.

"We're going to be all right," Amy said.

"I'm scared," Caitlyn said quietly.

"We'll just be careful with our water," Amy said.

They rested for a few minutes more and then started up again. They were getting tired, their leg muscles began to throb. Amy wondered what would happen if they didn't make it out. How would the spa staff find them? Would they know how to get hold of Eric, or would he just show up at the airport in a week and not find her?

Poor Eric. He would be so devastated. What an ass she'd been, sending those e-mails to Brent.

Amy was scared to drink any more water. She didn't want to run out and get heat stroke beneath the searing sun. Her sunscreen dripped into her eyes, stinging them.

She was just about to ask her friends how their water supplies were holding up when it happened, fast as a stone skipping over water, bam bam bam. She felt a sharp jab just below her eye, swore as she swatted at what felt like a bee, knocked her glasses off, and then heard the crunch. Still holding the stung eye with one hand, Amy looked down to see her glasses half crushed beneath one of Leah's hiking boots.

"Are you okay?" Leah asked.

"I was until a bee stung me and you broke my glasses."

Leah looked down. "Oh. I'm so sorry." Leah stepped carefully back and handed Amy the mangled glasses. "Really, I'm really sorry."

"It's not your fault," Amy said. The bee had stung her on the tender skin just below her eye, and it burned as though she'd been jabbed with a branding iron. She looked at her glasses, which were now missing a lens. The left lens had been knocked out. Amy did her best to straighten the thin frames out, but she couldn't get the lens back in. "At least you only crushed the side I couldn't see out of anyway." She attempted to keep her tone light, but fatigue edged its way into her voice. She pocketed the lens and put the crushed glasses back on. She knew she must look ridiculous with her left eye all puffed up, the frames on the left side bent upward, and her other eye red and teary from the sunscreen. She could only look out with the slightest slit of her right eye open.

Again they fell into silence. Leah led, Amy followed, and Caitlyn trailed behind, her thoughts running rampant.

If I die, who would miss me? Caitlyn thought the notion held promise as a title to a poem, but it was a depressing question to ponder as she marched through the woods, not knowing where they were or where they were going. She didn't have any close girlfriends except Amy and Leah, and no family except her mother and a few distant cousins. She had some acquaintances she knew through literary circles and the three guys she held at arm's length that she'd been seeing for a few months, juggling them so that if one of them broke up with her, there was always somebody else to take his place.

She'd always thought her legacy was her poetry, but suddenly, despite her awards, that didn't seem like very much. She was a poet in a world that didn't read poetry. What was the point?

She thought of what she'd said to Amy, that if you wanted to know whether your spirituality was in good shape, you simply needed to look at how healthy your relationships were to your friends and family. The three people she spent the most time with were Reg, Sean, and Kyle, and she was lying to all of them. *God, I promise that if you help me get out of these woods alive, I'll break up with them. I'll even start going to church again.* She walked a dozen yards. She wanted to cry, but the tears wouldn't come. *Okay, you know and I know that I was lying about that last part, but really, who can wake up early enough on Sunday morning to make it to church? Be reasonable. But I will break up with them, I promise.*

Caitlyn simply couldn't die today. Her mother needed her. For all the fights they'd had over the years, through all the men that had come and gone, it had always been Caitlyn and her mother, a team, two women against the world.

She couldn't die before she learned who her father was. She shouldn't have stopped asking her mother about it. It was true that her mother could be exhausting when she was angry. Over the years, Caitlyn had learned to gauge her mother's mood as a meteorologist would attempt to predict the weather. Caitlyn would keep quiet when there was an ill wind blowing, but, as with the weather, nothing could be predicted with one hundred percent accuracy. When Caitlyn asked about her father, she knew an emotional tsunami was headed her way—her mother would begin screaming and ranting and crying. Caitlyn couldn't let her mother's tantrums stop her. Life was too short; it was time she learned the truth.

Caitlyn couldn't bear the idea of never knowing who her father was. Maybe it was a one-night stand, maybe it was something far more terrible, but Caitlyn wanted to know the truth. If she'd come into this world after a violent night of nonconsensual sex (somehow, she couldn't even bring herself to think the "R" word; it was too horrible to contemplate), she wanted to know that. Maybe knowing where she came from would help her figure out who she was.

*   *   *

As Caitlyn sent her silent prayers, Amy walked just behind her. Amy knew exactly what hours of strenuous exercise in the sun could do to a person. How many times had she read about football players dying during a practice even when they were surrounded by coaches and other teammates? Heat stroke could kill in no time at all. She had no idea how long they'd been walking. She just knew her leg muscles were quivering, she was exhausted, and she didn't see the spa anywhere ahead of them. The more they walked, the more fearful Amy grew, not just for herself, but for Caitlyn and Leah as well.

They found a place where they could descend the mountain. It was much harder going downhill than walking on the flat plateau because it put such a strain on their quadriceps. At least they had the force of gravity to propel them on.

They reached flat ground relatively quickly, but Amy didn't recognize where they were.

She couldn't take it anymore. Her mouth was parched. She needed water desperately. She paused a moment, unscrewed her bottle of water, and held it to her lips. Only a few tiny drops fell to her tongue.

"Amy," Caitlyn said.

"What?"

"It's Leah. She's not looking well."

Amy turned around. Leah trailed behind them, moving slowly, weaving as if she were drunk. She looked disoriented and weak. Her face was pale and clear of the sweat that not long ago had glistened off her skin.

"Are you okay?" Amy asked.

"I don't feel very well," Leah said.

Leah stumbled. Amy caught her, gripping her in an awkward sort of side hug.

"Come on, you're okay. Lean on me," Amy said. Caitlyn got on the other side of Leah, and together she and Amy helped support her as she walked slowly on. Caitlyn gave

Amy a what-the-hell-are-we-going-to-do? look. Amy shook her head. She had no idea.

Leah walked so slowly, it was hard to make any progress. They continued on for fifteen minutes, half an hour, and still, nothing. The woods stretched on and on in front of them. Amy kept hoping that right around the next turn, they'd see the spa grounds. But after each bend, she'd see only another long, desolate stretch of trees.

Stay positive, stay focused, Amy told herself. *You can keep going. Just think of this as another workout.* Sometimes at the gym she'd feel tired after running for only a few minutes on the treadmill, but her goal was to jog for twenty-five minutes. She would play games with herself to keep going. She wouldn't let herself glance down at the big red digital numbers on the monitor in front of her until two songs on her iPod had gone by, and then she would do the same thing again and again until she had only one hundred and twenty seconds to count down. Breaking it into minigoals made it manageable. Life was much harder without any goalposts in sight. When you didn't have direction, you got frustrated or tired and feel as if you couldn't possibly go another foot. But when you could see that you were making progress toward your goal, you were renewed.

Here, though, there were no goalposts. For all she knew, they were going in the completely wrong direction.

She eyed the next bend. It absolutely had to be the last one. They had to be at the end. This had to be it.

But when they came up over the bend, the spa was still nowhere in sight. They hiked and hiked. Amy could tell by the position of the sun it had to be mid to late afternoon. They'd been lost in these woods for at least six hours.

Amy staggered on, one foot in front of the other, helping Leah walk. Amy's mouth and throat were parched. She fantasized about a chilled liter of bottled water, imagined the liquid rushing down her throat and swallowing large gulps of it until every last drop was gone. She could see the condensation on the outside of the bottle, feel how wet and cold it would be when she brought it to her lips, feel the wetness against her tongue as it slid down her throat.

Another bend. This had to be it.

When the spa wasn't in view, when all she could see were more and more trees, her spirits plummeted like a broken elevator. She knew she had to stay alert and positive for Leah's sake, but it was getting harder and harder.

Her tongue felt like chalk. Water. A large, chilled liter of water. She could feel the cold water on her tongue, running down her throat. She thought she might very well go out of her mind with want.

"There it is!" Caitlyn called.

Amy looked out and, squinting, made out the sun-splashed cottages of the spa. Her heart lightened with hope, but only for a moment. At least now they knew where they were going, but they still had at least half an hour until they got there. Amy wasn't sure how long it took for heat stroke to set in. Already Amy's arms were tired from supporting Leah's weight.

Leah stumbled. Amy and Caitlyn tried to catch her, but she was too tall, the balance was off, and all three of them fell to the ground.

"I can't go on," Caitlyn said, her breath ragged.

"We're almost there," Amy said.

"Let me rest."

"We don't have time."

Caitlyn nodded. She knew Amy was right. Together they struggled to get Leah standing. "Come on," Amy coaxed. "We're almost there. Leah, please, we're not strong enough to carry you."

At last Leah staggered to her feet. Tears of fear welled in Amy's eyes. The spa grounds were in sight, and yet she was more afraid than ever.

Every few feet they moved forward seemed like climbing a mountain peak. They didn't appear to be getting any closer.

Amy hoped it was a trick of her messed-up depth perception, her broken glasses making their goal seem ever more elusive.

"Jim!" Caitlyn yelled. "Jim!"

Amy saw a dark-haired man in the distance. He turned and ran toward them.

"Oh, thank God," he said. "I was just about to send out a search party for you. Leah, are you okay?"

"I think she's got heat stroke," Amy said.

"What happened to you?"

"I got stung by a bee. I'm fine."

"The bee broke your glasses?"

"No, it's a long story."

Leah's legs gave out. Before she hit the ground, Jim caught her. He carried her to his cottage, his arm muscles bulging with effort, the veins in his face and neck straining.

"The keys are in my pocket," he said.

Amy looked at him wide eyed, then turned her panicked gaze on Caitlyn, who reached into Jim's pocket, fished out the keys, and unlocked the door to his cottage. He rested Leah on his bed. Amy and Caitlyn collapsed on the edge of the bed beside her, studying her face to see how she was doing. She looked as if she were trying to wake from a dream, foggy and disoriented and unfocused.

Jim retrieved a pitcher of water from the bathroom. "Sit up," he instructed Leah.

"Mmm?" With Jim's aid, Leah sat up. He helped her drink some water. Amy and Caitlyn watched enviously. For a moment Amy had the fleeting thought that she wished she could have been the one who got sick so she could have water first. Then a flush of guilt gripped her. It made her want to suffer through more endless seconds of her chalky, dry mouth, aching for a sip of water as punishment. To distract herself from her intense craving, she unlaced her hiking boots and peeled her sweat-soaked socks off her feet. She took her mangled glasses off and set them on the bedside table. At last Jim passed the glass of water to her. She drank it in a gulp.

"Is Leah going to be okay?" Amy asked.

"I think so. I want to take her temperature and get you something to bring down the swelling in your eye. I need to get the first aid kit from the office. How are you guys feeling? Are your muscles cramping?"

Amy and Caitlyn nodded.

"You may have mild heat stroke, too. Do you feel disoriented? Nauseous?"

"I just feel very, very tired. Do you mind if I just lie down next to Leah?" Before Jim could answer, Amy lay beside her friend. Fortunately, Jim had a queen-size bed. There wasn't much room, but it was enough.

"I'll be right back," he said.

When he returned, Leah and Caitlyn were asleep. He hated to do it, but he shook Leah awake to take her temperature. It wasn't dangerously high. After he treated Amy's eye, she promptly fell asleep, too.

He let them rest, waking them briefly twice to have them drink more water, then let them alone. He left the cabin and returned with fresh fruit and bread.

Amy was the first to wake. It took a few moments for her sleepy brain to put the pieces of her day back together.

"How are you feeling?" Jim asked.

She thought a moment. "Hungry." She looked at Leah. "Is she okay?"

"She'll be fine. I brought some fruit and bread for you. And if you want it, I have my own secret stash of tuna."

"Tuna! Yes, please."

He opened a can of tuna and gave her a plastic fork. She wolfed it down plain; even plain, a can of tuna had never tasted so good. He held out the tray of fruit and bread, and she grabbed a slice of papaya. It was perfectly ripe, and its juices dripped from the corners of her mouth; she licked the juices clean and grabbed another slice and another.

"Slow down. You want to eat small meals for the next twenty-four hours. Don't go crazy."

"Jim, I'm so sorry about what happened."

"No, I'm sorry, it was my fault. I shouldn't have let you go up ahead. I feel terrible."

Their conversation woke Caitlyn. She sat up and looked around. "Is Leah all right?"

Jim nodded. "She'll be fine. Do you want something to eat?"

Caitlyn nodded. She had a few pieces of fruit and a couple of forkfuls of tuna. "Thanks, Jim. For everything. If you're sure Leah's going to be all right, do you mind if I go back to our cabin and take a shower?"

"She'll be okay. She can spend the night, or if she wakes up later, I'll walk her back to your place."

"Are you sure?" Amy said.

He nodded.

Caitlyn and Amy stood. Jim walked them to the door. Caitlyn hugged Jim tightly. Caitlyn didn't let go for several moments. When she broke away, Amy hugged him, too. "Thank you. You're a good man."

"But not a very good guide, unfortunately."

"It wasn't your fault," Amy said. "It was mine. I'm impatient and I like to do things my own way."

"We're okay," Caitlyn said. "That's what matters."

Amy and Caitlyn left together. Jim returned to his seat on a wood chair beside the bed and watched Leah sleep. One of her hands rested by her cheek, curled gently in pose like a swooning maiden from a Renaissance painting. Her other hand rested on her stomach just beneath the gentle curve of her breasts, which rose and fell with each breath she took. Her fingers were long and thin and delicately beautiful. Her cheeks were lightly flushed, and her pale skin contrasted with the pink of her cheeks and her dark hair, which curled around her face.

Leah's eyes fluttered open, her dark lashes blinking like the wings of a butterfly. "Hi." Her voice was raspy and rough. "What happened?"

"I think you had the beginnings of heat stroke. We got some water into you. I think you'll be okay. You just need to keep drinking water and get a little food in you."

She nodded as she remembered the events of the day. "You carried me into this room, didn't you? And I remember you waking me to take my temperature."

Jim didn't answer. He felt embarrassed, though he wasn't entirely sure why. "Why don't you try to eat something?"

Leah nodded and sat up. She took the glass of water he offered, and when she'd drunk it, she set the glass down and took the food he held out for her.

"I'm so sorry about what happened," he said.

Leah swallowed a piece of papaya that was so soft it melted in her mouth. "Don't be sorry. It wasn't your fault. It just happened. We got caught up in our conversation. We weren't paying attention to where we were going. We knew how difficult the woods were. You warned us, too."

"I was your guide. I let you down. I shouldn't have let you go on up ahead. You sure you're okay?" He reached out and touched her cheek with the back of his fingers and stroked her skin lightly. She enclosed her fingers around his hands and kissed his palm. He jerked his hand away.

"I'm sorry, I didn't mean . . . I think you're a really beautiful woman. If things were different . . . It's just, I wasn't lying to Caitlyn when I told her I don't do flings."

Leah studied the remnants of food clinging to her plate. She wanted to crawl under the covers and hide. But in addition to her embarrassment, she felt anger and confusion. "Jim, you work at a resort in Mexico. You said yourself that you barely speak Spanish and you don't leave the spa much. That means the only women you'll ever meet are the women who work here, most of whom barely speak English, or the women who come through here for a week or two before going home again."

"I know."

"So you're just never going to date?"

"Not forever. I just need some time to think. Or maybe not to think." For a moment, neither of them said a word. Then gently, he said, "I'll walk you home."

Leah nodded, and wordlessly they left his cabin and went into the dark night. The howls of wild dogs filled the chilly air like the moans of unhappy ghosts.

When they got to the door of his cabin, she looked up at Jim; their gazes locked. Her body was electric with energy and desire and attraction . . . and confusion. She thanked him once again for his help and wished him a good night.

Chapter 14

Day Eight

T he next morning, Caitlyn, Amy, and Leah were sore but otherwise okay. They sat at the breakfast table over plates of fruit and yogurt. Fortunately, Amy had brought her contacts along. She didn't like wearing them, but they would do until she could get home and buy a new pair of glasses. At least she could see.

"Leah, are you feeling all right?" Amy asked. "You seem down."

"I'm fine. I feel fine."

"Something happened with Jim last night after Caitlyn and I left, didn't it?" Amy said.

Leah studied her plate.

"Come on, spill," Amy said.

"Well, Caitlin I took your advice and tried to be forceful. I kissed his hand."

"You kissed his hand?" Caitlin asked, perplexed.

"It made sense at the time. Anyway, he said he hadn't been kidding when he told you that he doesn't believe in one-night stands."

"See, he's gay. I told you," Caitlyn said. "There's no possible way a heterosexual male would ever say that."

"Maybe he's just playing hard to get," Amy said. When

Leah didn't say anything, Amy said, "So what should we do today? I say we skip the hike."

Caitlyn laughed. "I guess you're going to have to twist my arm." Caitlyn pretended to twist her own arm about a millimeter. "All right, I'm convinced. Actually, I read in the pamphlet that Sunday are market days in town. The spa will bus guests who want to go into town for the day. The flea market is known for its glasswork and bargain prices."

"That might be fun," Amy said.

"I don't know. You know I've never been into shopping." Leah ate ravenously.

"I know, I've always thought you were weird that way." Caitlyn shook her head. Then, with a smile and a cocked eyebrow, she added, "I heard that Jim is the one who drives the guests into town."

"Really?" Leah said.

"Then we're definitely going," Amy said. "We're going to change his mind."

"I don't think so. I don't think I can face him again. It was humiliating to throw myself at him and get flat-out rejected," Leah said.

"We're leaving soon. Who cares if you embarrass yourself in front of him?" Amy said. "Besides, if I can do a topless water ballet in front of half a soccer team and live to tell the tale, and if we can survive nearly dying in the woods, I think you can take trying to hit on a cute nature guide one more time."

After breakfast, Amy, Caitlyn, Leah, and two fifty-something women who had just arrived at the spa two days earlier gathered by the office, waiting for Jim to pull around with a battered old blue van.

As everyone climbed into the van, Leah felt a stab of anxiety about where she should sit. Should she climb into the back with everyone else? Should she get into the passenger seat next to Jim? Would that seem presumptuous and overly forward? The fifty-something women in their flowing linen pants and tops took the seats in the far back. Amy and Caitlyn slid into the seats in the middle. Feeling nervous, Leah sat next to Caitlyn. For a moment she was annoyed with herself for not being more bold, but then she realized she could stare at Jim for the entire ride in the rearview mirror, so it wasn't so bad after all.

They had to bounce along the cobblestone and dirt roads to get to the highway. As they bounced along, Caitlyn began talking with the women in the back. The woman, Lois, had thick thighs and small breasts and a beautiful face. She was certified in homeopathic medicine.

"That's cool," Caitlyn said. "I wish more people tried natural routes to health. I think people are too dependent on drugs. Do you have any treatments you swear by?"

"Have you tried ear candles?" Lois's friend Roseanne said.

"No, what's that?" Caitlyn said.

"They are hollow candles that you put into your ears. You light one end and it sucks all of the ear wax right out," Roseanne explained.

"You light a candle on your head?" Amy asked.

"It works like a charm. You can go to a salon and have it done professionally for about forty bucks or you can buy them at health food stores and do it at home," Lois said.

"I do it, and you can hear so much better when you're done. I still had fluid seeping out of my ear onto the pillow that night," Roseanne added.

Would you shut up? Leah thought. *Look at the gorgeous man we should be talking to in the front seat. We should take this opportunity to ask him about Mexico and why he's so gorgeous and why he doesn't believe in one-night stands, not about earwax, for God's sake.*

Periodically Jim would glance in the rearview mirror and smile at some of the more wacky comments flying around in the back seat. When he did, Leah would quickly turn her head and pretend that she was very interested in the conversation and wasn't staring at him.

"How about a Neti Pot? Have you tried that?" Lois said.

"Never heard of it," Caitlyn said.

"It's like a little tea kettle that you put lukewarm water into; then you pour it into one nostril and it comes out the other. It cleans out all the dirt and pollution you breathe in and helps you avoid colds and sinus infections."

There wasn't much that grossed Leah out, but Lois's description of the uses of a Neti Pot made her blanch. There were just some topics that she would prefer not to discuss in the presence of a hunky male.

As they got closer to town, the conversation quieted as everyone eagerly took in the sights: the brightly painted buildings with bold murals, the billboards, the people. They saw small children doing headstands in the middle of the street at intersections.

"What are those kids doing?" Caitlyn asked.

"They're trying to earn a few pesos by doing tricks," Leah said.

"In the street? They're little kids! Where are their parents?"

"Probably begging on a different street corner," Leah said.

"Oh."

Jim parked the van on a street in front of a touristy restaurant. He said they were free to wander on their own for the next several hours, but they had to be back here by four o'clock so they could drive back to the spa.

"We're having another campfire tonight and we don't want to be late. If you get lost, just ask someone to tell you how to get to Casco Viejo." Jim pointed to the restaurant behind them and walked the five women to the heart of the flea market. Lois and Roseanne waved goodbye and took off on their own.

"Are you going to be joining us today?" Leah asked, hoping he couldn't hear the thumping of her heart from where he stood.

"Usually I just go back to the spa and come back around four."

Leah nodded.

"But I don't have much else to do today . . ."

Leah smiled. "We'd love for you to tag along."

"Sure. Why not?"

The flea market teemed with people who shuffled slowly through crowded, narrow paths. Their ears buzzed with the sounds of babies crying and shoppers bartering. Goods were laid out on tables covered by tent-like roofs propped up by wood poles. It was a smorgasbord of consumerism. There were glassware, furniture, jewelry, cheap bras and underwear, shoes dangling from hooks, leather goods, salt shakers, dishware, and bark paintings. There were obviously bootlegged copies of American movies on DVD—some of the movies had been released just that week in theaters. Clearly someone had taken a video camera into the theater with them and made copies.

The prices were ridiculously cheap. Right away Caitlyn found bracelets in a variety of colors that she simply had to have. They were only two dollars each. In the States, they would have been at least twenty bucks.

A number of vendors sold all sorts of foods that looked delicious, and the smells of fresh fruit, fried dough, and spiced meats were tempting, but Leah cautioned Amy and Caitlyn not to eat any of it, no matter how innocuous looking.

"What do you think of this?" Caitlyn asked Amy as she held up a cornhusk doll.

"It's pretty, but what would you do with it?"

"Decorate my apartment?" Caitlyn pursed her lips and squinted at the doll before setting it back down. "You're right, it doesn't go with my décor at all."

A few stands back, Leah ran her fingers over a beautiful vase.

"I love this glasswork," Leah said to Jim, "but I'd never be able to get it home in one piece."

"Maybe if you come back next year, you can bring an empty suitcase to take home all the stuff you buy."

Leah looked at Jim, his thick, shiny black hair pulled back into a ponytail, his black T-shirt stretched taut over his chest, his powerful arms with their prominent veins. She longed to reach out and touch the medallion that he wore around his neck, to stroke the top of his chest. Finally she realized she hadn't answered his question yet and quickly said, "I don't actually like shopping much. I would never use this stuff, so there is no point in buying it anyway."

Leah picked up a margarita glass. On the edge of the glass was a clay figure of a drunk man with his pants down. She inspected the sombrero-wearing man for a moment before she realized that the guy was taking a pee. "Now, that is class," she said.

Jim chuckled. "It's what every household needs."

"Every college frat house, maybe."

Leah held up a pair of black thong underwear. "How about this, is it me?"

"I don't know, is it?" The flirtatious way he asked made Leah's heart beat double time. His coy smile and teasing eyes rattled her. He said he didn't want a fling, but his eyes and smile said otherwise. Why was he confusing her like this?

"To be honest, not really. But I figure animals in nature have been successfully reproducing for years without the benefit of black lace lingerie, so I'll probably be okay."

Jim laughed. Leah smiled. For a moment, her gaze became ensnared in his. She couldn't break away. Their eyes were locked intently for several moments until a passing shopper bumped Jim's arm and he stumbled a step or two forward.

All afternoon, the four of them wove their way through the seemingly endless shops and stands. Sometimes they stuck together and other times they paired off, Amy with Caitlyn and Leah with Jim. Leah had never enjoyed shopping so much.

Just being around Jim was enough. It was easy making conversation with him. Chuck had been much more reserved. She realized she had missed this aspect of dating: learning how different people could be.

When it was getting close to four o'clock, Leah saw Amy looking around and gave her a wave. There weren't that many five-foot-ten white women around, so it didn't take Amy long to spot her and smile, and Caitlyn and Amy quickly caught up to them. Caitlyn had a number of bags dangling from her arms.

Lois and Roseanne were already waiting in front of the restaurant. The whole way home, Lois and Roseanne showed off all the things they'd bought that day.

When Jim pulled up, to the main office at the spa, Leah unbuckled her seat belt to get out of the van.

"I had a lot of fun today," she said.

"I did, too."

"I guess I'll see you tonight?"

"Count on it."

Leah followed Caitlyn and Amy back to their cottage.

"I need a nap," Caitlyn said. "Spending money is exhausting."

"That sounds great," Amy said.

As Amy and Caitlyn napped, Leah lay on her bed, reviewing everything Jim had said to her at the flea market.

Leah had once written an article explaining that birds, like planes, could fly because the shape of their wings caused the air pressure above the wings to be lower than the pressure underneath. The difference in pressure was the force that kept the bird airborn. It was simple, really. Right now, Leah felt that she, too, was flying, that she was being lifted from below by an unseen force that kept her soaring above the earth's crust.

She was so happy floating in her little fantasyland that she was disappointed to have to quit daydreaming and wake up when Caitlyn and Amy awoke and started getting ready for dinner.

"Come on, Leah, I'll help you get glammed up for dinner," Caitlyn said. "With my help, Jim will throw all his rules and morals out the window and you'll be screwing in no time."

Leah rolled her eyes. "What do you want me to do?"

"Let's start with clothes. Do you have any skirts or dresses?"

"I think I have a couple . . . back in Portland. I wasn't planning on having to seduce a nature guide while I was here."

"You can borrow one of mine."

"Perhaps you haven't noticed that I have the kind of hips that were made to birth babies and you have the kind of hips that are made to look good in tight skirts."

"Maybe Amy has something you can wear."

"You can borrow anything I have, but I'm five inches shorter," Amy said. "What would be a short skirt on me would be pornographic on you."

"You know, let's forget the skirt. Leah, open your suitcase. I need to see what I have to work with."

Leah did as she was told. As Caitlyn surveyed the contents, her expression skewered. Finally she selected a pair of tan shorts and lent Leah a white cotton shirt. Leah reached for a white cotton tank top.

"No, no tank top."

"Caitlyn, the fabric is see-through. You can see my bra," Leah said, inspecting her image in the mirror.

"That's the point. That's the look."

"Are you sure?"

"Trust me."

Leah sat in a chair and allowed Caitlyn to flit about her, dabbing lipstick and eyeshadow and mascara on her.

"Don't go too crazy," Leah cautioned. "I don't want to look like a drag queen."

"Don't worry, I'll be subtle."

Caitlyn finished by giving Leah's hair extra volume with well-aimed douses of hairspray.

When Leah regarded herself in the mirror, she had to admit she looked nice. The lipstick and eyeshadow brightened her face.

"Ready?" Caitlyn asked.

"I guess."

"Okay. Let's go. Be sure not to sweat as we walk up the hill to the fire."

"I'll do my best."

Once again dinner was outside by the campfire, and again they were given Tofu Pups to cook over the flames. As Leah took her skewer and Tofu Pup from the Mexican girl who worked for the spa, she looked around for Jim. She saw no sign of him.

Leah sat down by Caitlyn. When Amy sat on the other side of her, Leah said, "Sorry, Aim, would you mind sitting by Caitlyn? Just in case?"

"Oh, right. Of course."

Leah threaded her Tofu Pup onto the skewer and did her best to listen to Caitlyn and Amy's conversation, but she was too busy trying to spot Jim to focus on what they were saying. She ate her Tofu Pup on a whole wheat bun with fruit and organic potato salad. At least it wasn't soup and salad.

It wasn't until she stood and walked over to the garbage can to throw her paper plate away that she saw him. He wore his hair down tonight, and the sight of his thick shoulder-length hair made her heart flip. She watched his lips pull into a smile, his hair swinging slightly as he walked. His white T-shirt contrasted with his dark hair and the sharp lines of his eyebrows.

"Hey," Leah said, looking at his full, pink lips. Bad idea.

"Hi. Have you already eaten?"

She nodded.

"Me, too. I had some tuna. I think I've had my fill of Tofu Pups for the season. I was just going for a walk. Do you want to join me?"

Leah looked over her shoulder. Sure enough, Amy and Caitlyn were gawking and smiling. Caitlyn gave her the thumbs-up signal. Subtle.

"As long as you can promise me we won't get lost in the woods for nine hours."

"We won't even go into the woods, so the odds that we'll get lost in them are really low."

Leah and Jim walked along the border of the spa beneath the moonlight, not speaking. They moved past the organic garden—a sea of leafy greens—along the Montezuma pines and palm trees. When they were well away from everyone else, Leah turned and looked at Jim. What she wanted to ask was, *Why the hell don't you believe in flings? What kind of heterosexual male are you?* But instead she asked, "So, tell me, what made you interested in studying nutrition?"

"When I was a little kid, I had a lot of food allergies, except for a while, we didn't know that; we didn't know why I kept getting sick. Once I ran up to my dad when he got home from work to hug him, and the second he hugged me back, I puked all over him."

Leah smiled.

"Finally a doctor identified the foods I was allergic to. Strawberries, nuts, a whole bunch of things. I had to really watch what I ate so I wouldn't get sick. Of course, it's not cool for a guy to pay any attention to his diet, but fortunately I was a jock, so people just passed it off as, you know, I was an athlete in training. And if the guys ever gave me a hard time about studying nutrition, I just pointed out truthfully that all my classes were filled with pretty, healthy women. I think diet is a really important part of how you feel. You have more energy when you eat well."

"I know. I've had tons of energy all week. It's amazing."

"See?"

"But I have to say I miss cheeseburgers."

He smiled. "If it's done in moderation, it's not a problem. I think Americans overeat for the same reason they drink or do drugs—they are trying to fill some void that food, alcohol, and drugs can't fill."

"You sound much too advanced to be a bachelor. Are you sure you're straight?"

"I am, I promise."

For a moment, Leah was certain that he was going to lean in and kiss her. Then he abruptly said, "We should probably get back to the others."

Leah exhaled. She was out of practice with the whole dating-sex-romance thing, but she really thought he wanted to kiss her. Was she way off base? Or did he want to kiss her, but forced himself to resist the urge? If that was the case, why was he stopping himself? Why had he asked her to walk with him and then cut it off in just a few minutes?

Jim dropped her off at the campfire.

"Good night," he said. "See you tomorrow."

Chapter 15

Days Nine, Ten, and Eleven

Amy was glad she'd waited to get her facial and massage toward the end of her trip. She had good skin, and she worked hard to keep it that way by slathering lots of eye cream on every morning and night. Amy desperately wanted to believe any claims made on the packaging of obscenely overpriced lotions and creams, and she willingly parted with her hard-earned cash to buy them. Her bathroom was like a museum for hair tonics, make-up, cleansers, and moisturizers. The cabinet beneath her sink looked like a graveyard for beauty products of yore. Some women believed in psychics and astrology; she believed that if she applied antiwrinkle cream by the gallon, she could stay forever young looking. She rationalized the tanning she was doing on this trip by telling herself she was being careful about it, wearing sunscreen, and only getting color slowly but surely.

She got a moisturizing facial in the morning and then had an hour-long massage by a muscular man named José in the afternoon. José helped work out the soreness in her muscles from the hours she'd spent lost in the woods. Her entire body relaxed as his hands melted away her tension, both physical and mental.

As José's hands kneaded her muscles, she thought about Eric. For the first week she'd been here, it had almost been a relief to get away from him. It felt strange not to fall asleep in his arms and go to bed without a good night kiss from him, but she'd been unable to tell if she missed that out of *habit* or because she missed *him*. Now, she realized she truly missed him. But then she thought about sex with him, and the thought didn't bring about a carnal wave of lust as thoughts of Brent did. She realized it had been silly for her to think that going away for two weeks would bring back the spark to their relationship, but she wasn't sure what else to do.

Leah spent her day alternately working on her articles and thinking about Jim. She wasn't sure why Jim not kissing her was bothering her so much. She was leaving in a few days; she would never see him again. Making love to him would be nice, but it would only make going home to her solitary life that much bleaker. She didn't need Jim anyway. She had Russ Evans and that guy Lindsey wanted to set her up with. She had plenty of options.

What was bothering her about Jim, she decided, was that she wanted to know the truth. If he wasn't attracted to her, fine. If he was attracted to her but refused to even kiss her, she wanted to know what was stopping him. She was a curious person by nature. She needed answers.

After dinner, Leah went to Jim's cabin. He opened the door and smiled. "Leah. Come in."

Leah walked in the room and pivoted to face him as he closed the door behind them. "I'm sorry to bother you."

"You're not bothering me. What's up?"

"I just . . . I was curious. Last night . . . I mean, I could have been totally wrong. If I was, that's fine, I just wanted to know . . ."

"Leah, I have no idea what you're talking about."

She exhaled and tried to summon her composure. She looked

him straight in the eye. "It's just that—last night I thought you were going to kiss me. Am I crazy? It's okay if you're not attracted to me, I just . . ."

Jim sighed. He gestured toward the bed, indicating that she should sit down. He sat beside her. "Leah," he said at last, "the reason I came out here was that I needed to get away."

Leah waited for him to continue. When he didn't, she prodded, "Did you break someone's heart? Have your heart broken? Did you get left at the altar? What?"

He blinked his eyes, closing them for a long moment. "I'm not really sure where to begin."

"Why don't you start with the beginning?"

He exhaled, nodding. "About two and a half years ago, a girl I was dating broke up with me in favor of a guy who made a bunch of money, a lot more than I make. I was feeling really low and discouraged about dating and relationships. I went to a pool party at my friend's house. There was a girl there who flirted like crazy with me all night. She was cute, not gorgeous or anything, but cute. She kept telling me what great shape I was in, that sort of thing. There were drinks, bathing suits, all this flirting. We slept together. I felt bad about it because I knew I wasn't interested in seeing her and I normally don't sleep with someone I don't care deeply about.

"I gave her my number out of guilt, but I was relieved that she never called me. Except, about two years later, she *did* call me. I didn't even recognize her name. It wasn't until she said the words 'pool party' that I remembered that night at all. You can imagine how surprised I was to hear from her. She asked to meet me. I agreed because the first thing that popped into my mind was that maybe she'd found out she had AIDS or some other disease and she needed to tell me. So I met her at a café. She was sitting at a table outside. It took me a moment to recognize her. She had this cute little baby boy with her."

"Oh," Leah breathed.

Jim's face tightened. Leah reached out and gently squeezed his forearm.

"Naturally, I was reeling when she told me I was the father. It was so out of the blue. If she'd been pregnant, I would have had some time to get my mind around the idea of being a father, but here she was with a fifteen-month-old child. She said she'd originally thought about giving the baby up for adoption, which is why she didn't tell me about it in the first place. She said I didn't have to be involved in the child's life if I didn't want to be, but that if I did, she didn't want to deny me that right."

"What did you say?"

"At first I had a hard time coming to terms with the idea of being a dad. I asked to do a paternity test and we did, and it confirmed that I was the father. So Molly and I got together every now and then, and I'd spend a little time with Dennis. At first I felt really awkward, like I was playing the role of father, like I was a part in a play or something. But then one day Dennis and Molly and I went out for ice cream. He had a little taste of banana ice cream, and he made this face, this smile that . . . It was a small, silly little thing, but in that moment, I realized that being a dad is the best thing on earth. I felt this joy that was just so . . . intense. I'd never felt anything like it. Over time, Molly and I became friends. We knew that friends were all we'd ever be. We were just way too different. But we talked about me getting custody of Dennis on alternate weekends."

"So what are you doing here? Why aren't you back in Seattle with Molly and Dennis?"

He looked away. His lips became thin white lines. "A few weeks after that day when we got ice cream, Molly and Dennis were killed as they crossed the street by a driver who was talking on a cell phone. It was the middle of a bright, sunny summer day and . . ." He just shook his head, unable to finish.

Leah exhaled. "Jim, I'm so sorry." She leaned forward and hugged him.

"I came out here a few months ago. Back in Washington, I just felt like I was going crazy, like nothing made sense anymore. I thought I could come out here and hide out from the real world."

"Did it work?"

He shrugged.

Leah nodded. "I guess you have a good reason for not doing flings."

He smiled a sad smile.

"I respect that. Really." Leah studied his pained expression.

"Leah, would you mind not telling your friends?"

"There's nothing to be ashamed of."

"You're the only person I've told."

"You mean besides your family?"

"I hadn't told them yet. I'd been trying to get used to being a parent, and then by the time I did . . ."

"Oh." Leah shook her head, stunned.

"I just wanted you to know that I think you're an amazing woman. If things were different . . . ," he said again. "The thing is, just talking with you on our hikes has made me remember . . . It's just made me think about going back to the real world. But I can't possibly make love to you and then have you go home . . ."

"I understand. Thank you for telling me." Hearing Jim's story only made Leah like him more. He must have been so badly hurt to run away.

Leah did not believe in fate, or karma, or divine intervention, but the events of the past two weeks *had* been strangely coincidental. As she'd been leaving for a two-week trip with her college girlfriends, she'd run into a guy who looked just like her college boyfriend. Seeing the David lookalike had reminded her of the person she'd been before she'd allowed her

job to become her life. Then she met a man who was as de-
voted to hiding from his emotions as she was from hers.

Leah and Jim fell asleep side by side. In the morning, Leah
sheepishly said her goodbyes. She felt that the conversation
they'd had was more intimate than if they had taken off all
their clothes and slept together. Leah returned to her cabin
where she was greeted by Caitlyn, who was dressed and
putting her makeup on. Amy was on her bed putting her hiking boots on.

"Get laid?" Caitlyn asked.

"No. Not even a kiss. We just talked and then fell asleep."

"You're lying, right?"

"Why would I lie?"

"Good point. What did you talk about?"

Leah tried to think quickly. Then she decided she'd be
honest—mostly honest, anyway. "I asked him if he'd wanted
to kiss me."

"You did not! What did he say?"

"He said he did want to kiss me the other night."

"So? Why didn't he?"

"Basically, he's getting over a heartbreak." It wasn't a lie,
Leah reasoned. "Things ended badly."

"Well, shit."

Leah nodded.

Amy, Leah, and Caitlyn met for a hike. Leah and Jim smiled
shyly at each other. For two and a half hours, the group walked
uphill, downhill, through trees. Sometimes Leah would ask Jim
a question about the vegetation and foliage, and he would
tell her what he knew.

After an hour of yoga and an afternoon in the sun (or
shade, in Leah's case), Leah, Caitlyn, and Amy went to the
dining room where, surprise, surprise, they had soup, salad,
and whole-grain bread that was the weight, density, and fla-
vor of plutonium.

As Amy listlessly poked at her naked salad greens, she

thought about how she was actually looking forward to the seminar tonight. It was on reducing stress by living in the moment. Maybe if Amy could learn how not to get so stressed out with work and wedding plans, she could relax and enjoy sex with her husband-to-be again.

Amy was sighing as she ate yet another taste-free carrot slice when Devin approached their table. "It's Jenny's birthday tonight."

"Jenny?" Amy asked.

"One of the social workers from California," Caitlyn said.

"Oh. Um, that's great."

"There's cake," Devin said.

"Cake? Where?" Amy looked around and saw the group gathered at the large table in the corner. She leapt out of her chair and sprinted over, nearly plowing down an old lady who got in her way.

Amy watched the cake being sliced into pieces as thin as Kleenex tissues. She glanced around, calculating the number of grubby hands waiting for cake versus the ever-diminishing supply. Each time a slice was gently laid on a plate, it was savagely snapped up by a salivating guest. At last it was Amy's turn. The cake was as thin as a communion wafer, and it evaporated almost the second in hit her tongue. Still, she got tiniest taste of chocolate cake with a vanilla pudding middle and a creamy frosting on top. She closed her eyes and let the taste roll over her tongue. She wasn't sure anything had ever tasted quite so exquisite. After Leah and Caitlyn had had their slivers of cake, the three of them headed next door to the events building for the seminar.

As they walked out of the dining room, Leah saw Jim. "Guys," she said to Amy and Caitlyn, "I want to . . . I'll meet you . . ."

"Go," Amy said.

Leah smiled at them and jogged toward Jim. Amy and Caitlyn went into the cabin where the seminar on the importance of living in the moment was being held. Their yoga instructor Kiera led the workshop.

Fourteen women sat on uncomfortable wood chairs, and Kiera paced back and forth at the front of the room. She wore a long, loose white linen dress.

"We are all on a path," she began in that feathery-light voice of hers. "We want our lives to go one way—we want a new job or a new boyfriend and to always be healthy and never get sick—but you need to understand that while it's important to strive toward your goals, when obstacles get in your way, it's not because you are being punished. These obstacles are your life. They are there for you so you can learn and grow. So don't fight them. Don't get angry. You can think of anger as a very heavy weight. You can either hold on to anger and carry it around with you all the time or you can do the work it takes to let go of that anger and spend the rest of your life free of that heavy burden. Either way it takes effort—you may as well let go of anger and embrace peace. Sometimes the things that happen in your life that seem bad can be the things that transform you into the kind of person you want to be. Things won't always go the way you want or planned, but life is like the weather, you can't control it, so you may as well just enjoy the rain as much as the sun, because you need both."

For once, Amy paid attention during the seminar. Though Kiera seemed like something of a wack job, there was a peace about her that Amy wanted. Plus, everything Kiera said made so much sense. Amy had been holding on to anger for so many years—anger toward her brother for stealing all of their mother's attention and being endless fodder for gossip hounds, toward her mother for spending all her energy on the black sheep and none on the golden child, toward the girls Amy had gone to high school with who'd called her a slut because of her natural double Ds, toward her father for spending so much time on work and his disposable blondes.

"Anger is really just fear," Kiera continued. "When you get angry about your spouse flirting with another woman, you're really afraid that he's no longer attracted to you. You're afraid that you're going to lose him."

Anger is really just fear. It made sense. Maybe what was keeping Amy so unhappy was fear masquerading as anger. Fear that Eric might abandon her as her parents had done. Maybe that was why, in the past, Amy had always chosen men who didn't really excite her. Then, if they left her, she wouldn't be devastated. Eric, she truly cared about. The stakes were much, much higher. Maybe she was trying to sabotage it to save herself the pain of possibly getting hurt.

"Just like you can't control the weather, you can't control other people. You can't control the economy, or who the president elects to the Supreme Court, or whether another person keeps his or her word. All you can control is yourself, and sometimes you can't even control that." Kiera stopped pacing for a moment and faced her audience. "Let me explain. You can't control whether you get a new job, for example, but you *can* do your best to get the job by looking your best and being prepared for the interview. If you do get the job, you can't control whether your coworkers do their work well or on time, and you can't control whether your boss is nice or a jerk. What you can do is your best—you can show up to the office on time and try your hardest. You can choose not to waste time gossiping about coworkers, that sort of thing. What I meant when I said that you can't always control yourself is this: Sometimes you're to have every ambition of waking up in the morning and going into the office and working hard and getting a lot done, but it turns out you got a terrible night of sleep and you're exhausted, so your thoughts aren't as sharp and focused as they could be. Or you might wake up feeling under the weather, with a headache and a sore throat and the sniffles, which keep you from doing your best. My point is that the vast majority of things in this world aren't under our control. Not our spouses, not our kids, not even whether our car starts in the morning. All we can do is our best. For this reason, you can't decide that you'll be happy only if you get a new job or if your boyfriend finally asks you to marry him. You can't base your happiness on things that are out of your control, because that's a recipe for unhappiness.

"You can't be happy all the time," Kiera continued. "If you were happy all the time, it would be like eating chocolate cake for every meal. It might be 'fun,' but having fun all the time only gets you fat. But we can't always being eating broccoli either. You need some broccoli and the occasional dessert."

Across the spa grounds, Jim and Leah were walking and talking. They stopped in front of a bougainvillea.

Jim leaned in close. "It's driving me crazy to be hanging out with you," he whispered.

"Do you want me to go away?"

"No. It's just that . . . For these last six months, I've tried to run away from my feelings by exercising my body as hard as I can or spending so much time working I don't have time to think or feel. Being around you reminds me of what I've been missing."

"So basically, I've got you all hot and bothered."

He smiled.

"You know, there are other things we can do besides sex," she said.

"That's true."

"It could be fun. It'd be like a return to high school. We could, you know, stop at third base."

"What is third base, anyway?"

"I don't actually remember. It's good stuff, though, I'm pretty sure."

He looked away. "What am I going to do with you?"

"Anything you want?"

He turned to face her again. His eyes studied hers.

"We could start with a kiss," she suggested.

He nodded. "We could."

She was supremely aware of just how close he was to her. She could feel the warmth of his skin against hers, the energy of their hearts and bodies pulling each other closer. Her pulse rocketed. At last his soft lips descended on hers tentatively, questioningly, as a chef might taste just a tiny drop of sauce to see if it was ready. His kisses grew more assured, and his tongue and lips delved into her mouth with burning exploration. He wrapped his arms around her. She returned the embrace, pulling him closer, feeling the swell of muscles in his arms and chest.

Breathing heavily, Jim pulled away. "I might get in trouble if I'm caught with tongue down a guest's throat."

"Maybe we should go to your cabin."

Jim waited a beat. Then he grabbed her hand and started running. "Let's go!"

Leah laughed. When they got to his cabin, he fumbled with the key to unlock the door, and they stumbled inside, their arms around each other as Jim crushed his lips against hers. He kicked the door closed behind them.

Jim's hands found their way beneath her shirt to her back, which he caressed gently. His touch was so delicate, like a leaf floating lightly on the surface of a clear blue pool. His hand on her was as warm and comforting as being bathed in sunlight.

He unbuttoned her shirt slowly, nibbling at her white cotton bra, squeezing her breasts gently. He used his fingers to pull her bra down enough to suckle her nipple and reached around to her back to snap her bra off.

"Hang on," Leah said. She sat up and wrestled with the knot on her boots. In her haste to get her boots off, she inadvertently tightened the knot, and she struggled awkwardly for a few moments to untie her laces and kick her boots and socks off. Jim took the cue and kicked his boots off and pulled his shirt over his head.

Leah drank in the sight of his naked chest and stomach before Jim fell back against the pillows with her. Jim proved expert at finding seemingly innocent spots on her body that sent shivers through her, tracing his fingers gently across the hallow of her neck, the crook of her elbow, the underside of her silken breast. All of the nerves in her body were taut with excitement.

At last Jim pulled her shorts and underwear off. He explored her inner thighs with gentle kisses until she was lightheaded with longing. Finally he plunged his fingers inside her. Leah was so worked up she came almost instantly, her body exploding with release.

Quickly she turned to her side, pushing him on his back. She sucked his nipples, sneaking a glance at his face to watch his breath deepen, his eyes close. She trailed her tongue down his hard stomach. He shuddered moments after she took him into her mouth.

She lay beside him, resting her head on his chest. "God, that was embarrassing," he said.

She laughed. "It's been a while."

"I know."

"We'll be less overexcitable next time."

They didn't say anything but simply held each other. Leah traced her fingers across his chest, watching it rise and fall. The motion put her into an incredibly calm, almost meditative state. He had one arm around her, and his other hand lightly stroked her arm.

She touched his medallion. "Where did you get this?"

The silver medallion looked like a sundial. In the center was something that looked a little like a sideways treble clef. Intricately knotted pieces of silver fanned out from the clef to form a circle.

"I got it when I was in Central America."

"What were you doing in Central America?"

"I worked with the Peace Corps for a couple of years after college."

"That's cool. What was it like there?"

"It was different. Very different. Especially because I was in the small towns mostly."

"Different how?"

"Poverty is rampant. There isn't much clean drinking water. Their culture is very traditional. Men would never *think* of helping with the cooking or raising kids."

"Sounds like my family. We had this rule that there had to be a jumper for every meal. The jumper sat close to the kitchen door, and if someone needed extra mashed potatoes or more milk, the jumper jumped up and got it. It was always my sister or me who had to be the jumpers because we were girls, and I have to say that if you give a young boy power, it'll go straight to his head. My family was really traditional that way. The women cooked and cleaned and sewed. The men pretty much didn't have to do anything but take the garbage out and mow the lawn. I think that's part of the reason I became a tomboy."

Leah gently twirled Jim's chest hair with her index finger. "I don't think I've ever told anyone that before. It's really easy to talk to you."

"I feel the same way."

Leah felt incredibly happy and sad at the same time. She was happy that she'd been able to meet Jim but sad that she'd met a guy unlike anyone else she'd ever known and would soon be leaving him.

In the morning, she and Jim had everything-but sex again. It was wonderful, but Leah ached to have him inside her. They held each other for just a few minutes before Jim looked at his watch and said, "We should get going. I need to get something to eat before I lead the hike today."

Leah wanted to clobber him in the head with a baseball bat. She knew he was right: they'd talked until late into the night, and they'd used every last free moment of their morning touching and exploring each other, but she hated the idea of leaving. Reluctantly, she got dressed and put her shoes on.

Jim walked her to the door and gave her a soft, tender good-bye kiss.

"Well, well, well," Caitlyn said when Leah unlocked the door to their cottage. Caitlyn's hair was wet from her shower. Dressed in a pale pink bra and matching underwear, she sprawled across her bed and filed her nails. Amy was fully dressed and had already finished drying her hair.

"Look who's home," Caitlyn said without looking up from her nails. "We were worried that you'd been eaten by wolves or something. So were you? Eaten, that is?"

"Caitlyn!" Leah tsked. Then, a smile lighted her face. "I was, actually, and it was wonderful. We did everything but have sex. It was great but also . . . It also left me wanting more."

"Why didn't you guys have sex?"

"Because I fell for the one straight male on the planet who has principles, damn it."

"He still doesn't believe in flings? That guy is a unicorn. Men like him just don't exist." Caitlyn was adamant.

"Are you guys up for a hike today?" Leah said.

"You're kidding, right? I'm spending the rest of this trip with my ass firmly planted in a lounge chair by the pool," Caitlyn said.

"My legs are still sore from the other day, but I'd be up for going," Amy said.

"You guys can't leave me alone," Caitlyn whined. "What if something exciting happens?"

"Like we get lost in the woods?"

"Exactly."

"You don't have to come."

Caitlyn sighed. "If you're going, I'm going."

After Leah showered and changed, they got some breakfast in them and gathered by the pool with the other hikers.

"Aren't you the girls who got lost in the woods the other day?" one of the women asked. She was thin with toffee-colored skin and short dark hair. She was cute, but her nose and facial features had a somewhat smooshed look to them, like a clay mask that had been dropped before it had a chance to harden.

"That's us," Amy said.

"I can't believe you're brave enough to go back out there."

"Was it scary out there?"

"A little," Amy confessed.

"You girls are so brave."

"Not really. We didn't have any other choice but to go on.

"That's not true. Some people break under the stress. Keeping your wits about your shows just what you're made of."

Amy hadn't considered this. Maybe this woman was right. Amy had gotten through a lot of tough things in her life. She had two parents who'd never really been there for her, and she'd been teased mercilessly all through her school by her classmates about her lawless brother, and not only had she survived getting lost in the woods, but she'd helped her sick friend make it out alive, too.

When Leah saw Jim, a smile lit up her face.

"How are you?" he asked, smiling.

"I'm a little tired, actually. I didn't get much sleep last night."

"Shame."

"I know, I know. Poor me."

Jim got the hike started. As the guests followed behind him, Leah walked beside him. As they walked, she learned that he had gone to Berkeley on a football scholarship, but he was sidelined with a bad knee for most of his sophomore year. He'd had surgery, but his knee was never the same. His doctor warned him that another injury would likely mean that Jim would never walk normally again. That was enough to convince Jim to say goodbye to football.

She told him about they years she'd spent doing field research for the Oregon Fish and Wildlife department. "I spent most of my days counting fish in rivers," she said. "The research project I was working on looked at the environmental impact of global warming and pollution on fish and, by extension, tried to figure out what impact that would have on people."

"What did you learn?"

"Nothing good, that's for sure. Anyway, the funding for that project was pulled when the new administration came into office. Their philosophy is to be ignorant of how pollution and global warming are slowly killing us. Ignorance is bliss, right? At least that way we don't have to do anything about it. Even before the funding was cut, the pay we researchers were getting was embarrassingly low. That's why I started freelancing articles for *Our World*. It was a part-time thing I did at night and on the weekends. Fortunately, a full-time position opened up shortly after I'd been laid off from my state job."

Leah asked Jim more about his experience in the Peace Corps. He explained that his job was to educate people about proper nutrition in an effort to prevent disease and reduce infant mortality rates. "It's kind of funny," he said. "I stayed with a family for a while when I was down there. They would make vegetables, but they would add a huge spoonful of lard when they were cooking them. They need fat in their diets, I get that, but lard is not butter, it doesn't help the taste, and that much of it . . . Uh, just thinking about it can still make my stomach queasy, and that was a decade ago. I'd see these fresh crisp vegetables, and seconds later they were being cooked in scoops of lard. I begged them to just let me eat the veggies raw, but they didn't think I'd get enough calories to survive. I couldn't win."

When they were getting close to the spa again after the hike, Jim asked her, "Do you want to stop by my cottage after dinner?"

"I'd love to."

"I didn't even say what we might spend the evening doing."

"Doesn't matter. It sounds good to me."

"Come to my cabin and I'll make us dinner."

"Please tell me it will involve a cheeseburger, fattening dairy products, and noncomplex carbohydrates."

"Sorry, it won't. But it will be as yummy as I can do with organic greens and contraband beer."

"Ooh, beer. I'm definitely in then. I'll see you later."

He looked at her with smiling eyes. "Later."

Chapter 16

Day Twelve

Caitlyn woke up feeling blue. Unlike the stereotypical angst-ridden poet, Caitlyn was generally a happy person, so she wasn't used to feeling glum. Maybe a walk would help her clear her head.

She told Amy and Leah that she was going to take a stroll and maybe write in her journal a little. Journal writing was the only writing she'd done in months. It didn't require her to be creative, she merely reported the who, what, when, where, and how of her life.

She thought about all the boyfriends she'd had over the years, all the day jobs she'd experimented with—cocktail waitress, English tutor, bartender, retail clerk, administrative assistant. She thought of all the hair colors she'd tried out and the fashions she'd experimented with. The only constants in her life were her writing and her friends, except lately she hadn't been writing much, and Amy and Leah lived far away. As much as they loved each other, they just weren't the same support system they'd once been.

Maybe it was time to stop moving from apartment to apartment, from job to job, guy to guy. Maybe some roots wouldn't be such a bad thing.

Caitlyn found the river and walked along it. She thought

about their getting lost in the woods. If they'd made just one more wrong turn, it could have cost them another critical hour or two before they reached water, an hour or two that could have cost her her life.

She figured as long as she stuck by the spring there was no way she could get lost. She walked until she came upon a waterfall. Because it was a formed by a hot spring, steam rose out of it. Beams of sunlight streamed through the steam.

Caitlyn stopped dead. How amazing the world was. She thought of all the hours she spent locked up in front of her computer or her TV while nature was putting on a spectacular show right outside.

She sat beside it on a large flat rock. She inhaled, exhaled. She tried to clear her mind and feel the primordial energy of the earth. She listened to the wind creaking through the trees.

For no reason she could understand, tears pooled in her eyes and slid down her cheeks. She watched the hypnotic lull of the river burbling gently by. Caitlyn wiped the tears from her face. It felt strangely good to cry. Was she crying out of relief that she was still alive?

The tears continued to fall so quickly she couldn't wipe them away fast enough. Even though she wanted to open herself up to true love, even though she had promised that if she made it out of the woods alive she would break up with Reg, Sean, and Kyle, thinking about having to actually go through with it terrified her. Maybe, she thought, she could just break up with one of them. Then, after a few weeks, she could break up with the second one. Then, a few weeks after that, she could sever the ties with the third one. Ideally, of course, she would have met the man of her dreams by then. But if she didn't, she would be okay.

Yes, that was what she would do. Who broke up with three people in a matter of just a few days?

Even as she tried to convince herself that she was still living up to her promise if it took her a few months to break up with her bevy of boyfriends, she knew she was doing what she'd done for years—lying to herself. She just had to be brave. It would be okay. No problem. She was a strong woman. She was smart. She was capable. She'd be fine.

Caitlyn opened her journal. For the next half hour, she recounted the details of the day she'd spent lost in the woods. At first, she kept her tone light and joked about what "dorks" and "idiots" Leah, Amy, and she were. She even kidded about the fact they could have died in a national forest in Mexico:

> *Most tourists are killed by rapists and bandits. Us? We were almost done in by some trees!*

Caitlyn stopped writing. She bit her lip and thought a moment, and then began writing again:

> *Now that I know everything turned out okay, I can joke about what happened, but the truth was, it was really scary. It got me thinking. It got me into one of those existential, what-is-the-meaning-of-my-life sort of mood, that whole what-if-I-die-today sort of mood that forced me to think about what I'd regret if I didn't live to see the morning. I thought about how much I want to be around to see Amy's wedding, and Leah's for that matter, whenever that should happen. I want to find out if I'm awarded the grant to work in France. I want to see what other poems I have in me. I know they're inside me; they've just been hibernating for a while. I want to fall in love. Whether it happens next week or next year or sometime in the next decade, I want to be open and ready for it. I want to know who my father is. I understand that I'll probably never meet him; I just want to know a little about him and who he was.*

The tears came again, faster this time. They fell to the ground beside the waterfall that was hidden beneath a veil of steam that rose up from the hot springs buried deep within the earth.

Though Caitlyn normally used a different notebook to jot down ideas for poems, she didn't have any paper besides her journal with her, so she flipped to a blank page.

For many years I marched ahead
Though I found myself in a different place, the scenery
stayed the same
Just when I thought I was coming to the crest
Just when I thought the end was just around the bend
I realized that the journey wasn't over

All I saw was trees ahead of me, beside me, behind me
Though I found myself in a different place, the scenery
stayed the same

I just kept going, one foot in front of the other
Always looking forward and backward, but never
looking in

A new job, a new apartment, a new boyfriend
A new outfit, a new pair of shoes
Ten pounds lighter, ten pounds heavier
Though I found myself in a different place, the scenery
stayed the same

Chapter 17

Days Twelve and Thirteen

Jim's hand was on Leah's breast and his lips were kissing hers. His penis was on her thigh, perilously close to where she truly ached for it to be.

Jim moaned. In a husky voice he said, "God, this is driving me crazy. I want to be inside you."

"I want you inside, too."

"I know we've only known each other a few days, but I really like you."

"I know."

Does this mean we get to have sex? she wondered.

His fingers trailed gently from her breast down to her stomach. She waited for him to enter her. To say something about getting a condom. Anything. But he didn't.

"Jim," she said in a whisper, "humans are meant to mate. The desire to have sex is incredibly powerful. It has to be. We need to keep producing babies somehow."

He smiled. "I know. I just . . . can't."

Leah smiled a sad smile. "It's okay," she said. She kissed him again. On most vacations to hot, sunny climates, eating decadent meals and having cheap sex with a hot guy was part of the package. Here she'd been tormented by alfalfa sprouts and broccoli soup and a hot guy who wouldn't go beyond third base. Leah had no experience whatsoever with a grown man saying no to sex. Despite the powerful orgasm he brought her to using his fingers, their lovemaking felt incomplete. Leah felt as though she'd eaten a tasty appetizer that whet her appetite, but was never given the main course.

Again, he began kissing and touching her. In moments, their breathing was harried, their kisses and touches frenzied.

"Aaagh," he groaned, pulling away from her.

"What's wrong?"

"I want to be inside you."

"So what's the problem exactly?"

He didn't say anything for a moment.

"I don't have any condoms."

"So are you changing your mind?"

"I'm terrible. I have no willpower."

"It's not you. You're a victim of biology. It's only right that we celebrate or humanness by mating like crazy. Except I don't have any condoms either. I can ask my girlfriends if they brought any. Caitlyn might have some. I'll ask her in the morning."

They continued touching each other, sometimes sensually, sometimes playfully, until they were both sated and they fell asleep.

When Leah awoke, she watched Jim sleep. Part of her wished she'd never come here. Jim had awakened so many feelings in her that she hadn't even realized were asleep. For the last few years, she'd been so safe in her routine. She would wake up at around eight in the morning, shuffle down the stairs of her town home and grab a Diet Coke (she'd never been a coffee drinker), then go to her study and read her e-mails and the on-line newspaper. She would go to her living room and spend half an hour jogging on her treadmill while watching the morning news. She'd shower, eat some cereal or some frozen waffles or a Pop Tart, and she'd start work at her desk. She did most of her interviews over the phone, so there were many days when she never had to leave the house at all. When she actually had to change out of her sweats and PJs and put on actual socks and shoes, it was almost jarring. Except for grocery shopping, she did all of her shopping on-line, buying her clothes, books, and CDs and DVDs over the Internet. There was so much beauty in this world, and yet she spent her days voluntarily locked up inside, chained to her computer. She wrote about science and nature but spent very little time exploring nature in the real world.

Leah stroked Jim's chest. He opened his eyes and smiled at her. She cupped her hand around his flaccid penis. Within seconds it grew hard.

"It's like magic," Leah teased.

He nodded. "It's like a magic lantern. Stroke it a few times and all your wishes come true."

Leah laughed and groaned, burying her face in his chest. He laughed.

"I should go," Leah said. Jim nodded. She kissed him goodbye and quietly dressed. She returned to her cabin where Caitlyn was wrapped in a towel, combing her wet hair, and Amy was dressed and blow-drying her hair in the bathroom.

"Hey, stranger," Caitlyn said. "How's loverboy?"

"Great. And things are looking even better. He finally caved and wants to have sex-sex."

"Congratulations!"

"The problem is, neither of us has any condoms."

"I have a few I can give you."

"Really? Caitlyn, I could kiss you."

"That won't be necessary." She set her comb down on the desk and riffled through her suitcase until she pulled out four condoms strung together, four squares of joy wrapped in plastic.

Leah and Jim had a mere two more days left together. Two days and four condoms.

The thought tempered her happiness. In two days she would be leaving a guy who brought alive feelings and emotions like no other guy she had known. Why did life always work this way?

After breakfast, Amy, Caitlyn, and Leah met Jim and the others for another hike. All through the hike, Leah and Jim exchanged smiles and secret glances. Leah couldn't wait for the night. Snapshots of them together flashed in her mind: him kissing her, him touching her, him smiling at her . . .

Leah realized Amy had said something. "What?" Leah asked.

"I said I think I lost another couple of pounds," Amy said. "I think it's thanks to the day we spent lost in the woods. At least something good came out of our brush with death."

"Way to have a positive attitude," Leah said.

When the group returned to the spa, Jim and Leah lingered behind the rest of them. "See you tonight," he said. "Six?"

"I'll be there."

Through yoga, lunch, and an afternoon in the sun, Leah glanced at her watch every few seconds. She was convinced that, defying all laws of logic and reason, time was actually moving backward. Time had never gone so slowly.

At five, Leah showered and tried to look as cute as possible working with the limited wardrobe she had. She wished she'd brought something besides boring white bras and underwear, but that's all she had. Caitlyn helped her with her make-up. Leah looked at her watch. Someone was playing a cruel joke on her. It was five-thirty-three.

Slowly, painfully, the minutes passed, and it was time to meet Jim. He opened the door with a radiant smile, wrapped her in his arms, and kissed her passionately.

He broke away for a moment. "I made a healthy Mexican dinner—"

Leah pulled the strip of four condoms from her pocket. "We can eat later." She pulled her shirt and boots off and went to the bed, giving him the come-hither sign with her index finger.

Their lovemaking was frenzied and urgent. Time, which all day had taunted Leah, suddenly lost meaning. Naked and sweaty and sated, smiling stupidly, Leah and Jim finally ate the dinner he'd prepared. It was cold, but they were so hungry it didn't matter.

Leah lay on the bed. Her mind was dreamy and unfocused.

Jim propped himself up on the one tanned elbow. His dark hair fell around his face. "Let's go for a steam."

"A steam? But we've just created our own steam for the last few hours."

"Steaming is good for you. It gets all the toxins out."

"I've spent two weeks eating tofu and lentil soup. I have no toxins."

"Come on," he urged, tossing her a towel.

Wrapped only in towels, Leah and Jim ran across the grounds to the steam room, which was near the pool. The room was nearly pitch-black. The only light was that from the moon sneaking its way in through an overhead window. The smell of eucalyptus from the leaves draped over the steam from the underground hot springs infused the air. Leah inhaled deeply, cleansing her lungs with the pleasing, pungent odor.

Within minutes, Leah was sweating so hard, droplets of sweat ran down her forehead and dripped off her nose. In the calm, dark silence, the happiness Leah had felt making love to Jim was interrupted by a sharp pain when she thought about how little time they had left. They had known each other only for two weeks, but it had been an intense two weeks. Each of their "dates" lasted for hours. But still, two weeks was hardly any time at all. And it hadn't been a real-life two weeks. She was on vacation. She had worked some on her article, but it hadn't been anything like her usual workweek. They hadn't had to deal with traffic or bills. She had no idea what their relationship would be like when they weren't in a beautiful fantasyland filled with relaxing hikes and energetic sex. She felt such a powerful connection with him. She wanted to see if things could work between them in the real world. Leah didn't want to move to Mexico. The spa was beautiful and wonderful and all that, but Leah loved her work, and she just didn't see how it would be possible to do it in the mountains in the middle of Central Mexico. If the spa had access to high-speed Internet connection, that would help, but the dial-up connection was so agonizingly slow and unsteady, she would never be able to access the information she needed in a timely fashion. And she didn't speak Spanish, so she couldn't interview local professors and scientists to get the information she needed. The cost of calling experts in the United States would be exorbitant—her magazine paid for most of her travel and phone expenses, but there was no way *Our World* could eat the cost of her constantly making international phone calls.

Jim had said that he wanted to move back to be close to his family at some point. If he moved back to Seattle, that would be only three hours away from where she lived. They could make the commute back and forth for a while. If things worked out, Leah was willing to move to Seattle. It was a great city. She would miss her friends in Portland, but she could make new ones.

These were the thoughts causing anarchy in her mind when Jim leaned over and stroked her sweating breast. She was instantly aroused, and as he leaned in to kiss her, pushing her on her back, spreading her legs . . .

"Couldn't this be a health risk?" she whispered as a smile spread across her face. "You know, intense exercise in intense heat and all that."

"Let's find out."

Chapter 18

Day Fourteen

"Good morning, beautiful."

Leah's eyes blinked open. When she saw Jim smiling at her on his bed, she instinctively smiled back. "Hi."

But the spark of happiness she felt was immediately tempered by feelings of sadness. She wanted to talk to him about all of her thoughts about their future, but every time the words came close to her lips, fear clenched her heart. What if Jim didn't feel the same way about her? What if these last few days had really just been a fling?

But she didn't say anything. She made love to him slowly, got dressed, kissed him goodbye and told him she'd see him in an hour for the hike.

When she got back to the cottage, Caitlyn extended her boots so Leah could perform her morning ritual of checking for scorpions. "Oh, good, you're just in time."

"All clear," she pronounced.

"How are you doing?" Caitlyn asked.

"I'll be fine. I knew it was just a fling. It was a fun few days of sex, that's all."

She could see that Caitlyn didn't buy it, and Leah didn't blame her.

The three friends grabbed breakfast and then met at the pool for their final hike.

Leah wanted to talk to Jim about whether she was ever going to see him again. Why hadn't he said anything to her this morning? Why hadn't he asked for her e-mail address, her mailing address, or her phone number?

All through the hike, Leah turned over in her mind what she should say to him. "Hi, Jim, I think I love you. Therefore, it would really be convenient if I could see you again someday."

Somehow that didn't seem quite right.

For two and a half hours, Leah plodded along, oblivious of her surroundings or the conversation going on around her. She wished Jim would tell her how he felt and that he wanted to see her again. Maybe he could ask her to come back for a visit sometime.

She and Caitlyn and Amy spent their afternoon lounging and reading, but Leah couldn't concentrate on her research.

Before dinner, they went back to their room to pack. As Leah folded her clothes, packing into her suitcase everything but the outfit she was going to wear home tomorrow, a dull feeling descended over her.

"I had a great time here, but I can't say I'm going to miss the food," Amy said. She was already packed and sat on her bed watching Caitlyn and Leah.

"I feel healthy and energized. But is eating well really worth the benefits? Are health and energy really that important?" Caitlyn said. Caitlyn's packing method was to hurl everything into her suitcase, tamp it down, and then sit on it to zip it closed. "Ready!" she said triumphantly.

For the last time they made their way up to the dining hall and served themselves dinner.

"I'm not going to eat soup for months after this," said Amy. She then noticed the distracted look on Leah's face. "You don't have to eat with us, you know. It's really okay. You can be with Jim."

"No. It's okay. Sorry. I'll be fine."

"Well, you can hang out with him when we're done. Really, Caitlyn and I don't mind."

"This is our last night together."

"That's okay. We had two weeks together. One night isn't going to hurt."

Leah smiled. "You two are good friends. What would I do without you?"

Wordlessly, Caitlyn reached out her hands and took Leah's and Amy's hands in hers, giving them a squeeze. "I missed you guys."

"I missed you, too."

"Me, too," Leah agreed.

"We have to do a better job of keeping in touch. I say that we force ourselves to write each other a quick e-mail every day," Amy said. "We'll do it first thing in the morning so it becomes a habit like brushing our teeth. And we'll have to plan on seeing each other at least every other year. No amount of e-mails or phone calls can make up for spending a few days together. Leah and I can come visit you in Chicago one year; then we can go to Portland the next. And every few years we need to plan a real getaway, to a spa or a beach someplace, no boys allowed."

"It sounds good, Amy," Caitlyn said, "but we always promise to write, and we do a good job for a while, and then inevitably we stop."

"We just have to try. There are three of us. If at least one of us keeps making an effort to keep each other in the loop, the guilt the other two of us feel will help us to keep trying, too. Trying is all we can do," Amy said.

Leah nodded. "I'm up for giving it a shot."

"Me, too." Caitlyn agreed.

They finished their meals and brought their trays to the counter by the kitchen. "You can go spend the night with Jim," Amy said. "Really. It's okay."

"You're sure? What are you two going to do?" Leah said.

"I don't know, Caitlyn, what do you think? Maybe one last purifying steam and one last soak in the warm pool?"

"Sounds perfect."

"You really don't mind?"

"Have fun," Caitlyn said.

"I love you guys."

"We love you, too."

Chapter 19

The final hours

It was hard to feel sexy in a white cotton tank top and loose blue linen shirt, but Leah had few clean clothes left, so she didn't have much choice. She knocked on Jim's door.

"Hey, beautiful."

"Hey."

She stepped inside his simple cottage. It was much like her cottage with red-tile floors and bark paintings on the wall, but unlike her room, his was neat and tidy since his cottage was Caitlyn-free. He took her in his arms and kissed her, guiding her toward the bed so she was on her back, he was half on top of her, half on his side, his arm draped over her.

"We don't have much time."

Ah. There it was. Finally. An acknowledgment that their time together was finite.

As they kissed, his hand found her breast. He pulled his lips from hers. "No bra." He raised his eyebrows, a hint of a smile on his lips.

"Is that a problem?"

"Are you kidding me? Bras are evil."

She laughed, and he crushed his lips against hers.

As it turned out, that was the last of their conversation for the night. There were no discussion of the future or of ever seeing each other again. They made love for most of the night, sleeping here and there. Leah awoke to his heavy arm over her. She tried to remember if she'd ever experienced such intense feelings for a man before. She could vaguely remember the feelings of happiness and excitement she'd felt in the first flushes of her romance with David and with Chuck, the powerful emotions she'd experienced each time she realized she was in love, but there was something different about what she felt for Jim.

With both David and Chuck, she'd found intellectual equals. She fell only for men who could keep up with her intellectually. But there were many other levels that she and Jim connected on.

She connected with Jim sexually in a way she'd never had with another man. She'd never felt such lust toward anyone like she did for Jim. David had been on the skinny side, and Chuck's arms had no definition and he'd had a slight potbelly. At the time she had been dating them, this hadn't bothered Leah in the least. But now that she'd run her hands over powerful, muscular flesh, she realized just how sexy it was to be enveloped by strong arms and a broad chest. It was such a turn on, and the fact that this amazing body was attached to a sexy, smart, caring man made it that much sexier.

She connected with Jim on an emotional level, too. He looked out for her needs as she looked out for his. She would never forget the way he'd cared for her that day she'd developed heat stroke when she'd been lost in the woods. She loved the way they laughed and teased each other. Leah was not a flirty, teasing type. At least she hadn't been until she met Jim.

Leah had never before believed in true love. She'd never believed that there was just one guy in the world who was meant just for her. She knew that finding a guy whom she really connected with and whom she was attracted to and who was equally attracted to her was no easy task, but she'd never thought there was just one guy in the world who could fit the bill. Still, as she lay beside Jim and watched him peacefully breathe in and out, his chest rising and falling, she couldn't imagine ever feeling like this with another man. She'd gone thirty-two years without ever feeling like this toward another person. Being with Jim made her realize that the love she'd had for David and Chuck had been a mere hint of what she was capable of feeling. Now she recognized real love; she could never go back.

For years, Jim had lived only three hours away from her in Seattle, but she'd needed to travel to the remote mountains of Central Mexico to find him working at a small resort. She'd never believed in fate or a higher power before, but watching Jim, she decided she might be persuaded to become a believer after all. If nothing else, she knew without a doubt that meeting Jim had been one of the best things to ever happen to her.

His eyes flickered open. "Good morning," he said.

"Good morning."

"What time is it?"

"I have no idea."

He kissed her, then rolled over and looked at the clock. "Shit, it's ten after nine. I have to get ready to lead the hike."

He hopped out of bed and immediately began pulling his clothes on. Leah lingered in bed, watching him. It took her a minute to find the will to leave his bed and dress herself.

"I'll walk you to your cabin," he said.

Leah longed to reach out and hold his hand, but she knew they had to be careful. There wasn't a policy against staff fraternizing with guests, but Jim had explained that it was tacitly understood that guests were off limits.

Jim walked her to her door and turned to face her. Leah's heart flipped—this was it. She was about to leave for Portland. If one of them didn't say something, they would probably never see each other again. This was their last chance. This was the moment they would talk about their future.

He pulled his necklace over his neck. "I want you to have this." She ducked her head, and he put it around her neck.

"Thanks." She touched the medallion with the pads of her fingertips.

"I have to run now. But I want you to know how much these last few days have meant to me."

"Me, too."

"Goodbye, Leah."

And with one last kiss, Jim Maddalena was out of Leah's life forever.

Chapter 20

Back to reality

Amy, Caitlyn, and Leah shared a taxi back to the airport. Their planes left within a couple of hours of each other. As the taxi bounced down the dirt road, Leah told them about how she and Jim hadn't exchanged contact information.

"Even if a guy has no intention of calling you, he always *says* he'll call you," Leah said.

"Why didn't you give your e-mail and phone number to him?" Caitlyn said.

Leah shrugged. "Maybe I was scared. The stereotype is that guys are commitment phobic. I didn't want to look pushy and scare him off."

"He lives in Mexico. How scared off can he get?" Caitlyn said. "Anyway, Jim is *not* a stereotype."

"I know. You're right. I guess I'm just out of practice with this whole dating thing. I really thought I would be fine with a fling. Getting into this, I knew the logistics of this relationship would never work out."

"I'm sure you could call the spa and get a hold of him that way," Amy said.

"You should," Caitlyn agreed.

"You think he'd like me to call?" Leah asked.

"I'm sure he would," Amy said.

"Maybe I will," Leah said. Even though she was with Amy and Caitlyn, she felt lonely already. She didn't want to go home to her empty town home.

When the cab arrived at the airport, Amy paid the driver, refusing the cash that Leah and Caitlyn tried to give her.

"I had a *great* time," Amy said.

"I did, too," Caitlyn said. "I do *not* want to go back to Chicago." She didn't say that it was more than the bad weather she wasn't looking forward to. Saying goodbye to Reg, Sean, and Kyle promised to be as much fun as getting dental surgery, and confronting her mother about her father yet again was going to be emotionally exhausting.

"I miss you guys already," Leah said.

"We'll see each other in just two months," Amy said. "And remember, the three of us are going to start e-mailing each other every day. We have to think of it as a New Year's resolution, except unlike eating well and exercising, this resolution is actually going to be fun."

Amy kissed and hugged her friends goodbye and headed through the airport to catch a flight that would stop in Dallas before taking her home to Denver.

Amy felt nervous about seeing Eric. She wanted to make love to him tonight, and she wanted it to be special; different. She had been contemplating some of Caitlyn's ideas that seemed slightly less terrifying than the others, but there was still a part of her that worried she was going to make an ass of herself.

If you can survive getting lost in the woods without any water and not completely losing your cool, if you can flash half a soccer team in a swimming pool, you can damn well experiment with your fiancé in the bedroom, she told herself.

When Amy's plane landed in Denver, she made her way down to baggage claim. Her bags were supposed to be at claim area number five, but the luggage hadn't been unloaded yet. Amy sighed. She checked her watch, shifting her weight from one foot to the other. She looked around. Checked her watch again.

At last the ramp began to turn. Black bags with wheels, duffle bags, sealed boxes, plaid suitcases and golf club bags—around and around it all went until Amy finally spotted her periwinkle blue suitcase and grabbed it.

Triumphant, Amy went sprinting through the airport.

When she saw Eric pull up to the passenger pickup area, she smiled. It was good to see his familiar smile that tilted just a little to the right, his short dark hair, his fit body.

Eric parked the car and got out, meeting her on the sidewalk.

She threw her arms around him, and he lifted her off the ground as he squeezed her. His body felt so wonderfully comforting and familiar. "I missed you," he said.

"I missed you, too."

"You look beautiful."

"Thank you." Amy grinned. It had been a while since he'd said that to her, she realized. In the next moment, she realized she couldn't remember the last time she'd told him what a sexy smile he had or how good he smelled or how attractive he looked in his new shirt. "You look good, too," she said. "I like your haircut."

He smiled. "Yeah?"

"Yeah."

Finally, he set her down and kissed her ravenously. Maybe a little distance was a good thing every now and then. It made things new and exciting again.

At last he pulled away and threw her suitcase into the trunk and got in the driver's side door.

"Are you hungry? Should we stop for dinner somewhere?" he asked as he buckled up and pulled into traffic.

"Actually, I have an idea for something I'd like to make at home, so I'd like to stop at the grocery store."

"Really? You want to cook?"

"There won't be any cooking involved."

"What are you planning?"

"It's a surprise."

He gave her a curious look. "All right. So, tell me everything that happened these last few days."

"Well, Leah fell for this hunky nature guide."

"Good for her."

"Yeah. Also . . . We kind of got lost in this vast national forest and Leah got heat stroke."

"*What?*"

"Yeah, but we're all fine now. No big deal."

"You almost died and you don't think it's a big deal?"

"I didn't come close to dying. It was just kind of scary."

"How long were you out there for?"

"About eight or nine hours. Something like that."

"Jesus. No wonder you look so skinny."

"I look skinny?"

"A little too skinny. I mean, you're always beautiful, but I like your curves."

"Excellent." Amy smiled. She decided not to tell him the part when she flashed the four-man soccer team while doing tequila shots. Instead she detailed how nice it was to see Leah and Caitlyn and spend time relaxing in the sun. She told him about the food and how it would be years before she could eat soup again.

When they got to the grocery store, Amy grabbed a red handbasket on the way in. She charged through the aisles purposefully, first to the dairy aisle to pick up a can of whipped cream, then to where desserts were to pick up chocolate syrup. She grabbed a pint of ripe strawberries and two green apples. Last, she picked up a loaf of fresh French bread—it was still warm—and some goat cheese and blue cheese and the priciest brie she could find.

"Looks like quite a feast," Eric said as they checked themselves out in the self-checkout lane.

"When we get done with everything I have planned, we'll be famished."

"Really?"

"Really."

At home, Amy asked him to pull from the fridge the champagne they had leftover from New Years and put it on ice and to open a bottle of red wine to let it breathe.

"I'll be back in a few minutes," she said.

"Where are you going?"

She put her index finger to her lips in the universal "Shhh" gesture. "No questions. Be waiting for me on the couch."

Amy ran upstairs and started the shower. She stripped out of her clothes and quickly washed beneath the wonderfully hot spray of the showerhead. She dried off, wrapped the towel around her, and blow dried her hair. As she brushed her hair, her towel slipped off. She looked at her body in the mirror. She had lost only a few pounds, but all that hiking, yoga, and water aerobics had firmed her up some; she liked the effect.

Amy changed into her see-through red lace teddie with matching thong and a red silk robe that she left open. She took one last look in the mirror. A tremor of anxiety flashed through her. She knew she was being silly. She was just having sex with her fiancé. She'd had sex with Eric a thousand times. Taking a deep breath, she went out to the hallway and turned out the light, descending the staircase halfway before she realized something was missing. She ran back up the stairs and grabbed a few candles from her bedside table and the box of matches that she kept in the top drawer. Then she returned halfway down the stairs.

"Eric?" she called.

"Yes?"

"Close your eyes." She waited a moment. "Are they closed?"

"Yes."

Amy walked the rest of the way downstairs. Eric was sitting on their couch. The champagne chilled in a bucket on the coffee table beside two wineglasses, a bowl of strawberries, and a plate of the cheeses and slices of bread. The bottle of Hershey's syrup and whipped cream were nowhere to be found.

"Keep 'em closed till I tell you."

"Amy—"

"Trust me."

She set out the candles, lit them, and turned down the lights. Then she retrieved the critical ingredients of Hershey's chocolate syrup and whipped cream from the refrigerator where Eric had put them away. She grabbed the red wine and wineglasses.

"Keep 'em closed," she said again.

"They're closed!"

Amy poured two glasses of wine and drank one quickly in an attempt to calm her nerves. Knowing her fear was ridiculous didn't make it go away.

Then she went to kneel down in front of him. Unfortunately, she knelt on her own robe, thereby tripping herself and careening headfirst into his lap.

Now, it had not been her sexy, seductive plan to headbutt her fiancé in his crotch. Fortunately, she somehow managed not to cause permanent damage to the area in question. After he yelped in surprise and Amy apologized, she tried again. Eric, ever the dutiful listener, didn't open his eyes even once.

She sat in his lap. At once his hands felt her bare thigh. "What—"

"Don't open them. You can touch but don't look."

She realized she was doing exactly what Kiera told her not to—she was trying to control the situation. Well, at least she was trying something new. Attempting to play a passive role would be an experiment for another day.

His hands hungrily explored her thighs, then slid up her stomach to her breasts. "You feel so good."

Amy let him touch and caress her for a few minutes until he tried to slip his fingers inside her.

"Ah-ah," she said.

"Off limits?"

"For now."

"Can I open my eyes?"

"Not yet."

Amy unbuttoned his shirt and, with his help, took it off. Then she unclasped his belt buckle and unbuttoned his button-fly jeans. She took off his pants and underwear. She was about to unleash the avalanche of chocolate syrup when she real-ized what it would do to her three-thousand-dollar couch. She hesitated. It would be completely unromantic to go grab a towel. Good sex was messy.

Then again, she could have good sex without ruining her couch. Hey, she couldn't change completely overnight. It was all about baby steps.

"I'll be right back. Don't move." She bounded up the stairs to the linen closet, grabbed a towel, and raced back down-stairs. "Okay," she said, a little breathless, "lift your butt up and move over about two feet."

"What—"

"Eric." Her tone was scolding and he obeyed.

Now that her couch was safe, she uncapped the chocolate and poured it over his erection. His eyes opened reflexively. He briefly became saucer eyed, and then, as he took in the sight of Amy dressed in transparent red mesh on her knees in front of him, he smiled. She licked a trail of chocolate off him. His eyes closed. He groaned.

"Hey," she said. "You came before we could get to the whipped cream."

He smiled. "Sorry. It's been a while. Give me a few min-utes. And we still have you to think of. What's gotten into you?"

"Nothing. I just missed you and I've been craving choco-late like crazy. I thought I'd combine my cravings at once." She had no intention of telling him that in the original fantasy, his part was played by Brent Meyer. If he fantasized about other women—and she was certain that he did—she had no desire whatsoever to hear about it.

"Chocolate? But you never eat chocolate."

"Two weeks at a health spa will do that."

"You didn't secretly go off to one of those places that trains you how to have all sorts of crazy Tantric sex, did you? Like one of those places that HBO's *Real Sex* would do a show on?"

"No," she said laughing. "It was a health spa, I promise. I just had a lot of time to think."

"Your turn." He gently guided her to the spot he'd formerly occupied on the couch, laying her on her back. He picked up the can of whipped cream and began shaking it. "Are you sure it's okay to have dessert before dinner?"

"Mmm-hmm. Besides, I've spent two weeks eating lentil loaf and carrot salad. I can eat dessert for every meal for at least a week."

As Eric licked the whipped cream off her, Amy lost herself completely in pleasure, and for the first time in weeks, she forgot her fears about marriage, the wedding, work—everything but how good she felt.

Amy and Eric showered together and then returned to the couch to eat bread and cheese and wine for dinner and straw-berries with champagne for dessert.

Amy took Eric by the hand and led him upstairs to their bedroom where they made love again. Afterward they lay side by side, looking into each other's eyes.

"So, what did you do with yourself while I was gone?" she asked.

"Worked. Played cards with the guys."

"How are the guys?"

"The same as always. Rex sent this e-mail out the other day with a link to an article about how Denver is the drunk-est city in the country. Of course his subject line was, 'We rule!'"

"How do they figure that we're the drunkest city?"

"They looked at things like the number of alcohol-related deaths and accidents, things like that."

"Well, that's not really fair. Denver doesn't have the kind of public transportation that other big cities have."

"True. Also, we are the microbrew capital of the world."

She saw their cat, Sir Galahad, jump on their dresser. Amy made a smooch-smooch-smooch noise to try to lure him to her lap, but he ignored her.

Amy and Eric had each brought a cat to the relationship. Amy brought Peaches, an aging, overweight heap of purring fur. Eric's cat, Sir Galahad, was an intrepid hunter and explorer. He liked to sleep up in their bedroom closet shelves, unleashing an avalanche of sweaters as often as possible. The obvious solution to this dilemma was to keep the closet doors shut, but Sir Galahad had snuck into the closet without Eric or Amy knowing it so many times, getting locked in for as long as ten or twelve hours at a stretch, it seemed safest just to let him plunder and pillage to his heart's content and clean the mess up later.

Amy watched Sir Galahad as he prepared to jump from the dresser to the closet shelf. He seemed ready to spring up a couple times, but they were false starts. Then he leapt up, landing perfectly on the bottom of the two shelves above where Eric and Amy hung their clothes.

"Isn't that amazing how he can land exactly where he wants without plonking his head on the higher shelf?" Amy said.

Eric looked as Sir Galahad strolled from one end of the shelf to the other before curling up on an old scarf of Amy's to take a nap.

"I know. It's amazing how cats can jump several times their height and have such accuracy. Well, except Peaches."

Eric and Amy smiled knowingly at each other. Peaches was such a fat old cat, she would routinely try to jump on something relatively low like their bed and misjudge the distance, landing a few inches shy of her mark. Using her claws like a rock climber scaling a cliff face, she would struggle the rest of the way up.

"Every now and then she'll come into the bathroom when I'm getting ready for work, and she actually jumps all the way from the floor to the bathroom sink," Eric said.

"Really?" Amy said, impressed. She hadn't thought the old girl still had it in her.

"I spot her, though. If she didn't make it, it would be ugly. I'm like the . . . Who was that famous gymnastics coach? Bella Karoli! I'm like the Bella Karoli of the bathroom."

For some reason, Amy thought this was hilarious. It felt good to be talking to Eric about something other than wedding plans. They were having the kind of conversation they'd had when they were first dating.

She'd missed it more than she'd realized.

Chapter 21

Home again in Portland

Though it was only three in the afternoon, it was so dark and gray out it seemed like ten at night. Fat raindrops plopped to the pavement as Leah raced through the parking lot of her town home with her luggage trailing behind her. Even so, the mad dash wasn't enough to keep her from getting soaked.

She unlocked her door. It swung open and she rushed inside, dumped her luggage, and locked the door behind her. She was wet and cold, and her hair clung to her face like a drowned rat. All the place needed was a few tumbleweeds rolling by. She couldn't believe how desolate it seemed. She'd lived here for three years and had never bothered to decorate. She'd never really noticed that before, how empty and barren everything seemed.

She peeled off her clothes, got a towel from the bathroom to rid her hair of excess water, then sat on the edge of her bed. She felt not-quite-there. Remote. Light-headed.

She wondered what Jim was doing right now.

For the moment, she was glad she was all alone, because she had the privacy to collapse on her bed and cry.

Chapter 22

Home again in Chicago

Caitlyn unlocked the door to her small, one-bedroom apartment and dumped her bags by the door. She'd deal with them later.

It was another cold, dark day in Chicago. Even the vibrant way Caitlyn had decorated her apartment couldn't lighten the mood. Her walls were all white, and she wasn't allowed to paint them, so she'd had to get creative with how she brightened the place. She'd managed to buy a used but modern-looking lime green couch, and she'd bought a used bookshelf and painted it light blue. She'd gotten end tables and a desk secondhand and painted them bright colors as well. The splashes of color helped liven things up, and the place needed it, especially on days like this one where the skies were overcast and gloomy.

The gray weather reflected the vague feelings of dread floating inside her. She knew that if she didn't break it off with her harem of men right away, she would lose her resolve. Without even taking off her coat, she called Reg and asked him if she could meet him for coffee.

"Why don't you come to my place? Or I can come to yours. I've missed you so much, babe."

"I'm really jet-lagged. I'm dying for caffeine. Meet me in an hour?"

"Sure thing, babe."

Caitlyn hung up the phone and walked next door to her neighbor's. Georgia had just recently graduated from college and reminded Caitlyn of herself. Georgia was rail skinny— she liked to joke that she was a buttless wonder—with short platinum blond hair. Georgia had been holding Caitlyn's mail for her while she was in Mexico.

"You look great," Georgia said.

"Thanks. You look cute, too." Georgia pulled off outfits that these days were too risky even for Caitlyn. Today Georgia wore a black knit ski hat, an olive green army jacket, a short jeans skirt, and fishnet stockings with holes as big as silver dollars. Caitlyn wouldn't even be able to get stockings like that on without ripping them, let alone go walking around in them. Not to mention they exposed Georgia's bare legs— not a good idea in the cold weather.

Caitlyn was dying to get back to her apartment to look through the thick stack of mail to see if there was any word on the grant. The biggest part of being a writer wasn't writing; it was waiting. Waiting to hear back from agents and publishers and grant committees to tell you your future. Finally Caitlyn decided she'd made enough small talk. She went back to her apartment and quickly looked through the mail. She didn't see anything from the grant committee. She looked again. Still, there was nothing. Oh, well, no news was good news, right? At least she hadn't lost on the grant yet.

Caitlyn always got her coffee at the same coffee shop. A quaint place with ripped couches and battered coffee tables, it was a quick bus ride away. Caitlyn got off the bus and walked the last couple blocks to the shop, pulling her jacket a little tighter around her. The smell of rain lingered in the moist air, and puddles pooled in shallow spots on the sidewalks, making the pavement darker than usual. It was such a change from the dry, sunny climate she'd just come from.

She pushed open the doors of the coffee shop and was immediately enveloped by a comforting warmth. Then she saw him. He smiled at her; his white teeth against his dark skin were so striking. He had no idea that she was about to break his heart. She hated this moment. This moment that she knew things were over but he didn't. She couldn't move forward. She stood in the entrance feeling leaden. She couldn't go through with it. He had been nothing but kind to her, taking her out to dinner, taking her to plays and musicals. He'd bought her flowers and a necklace and a beautiful silk scarf. All she'd given him was her company, and with the way she was feeling about herself right now, that didn't seem like all that much. She watched him come toward her; still, she wasn't able to move.

"Hey, beautiful." He wrapped his arms around her. Oh, how she would miss his powerful linebacker build.

"Hey."

"I got us a table," he said.

"Great."

Finally her feet came unglued from their spot and she followed him. A skinny cappuccino was already waiting there for her. Her heart sunk just a little more—he knew exactly what coffee drink she liked.

"Tell me all about your trip. You look absolutely gorgeous."

"Thanks. Ah, the trip was good. Look, Reg, I have to talk to you about something."

Immediately his bright smile faded. "Yeah?"

"This isn't easy for me."

His facial features suddenly softened into an expression of resigned disappointment. He knew what was coming. Caitlyn wanted to run. She didn't want to go on. She didn't want to have to look into his eyes and finish this.

"The thing is . . . I don't think we should see each other anymore."

He studied her for a moment. The tension of his silence was palpable. "It's because I'm black, isn't it?"

"What? No, don't be ridiculous. Reg, if skin color had been a problem, would I have dated you in the first place?"

"What is it, then?"

"Reg, you've been nothing but kind and wonderful to me. I've had so much fun with you—"

"Then why are you breaking things off?"

"I . . . I just don't see this going anyplace."

"If you want long-term commitment, babe, I'll commit. You're the only person I've been seeing these last few months anyway."

This was even worse than she thought. She was trying to break up with him, and he was offering a long-term commitment. She looked at the mug of cappuccino in front of her. She didn't need caffeine—her heart was already racing. "I just don't think you're the right guy for me."

"You don't see a future with me because I'm black."

"That's not it at all. I'm all for marrying a black guy, white guy, Hispanic . . ."

"Why are you suddenly talking about marriage? I thought you didn't believe in marriage. Is this from hanging out with your friend who's getting married?"

"No. Yes. Maybe. I don't know if I want to get married; I'm just saying if I do decide to get married someday, skin color isn't an issue."

He stared at her and shook his head. The look of anger and disappointment in his eyes seared her like a laser. "Caitlyn Blake, you amaze me. All you are is a user. You are a selfish, self-absorbed bitch. You use people to get what you want without ever considering their feelings."

"Reg, the reason I'm breaking up with you is because I don't want to be like that anymore. I want to be honest and caring. I want to be a better person than I am. If you want me to give back any of the gifts—"

He glared at her.

"I'm really sorry." She scooped up her coat from the back of her chair and put it on as she headed toward the door and back into the slate gray world.

Chapter 23

The first week back

After the great sex Amy and Eric had on her return from Mexico, Amy had thought that everything had magically been fixed between them. She thought two weeks away from him, two weeks of relaxing, was all she needed to get her sex back on track. But after just one day back at work, Amy was a walking experiment in anxiety. If her diligent if stress-prone administrative assistant and her harried coworkers were right, the company had nearly fallen apart in her two-week absence. Amy fielded no fewer than eleven messages from clients and five hundred and sixty-four e-mails. Though she put in a fourteen-hour day, she still made it home before Eric. She was so hungry she was ready to stir fry her cats, and she might have done it, too, except she was too tired to cook. The fact that she managed to order in Thai food seemed a major accomplishment.

After Eric came home and they gorged themselves on take-out, Amy could feel all the weight she'd lost rapidly make a comeback in that one single meal. When he tried to stroke her breast, she wanted to poke his eye out with a chopstick.

She gave him a kiss and told him she was beat.

Those first few days back, Amy worked such long hours

she was much too tired for sex. She and Eric had fun together over the weekend and even managed to find time to make love twice. On Monday morning, Amy awoke thinking about all the things she had to get done that week.

Amy looked at Eric and thought about her resolve to make sex a priority. She considered waking him with a blow job. It was something she'd often done early in their relationship, and she knew that it would put a smile on his face that would last all day. There was a part of her that thrived on seeing him happy, but there was another part of her that was irritated with him for reasons she couldn't fathom.

She decided she would crawl under the covers and wake him up that way, but first she wanted to get herself in a sexual frame of mind. She went through her mental index of things that usually turned her on; this morning, nothing worked, not even thoughts of Brent.

Amy decided to go for it anyway and hope she'd magically get turned on in the process. She went under the covers and took him in her mouth. Instantly he stirred and started to get hard. She looked up—he was smiling.

"Good morning," he said gratefully.

She tried to clear her mind. She'd stunk at clearing her mind when she was at the spa attempting to meditate, and she hadn't improved any since then. She tried to do what Kiera had advised and really be present in the moment, not thinking about anything else. She listened to how his breathing changed depending on whether she used her hand and how she used her tongue.

After a few minutes, Amy crawled up beside him and guided his fingers to her bikini underwear. She felt a few seconds of intense pleasure. After a minute or two, she thought about all the stuff she still had to get done at work that day, and how she had to meet Gretchen after work to look for a dress. *Stop it! Live in the moment! Don't worry about what you have to do later!*

Amy took deep, slow breaths and tried to think only sexual thoughts. She attempted to conjure memories of the first weeks in which Eric and she had made love, when touch was thrilling and new.

It wasn't working. *I have so much to get done today. I don't have time for this.*

"Come inside me," she said in a soft voice.

He climbed on top of her and pushed himself inside her. Amy glanced over at the clock and wondered what was taking so long. He came after a few minutes and collapsed on top of her.

"Now that's how I like to wake up in the morning," he said, smiling. "Were you close?"

Amy cast him a glinty look, but his eyes were closed and he didn't catch it. She had strong urge to take the lamp from beside their bed and clobber him over the head with it. *No I wasn't close. Not only wasn't I in the ballpark, I wasn't in the same* state *as the ballpark. I wasn't in the same* hemisphere.

This was the eternal mystery Amy had yet to understand: how men could be just fine with their partners having as much fun in the bedroom as they had when they were vacuuming the carpets. If it was the other way around—if Eric couldn't come for some reason—Amy would never live down the guilt.

But Amy didn't say any of this. She kissed Eric and told him she needed to hop in the shower.

As Amy got ready for work, she told herself she was completely over her crush on Brent. The only reason she was spending extra time on her hair and was wearing her favorite pale blue suit was because she felt better when she looked good. The fact that she happened to have a meeting scheduled with Brent was merely a coincidence.

When Amy went to Brent's office later that afternoon, she didn't feel the same flutter of excitement that she had the first and second times she'd met with him. When he smiled at her, however, she felt a rush. It wasn't as intense as it had been before; she decided she was making progress.

As she talked, she realized she was still trying to impress him. She was doing what Caitlyn had always done—trying to get the approval of every man she was with. In a way, Amy felt as if she were on a job interview, but in this case, she didn't want to be found just intelligent and talented; she wanted to be found pretty and sexy. She wasn't proud of it, and she couldn't explain why she felt that way.

When the meeting was wrapping up, Brent said, "So, how was your trip?"

"It was great."

"You look amazing. You look rested. Your tan looks wonderful."

"Thanks."

"I'd love to hear all about it. Would you care to join me for quick drink?"

"Thanks, but I have to meet my wedding planner. She's freaking out that I haven't bought my dress yet. I'm determined to make my final decision tonight."

"What time are you meeting her?"

"Six."

"It's not even five. We have time for one quick drink."

If Eric suddenly started going out for drinks with a good-looking female colleague, she'd want to beat him with a lead pipe.

What you are doing is wrong . . . But you're always being the good girl. Live a little. You're not married yet.

No! There's a difference between knowing how to have fun and get a little crazy and being a shitty human being. Going out for drinks with man other than Eric falls distinctly into the latter category.

"Brent, I appreciate the offer, but I'm sorry, I really need to get going. I'll talk to you soon."

*   *   *

Though Amy had spent nearly every Saturday of the past few months shopping for wedding dresses, she hadn't been able to commit to one. Her wedding planner, Gretchen, was nearly ready to go off the deep end. Amy had promised Gretchen that after she returned from the spa, she would be ready to commit to a dress and didn't mind paying extra for last minute alterations.

Even though she'd lost a few pounds and was a little firmer than she'd been a few months earlier, when she looked in the mirror, she still wasn't excited by her reflection. All she could see was extra flesh around her waist and hips and a stomach that wasn't nearly as flat as she wanted it to be.

She had narrowed her choices to two dresses at two different shops within a few blocks of each other. She tried on the more conservative one first. It was nice, but rather sedate. Amy wanted to be a knockout. She tried on a few more dresses just to see if she looked different in them now that she was a little slimmer. She looked all right, but nothing made her feel magical. She and Gretchen went to the other bridal shop down the street that had the other dress Amy liked. The only problem was that it revealed more cleavage than she was comfortable with.

"You look stunning," Gretchen said. Gretchen was forty-two years old, skinny as a twelve-year-old, and had more energy than a playground full of children. She'd gotten married for the first time when she was twenty and divorced for the first time when she was twenty-two. She was on husband number four these days, and her love of weddings—her own or her clients'—never waned.

"I don't even go around my own house showing this much cleavage. I don't want to look like a slut for my wedding. My grandmother is going to be there."

Gretchen rolled her eyes. She wore her white blonde hair spiky. Her skin was always tan no matter what time of year it was. "You don't look slutty. You look womanly. If I had your knockers, you'd better believe I'd show them off whenever I had a chance. I think this is your dress. You look curvy and yet thin. It's really only a hint of cleavage."

"I don't know." Amy appraised herself in the mirror again. She did feel beautiful. The dress was a silvery satin halter sheath with a beaded V-neck empire bodice and fishtail skirt. She'd opted against dresses with trains, fearing a train would make her butt look big.

"Amy, you don't have time to think. Your wedding is just a few weeks away."

Amy thought about how she'd been hiding her body behind baggy, conservative clothes for years. There had been so many rumors about her brother, and when she'd been growing up, she'd always gone to the opposite extreme. She hid her curves rather than flaunting them, and she never went to school dances, even though she'd been asked many times. She just got good grades and tried her hardest to be invisible. But in just a few weeks, she would be a bride. She would be the star of the show. Everyone there would be someone who cared about her and knew she wasn't a slut just because of her double Ds. Everyone there would know she was nothing like her brother. With her guests, she would be free to be herself. And maybe that person was just a little bit sexy.

"You know," Amy said at last, "I think I'll take it."

"Thank *God*."

When Amy got home, Eric was making dinner. It was such a relief not to have to cook, she kissed him all up and down the back of his neck and hugged him hard.

"Good evening, my lovely bride-to-be. How was wedding dress shopping?"

"A nightmare as usual, but I now officially have a wedding dress. Just a few alterations for obscene amounts of money."

He turned away from the wok where is was stir frying vegetables and skinless chicken—though he'd told Amy a thousand times that her body was beautiful just the way it was, if she was really determined to lose a few more pounds before their wedding day, he supported her being as thin as her curvy body could be.

While Eric finished dinner, Amy changed into pajamas and a robe and went to her study. She sat down at her computer and logged into her e-mail.

To: leahalbright1111@ourworld.com;
chameleon0306@hotmail.com
From: amyharrington@attbi.com

Hello my adopted sisters. I know you are both dying to know how things are going in the bedroom department for Eric and me. The answer is: it's very up and down. The other night we went out with another couple to a nice dinner and then to see a play. It was a really special evening. Eric looked sexy as hell. He was wearing a button-down shirt, and a little of his chest hair was peeking out the top of his shirt. It occurred to me that I would be the only woman on the face of the earth who got to stroke and kiss his chest for all eternity. All night Eric and I kissed and hugged and held hands. We were like teenagers again. Any time there was an intermission or a break in the performance, Eric would whisper in my ear how much he couldn't wait until it was over and he could take me to bed. I was really hot and looking forward to a romp in the sheets, but then we got home around eleven and all I wanted to do was sleep. When he started kissing and pawing at me, I wasn't remotely turned on, and in fact, I was just irritated. Early this morning Eric wrapped his arms around me in bed. I smiled and snuggled against him, feeling happy and in love and lucky. Then his hand started caressing my breast. That was fine, but then his hand reached down further. I locked my legs like a bank vault. I was still half asleep. I know he gets horny in the morning, but he needs to wait until I've had my coffee like a civilized human being. It's amazing to me how quickly my mood

could change from feeling happy and in love to irritated and completely not turned on. What's up with the erratic mood swings?
Love,
Amy

Amy wandered downstairs and set the table for dinner. As she and Eric ate, they talked about their plans for the honeymoon.

For the most part, Amy felt ready to get married and have kids and work on a happy, committed relationship. One minute she was sure that going forward with the wedding was the right thing to do, and then, suddenly, out of nowhere, she just wanted to run away and become a hermit who lived in a cave. Unfortunately, Amy couldn't imagine a life without microwaves, so living like a hermit in a cave wasn't a feasible option.

Just before bed, Amy checked her e-mail again.

To: amyharrington@attbi.com; chameleon0306@hotmail.com
From: leahalbright1111@ourworld.com
Amy, I read an article recently about how a large percentage of Americans go through their entire lives with low-grade depression. This depression rarely gets diagnosed because most Americans are so used to living with it. They think feeling that way is just the way it is and they never ask for help. This kind of low-grade depression can have a major impact on mood and sex drive. Another thing to think about is hormonal cycles. Women have twenty-eight day cycles; men have twenty-four hour cycles. With men's cycles, they often have high levels in the morning, so they are particularly randy then. If you wake up before Eric, you might consider getting up, getting coffee, and then having sex when you're a little more awake.

Amy, your job is stressful and you're about to get married and you're planning a wedding. Anyone of these things could send a person over the deep end.
Love,
Your friendly neighborhood biologist

Chapter 24

The first week back

As usual, Caitlyn awoke screaming obscenities at her alarm clock. She raced through a shower, threw some clothes and make-up on, sprinted to the elevator where she descended eighteen floors, and ran four blocks to where she caught the "L" to work.

Caitlyn's boss knew whether Caitlyn got in on time or not based on when she turned the computer on and logged on, so as soon as she unlocked the door to the store, she raced behind the counter and started up the computer.

That task accomplished, she pulled on the white lab coat she was required to wear, as if she were a scientist rather than someone who sold soaps and lotions.

The lotion store was a small boutique next to other cute shops like a hip furniture store, a clothing boutique, and a stationery shop. The store always smelled like a flower garden with a mélange of fragrances wafting in the air. They sold plain shower gels, soaps, and lotions, and had hundreds of fragranced oils a customer could choose from to create a personalized scent.

She turned the cash register on, ran a vacuum across the carpet, and, at ten A.M. sharp, she unlocked the door, and turned the "Closed" sign around so it read "Open."

Caitlyn had a steady stream of customers all morning. She'd just finished blending bergamot and lemon scents into shower gel for an attractive middle-aged woman when the bell rang as the door opened. Caitlyn poured the mixture into a bottle and looked up. When she saw who it was, she smiled.

"Hi, Frank."

"Caitlyn, darling, I've *missed* you." Frank Wright had just celebrated his fiftieth birthday. He looked just like George Carlin, with thinning white hair, a white beard, and dark, expressive eyebrows. Frank took off his coat and hung it up in the office in the back. He had majored in theater in college and had spent his twenties working various low-paying day jobs to support his real work of performing in plays. He still had that air of exaggerated theatricality to him, as if his facial expressions, hand gestures, and voice needed to be seen and heard by audience members at the back of the theater. When Frank was almost thirty, his lover died of Lou Gehrig's disease, and then, just five weeks later, his father passed away. That was when Frank left California and came to Chicago. He'd given up acting then, even community theater. Acting required getting in touch with one's rawest emotions, and Frank had spent enough time dealing with painful emotions to last him a lifetime. His father left him a modest inheritance, and Frank used the money to buy the lotion store.

"How was your trip?" Frank asked, joining her behind the counter.

"It was really good. For the most part."

"I had to run this store twelve hours a day, six days a week. It nearly *killed* me. You do look *fabulous*. There were many hot guys there, I take it?"

"Sadly no. Almost all the guests there were older women. We were graced with the presence of some cute soccer players, and I made out with one of them."

"Well of *course* you did. What else did you do?" Frank opened the cash register, quickly counted the money, made a few notes in his highly technologically unadvanced note-book, and closed the register again.

"We got lost in the woods. My friend got heat stroke."

Frank's eyes grew dinner-plate round. "Oh. My. *God*. You poor dear. What happened?"

Caitlyn told him the details of her adventure in the woods and how she'd decided that she was done playing the field.

"You broke up with all of them?" Frank asked, aghast.

Caitlyn nodded. "I broke up with Reg in person. It was so awful, I just called Sean and Kyle. Sean acted like it was no big deal. Then he called me a few later crying and begging me to go out with him one more time. It was *awful.*"

Frank held the back of his hand up to her forehead as if he were checking her for a fever. "Darling, are you sure you're all right? Are you sure you weren't the one who got heat stroke?"

"Frank, I thought you'd approve. You and Byron have been together since around the time Mary gave birth to Jesus. Don't you want to see me get married someday?"

Frank regarded her for a moment and smiled. "If that's what you want, darling, that's what I want. Are you sure you're really okay? No post-traumatic stress disorder, either from the near-death experience in the woods or from the near-death experience breaking up with those lovely young men?"

Caitlyn laughed. "I'm all right, I promise."

Frank restocked one of those shelves of scented soaps, then lovingly arranged the assortment of colored loofahs in a lavender basket. "All right, I guess I'll believe you. If you're really all right, I'm desperate to take a little time off. I've gotten used to you being my right-hand woman, and actually having to work for a living nearly killed me. You'll be all right if I take off?"

Caitlyn nodded.

"I'll be back this afternoon," Frank said.

"Have fun. I'll see you later."

Time passed quickly enough. Caitlyn enjoyed working at the store for a couple of reasons. One of them was that her energy and people skills served her well in this job, and she truly believed in the healing powers of aromatherapy and that certain scents worked better for some people than others. The other thing was that unlike other bosses she'd had, Frank wasn't intimidated by Caitlyn's intelligence. When she had ideas for how to improve things or cut costs, ideas for new products to sell or older products to eliminate, he thoughtfully considered her ideas and usually implemented them. Caitlyn felt as though she were part owner in the store. Still, she didn't think she was being challenged enough intellectually. When she'd been writing a lot, her poetry gave her the intellectual stimulation she craved. These days, however, she feared her brains were turning to mush.

When Frank returned that afternoon, Caitlyn gave him a hug and a quick kiss on the cheek before running out the door to catch the "L" to the beauty salon.

Once she'd been fitted in a black cape that would put Zorro to shame, Caitlyn sat in the black swivel chair, and her hairdresser, Mark, began applying the blond highlights. Spending one hundred and fifty bucks to get her hair cut and highlighted was perhaps not the best financial decision, but she figured if she was tan and had had a facial and a manicure and pedicure, she may as well top off the look with a new cut and highlights. The creditors were going to be calling soon, leaving bitchy messages any day now. If she was headed to debtors' prison anyway, she may as well look good.

Dozens of squares of aluminum foil were folded up in her hair, giving her a wild silver mane.

Caitlyn looked up from her magazine when she noticed a tall, handsome man enter the salon. Oh, dear. She knew him. He was Professor McKenzie, the head of the committee that was deciding who would win the Hayes Grant. Hayes Grants went to Chicago-area poets. Professor McKenzie worked at the university; Caitlyn had met him a number of times at poetry readings and various dinner parties over the years. The first time she'd met him she'd done the could-he-be-my-father? inspection, but then she realized he was, at most, only ten years older than she was.

She couldn't let him see her looking like this. She wanted him to think she was a serious scholar. A thoughtful creator of inspired art. Caitlyn sprung out of her chair, flinging her magazine down on the coffee table. She raced across the room and hid herself as best she could behind a large ficus. She peered through the leaves and saw him stride across the room. He smiled at one of the hairdressers and followed her back to the sinks, where she washed his hair. The stylist was smiling and flirting shamelessly with him as she worked, the trollop.

God, he looked cute. Had he always been that sexy? Damn. Brown hair, just long enough to fall into his eyes. Hard, lean muscles. A strong jaw and tender, highly kissable lips.

Caitlyn watched Professor McKenzie's hairdresser towel dry his hair, and then the two of them walked together toward her station, having to go straight past Caitlyn to get there.

Caitlyn tried to squat down even farther until she was balancing on her toes and her butt was resting on her ankles. Unfortunately, her balance couldn't hold this tenuous position for long, and she went toppling forward over the ficus with a crash—dirt exploded like fireworks. Perhaps she could invent a new sport: plant diving. Points would be awarded based on one's ability to keep flailing to a minimum and the execution of a clean dismount. Caitlyn would have scored low on both counts as she thrashed around, pathetically frolicking in the foliage. Branches and limbs tangled as if she were attempting to wrestled the ficus into submission.

"Ack! Ack!" she exclaimed. Her eyes were blinded by branches that seemed intent on penetrating her mouth and nose. She couldn't extricate herself from the plant's tenacious grip for several awful moments. At last she was able to roll free. She righted herself and stood as quickly as she could, coming face to face with Professor McKenzie, who was watching her in wide-eyed confusion.

"Caitlyn?"

She plastered on her best casual smile. "Professor McKenzie! Hi! It's so good to see you! How are you?" Her face shone bright, gilded with embarrassment.

"I'm fine. How are *you?*"

Caitlyn made a curious expression as if she had no idea what he was talking about. "Me? I'm fine."

"What's new?"

"Not much. I'm still writing, and during the day I work at this beauty store called Bodyrama. It's on Third. Um, I should probably get these things out of my hair before it turns green. It was good to see you! I'll see you around, okay?"

Caitlyn sprinted back to Mark. She determinedly did not look in Professor McKenzie's direction as her stylist removed the squares of foil and washed the dye out. Mark and Caitlyn walked from the sinks back to his station, where he gave Caitlyn a quick trim.

As Mark snipped away, Caitlyn sat steeped in embarrassment. When at last her most painful flames of humiliation flickered down to a low smolder, she thought again of how good Professor McKenzie looked. She kicked herself for not asking him what he was up to. He was probably dating someone, but there was the possibility, however slight, that he was a free man.

Not that she could do anything about it after thrashing around in a plant with her hair sticking out as if she'd been taking styling advice from Donald Trump, but still.

A fresh flush of shame burned its way from her cheeks to her toes.

"You don't need to dry it," she told Mark. "I'm kind of in a hurry. It looks great, thanks."

Caitlyn ignored Mark's perplexed expression, peeled off the black cape, and with her hair sopping wet, she scurried to the front desk, threw a wad of cash at the receptionist, and raced out the door without a backward glance.

She was still running when her cell phone rang.

"Hello?"

"Caitlyn, it's your mother." It was Frank. The frantic tone of his voice immediately put her on edge.

"Frank, what's wrong? What is it?"

"I'm not sure. I'm one of her emergency contacts. Apparently someone from her office tried to call you, and when she couldn't get a hold of you, she called me. Your mother's at the hospital. She's had a heart attack."

Chapter 25

The first week back

The house seemed unnaturally quiet. Leah went to her CD player and turned it on random rotation. These days she kept her CD player going all the time to fill the silence.

The cheerful yellow kitchen seemed to mock her as she got herself a Diet Coke. Sipping her soda, she walked through the town house to her study.

For the first time since she'd left the Oregon Fish and Wildlife Department to go freelance, she wished she worked at an office. She felt a depth of loneliness she'd never experienced before. She'd lived on her own for a few years in her early twenties, but back then she'd had an office to go to and coworkers to talk with during the day. Now she had all day and all night by herself in a too-big town home. It used to be that she could ignore life's disappointments by throwing herself into her work, but she was having trouble concentrating these days. Now all she could think about was Jim.

She had e-mailed all her friends to drum up lunch dates to give her an excuse to get out of the house. Fortunately, she was meeting Lindsey for lunch today. It gave her a reason to shower.

Leah spent the morning trying to get something accomplished, but most of the time she stared blankly at the Word document on her computer screen and absently fingered the medallion Jim had given her. She wondered if he thought about her. She wondered what he was doing right now.

Thinking of his kisses, she reflexively touched her lips with her fingertips.

At some point she dreamily came out of her fugue state and glanced at the digital numbers at the bottom of her computer screen. It took her a moment to focus.

"Shit!" Leah sprang up from her desk and bolted to the shower, where she took approximately three minutes to wash her hair and body. She turned off the faucet, toweled off, threw on some clothes, and raced out to the car, where she raced to Lindsey's office with her head out the window in an attempt to dry her hair (fortunately it wasn't raining).

She got to Lindsey's office only twelve minutes late. Her hair was nearly dry.

"Lindsey, hi, sorry I'm late."

Lindsey looked up from her messy desk and smiled. She had thick chestnut hair and a pretty face that was completely free of make-up. She and Leah had met working at the Oregon Fish and Wildlife Department. Now Lindsey worked at the Environmental Health Sciences Center at the University of Oregon.

"No problem. I always have work to keep me busy. How are you?"

"I'm okay."

"Are you seeing anyone?"

Leah paused. There didn't seem to be any point to mention Jim. "Not right now."

"I think I have a guy for you."

"Oh . . . Lindsey, thanks"—Leah shook her head—"but I don't think so." She hadn't told anyone about Jim. It hurt too much. Even though she'd known that their time together was short, and even though she knew Jim wasn't a fling kind of guy, in retrospect, it had fling written all over it. It stung that he hadn't asked her for her address or phone number or e-mail. Maybe she should have just given it to him, but then what if he didn't get a hold of her? That would be much, much worse. This way she could pretend he'd meant to ask but forgotten.

"Just come look. I have a picture of him. He's an old friend of Ray's. He just moved here. He's smart. He's pretty cute."

Reluctantly, Leah went around to the other side of Lindsey's desk and looked at the digital picture Lindsey had opened on her computer. He wasn't bad looking, it was true. He wasn't exactly smiling in the picture, but he seemed happy.

"He's six-two."

"Six-two, huh?"

"You might have fun."

It might help get her mind off Jim, at least for a while. If nothing else, it would get her out of the house. "All right."

"Great. Pick a place and time. I'll have him meet you there."

Chapter 26

Week Two

It was almost time to leave the office at the end of the day on Friday when Eric called her and told her he had a surprise and he was going to pick her up from work.

"Where are we going?" she asked when he met her at the front of her office building.

"We're taking a little overnight trip," he said. "Don't worry, I packed your bag."

"That's supposed to assure me?" she said with a smile.

When Amy realized they were headed to the airport, she looked at Eric.

"I got tickets as kind of a bonus from work," he said.

"Tickets to where?"

"Vegas."

As they waited in the security line in the airport, Amy leaned in to Eric. "I have a secret."

"Are you gonna tell me or do I have to guess?"

"I've never been to Vegas."

"Well, if you had fun when we gambled in Cripple Creek, you'll have a blast."

"This is just going to be a short trip, though, right? I still have so much to do for the wedding."

"Amy, relax. You're allowed to have a little spontaneous fun every now and then."

Amy smiled. "You're right."

When they arrived, Eric rented a car and they blazed down to the strip.

Since Amy had never been to Vegas before, she was eager to drink it all in. From the radioactive green MGM Grand to the gold pyramid of the Luxor hotel to the endless neon and frenetic energy of the pulsing city, the spectacle was awesome.

From the driver's seat, Eric turned and faced her. "What do you think?"

"It's like Disneyland on steroids."

He laughed. "We'll check in to the hotel and then go do some gambling. Sound good?"

She nodded. She loved the whirling excitement.

After they checked in to their luxurious room at the Bellagio, Amy took Eric's hand, and they made their way through the frenzied lights and sounds, the waitresses in tight shorts and fishnet stockings, the combination of opulence and kitsch. There was a blonde with magnificent fake breasts and long thin legs perched daintily on the edge of a stool at the bar talking with an ugly, ruddy-faced middle-aged man—was she a hooker? The possibility seemed somehow exciting to Amy.

"Let's play blackjack," Eric said.

"I'm no good at blackjack. I can never remember the rules about when you're supposed to stand and when you're supposed to hit. I'll just watch for a while, okay?"

Amy stood behind him and watched as he tapped his fingers to indicate he wanted the dealer to hit and waved his fingers from side to side to indicate he wanted to stand. When he won, Amy cheered. He won more often than he lost.

"You're my good luck charm, baby."

The first several hands were thrilling to watch. Amy soon found herself being entertained by people watching.

"You bored, baby?"

"Hmm?" Amy peeled her eyes away from a short Japanese man with greasy hair and glasses who had a statuesque blonde draped over him. "No. Well, maybe a little. I think I'm going to get some quarters and play the slots."

"Sounds good."

She got twenty dollars' worth of quarters and found a flashy quarter slot machine. She slid her quarter in, turned the dial and got nothing, but she didn't mind. If she'd lost a quarter to blackjack, she would have felt guilty because there was some element of skill to blackjack. But with slots it was pure luck.

Amy continued playing, and on her eleventh spin, she won twenty quarters.

"Whoo!" she yelled, clapping her hands together. She felt as though she'd won the lottery herself.

She continued to play, and though she didn't win again, she thoroughly enjoyed herself. She remembered back to her second date with Eric, when they'd gone gambling in Cripple Creek. She realized that letting herself fall for Eric in the first place had been a huge gamble. Yes, this marriage thing was terrifying, and she might not get lucky, but unlike gambling in Vegas, with marriage *she* had the advantage—she had Eric.

Amy was down only ten bucks when he came to get her.

"I have a surprise for you," he said.

"What?"

"It's a surprise. Come on. You'll find out soon enough."

Feeling heady she followed Eric to his car. When he pulled up to a place called Flyaway Indoor Sky Diving, her eyes grew wide.

"Sky diving?"

Eric parked the car and smiled at her, pleased with himself.

She hesitated just a moment. *Sky diving?* "What exactly is indoor sky diving, anyway?"

"A giant fan keeps you suspended in air so you can experience what it's like to fly. It's perfectly safe." He took her hand.

Amy inhaled deeply. What could be scarier than getting married? If she could take that leap, surely she could do this.

After signing up and vowing that they wouldn't sue should they get hurt, they listened as a muscular guy in a white T-shirt and navy athletic pants gave them brief instructions on hand signals and the proper form to enable the air to flow over them evenly.

Next they were given their gear: baggy flight suits, goggles, helmets, ear plugs, and elbow and knee pads. Then they were brought to the "flight chamber." Amy felt a tug of apprehension. Normally she loved spontaneity and surprises, but this was really getting her adrenaline pumping, which, she supposed, was the whole point.

The flight chamber was a small circular room with a mesh floor and ceiling. The fan roared to life, and they entered the chamber. Five people went out at once, each getting three minutes of air time.

Eric looked adorable even in goggles and an oversized flight suit. "You go first."

"No. I want to watch you."

"You sure?"

Amy nodded.

"Okay."

She watched as he did what the instructor had told them to do: he held his arms across his chest with his fist under his chin, and then he leaned into the room. The instructor grabbed him and helped him lie horizontally. Eric's hair flew up comically. After a moment, he seemed to get the hang of things. He looked like a windblown Superman. Amy clapped, smiling as she watched him give her the thumbs-up.

When Eric's time was up, he grabbed the door frame and pulled himself down.

"Whoo!" he hooted. When he managed to catch his breath and calm down enough, he grinned at Amy. "Your turn."

Amy's heart jackhammered. She walked to the edge of the platform, folded her arms across her chest, took a big gulp of air, and leaned into the chamber. The powerful air currents terrified her at first, and when the instructor tried to help her straighten out, her first instinct was to curl up. She wanted to be back on solid ground. Then she realized she wasn't falling; she realized she was . . . flying. What a rush!

She was soaring. She'd never experienced anything like it. Weightless. Free. She didn't know what an out-of-body experience felt like, but she imagined this must be close. Some of the other people who had gone had done spins and other stunts. Amy had barely gotten used to the feeling of suspended animation when the fastest three minutes of her life came to an end, and she pulled herself back onto the platform.

"That was awesome!" Exhilaration made her breathing as heavy as if she'd just finished a marathon.

"I thought you'd like it. Now, let's get into something a little less comfortable, and I'll take you out for a decadent meal."

She smiled and took his hand.

"I want to take a shower before we go," she said when they got back to the room.

"I'll be waiting."

Giddy was the only word to describe how Amy felt as she let the hot water pour down her soapy body. Life could be so surreal.

She shut off the water and wrapped a towel around her body. After squeezing the excess water from her hair, she wrapped another towel turbanlike around her head and emerged from the bathroom.

Eric was on the bed, lying on his side, his right hand cradling his head as if he'd been staring at the bathroom door the whole time, just waiting for her to open it. "Hello, beautiful."

"Hey, sexy." Her garment bag was folded over a piece of furniture. She bent over and unzipped it. "What should I wear?"

She felt him press up against her. Tenderly, he kissed the back of her neck, then slipped his hand through the top of the towel and gently squeezed her breast as the towel fell to the floor. "We could always order room service."

She turned, put one hand behind his neck, the other on his back, and brought her lips close to his as she looked into his eyes. "I'm not that hungry." Gently, she pulled him toward her.

They had the kind of sex that people had in the movies. Amy kissed her fiancé hungrily, letting herself go, losing herself in the moment. Nothing else mattered but her lover's touch. The sex was carnal, as if they were having an illicit affair. Maybe that, Amy thought, was the real secret to keeping sex passionate in long-term relationships—pretending that they were cheating on each other *with* each other.

Chapter 27

Week Two

"Jesus! What hospital?" Caitlyn asked.

"Evanston. Get there just as soon as you can," Frank said.

As the "L" rumbled on, Caitlyn stood up and looked at the map posted inside the train to figure out where she needed to get off to catch a train that would take her to the hospital. As she waited impatiently for her stop, she wondered why her mother's coworker hadn't gotten hold of her. Then Caitlyn remembered she'd changed cell phone plans more than a year ago. Though mom had been working part-time doing administrative work at the university for almost two years, she must not have updated her emergency contact information.

Caitlyn got off one train and, after waiting ten long minutes, boarded another. She was able to get a seat and was grateful for it—she was so nervous she wasn't sure she could stand. It was maddening to have so little information. How could her mother have suffered a heart attack? She was only forty-eight years old. She was thin and healthy. She exercised. She didn't eat fattening foods. It didn't make any sense.

When she finally arrived at her stop, Caitlyn sprinted all the way from the train station to the hospital. She raced into the emergency room and stopped, breathless, at the front desk.

"Excuse me," Caitlyn said to a plump Hispanic woman in scrubs who stood behind the desk. "My mother had a heart attack. She was brought here a little while ago." Caitlyn had to stop every few words to breathe. "Can you please tell me where I can find Bridget Blake?"

The Hispanic woman typed something into her computer. "We don't have a Bridget Blake on file."

"What about a Bridget Bloomwood?" Her mother had reverted back to her maiden name after every divorce, but Caitlyn had heard her mother complain countless times what a pain it was to always have to be changing her driver's license and tax forms after every marriage and divorce. Maybe she'd been brought in with an old ID.

The Hispanic woman shook her head again. "Who brought her in?"

"I . . . I . . . I don't know. Hang on a second." Caitlyn pulled her cell phone from her purse.

"I'm sorry," the nurse said, "but you can't use that in here."

Caitlyn went outside to the loading dock. The signs all explicitly stated that this area was for ambulances only. Just as Caitlyn was about to call Frank to see if he could figure out where the hell her mother, her cell phone rang. "Hello?"

"Caitlyn!" her mother sobbed.

"Mom? What's going on? Frank said . . ."

"It's Eddie! He's had a heart attack!"

"Eddie? I thought . . ."

"Caitlyn, oh, God."

"Mom? Mom? Are you still there? Mom, answer me. I'm here at the hospital. Where are you?"

All Caitlyn could hear was the sound of her mother sobbing.

"Mom? Mom? Where are you? What's going on?"

"I'm at hospital. It's Eddie. He had a heart attack."

"I'm here at Evanston Hospital. What room are you in?"

"You're here?"

Finally Caitlyn was able to get her mother to explain which waiting room she was in and what floor she was on. "I'll be right there."

The hospital loomed ahead like a rat maze. The signs seemed to only make things more confusing. Even after stopping for directions, Caitlyn took one turn and was lost again. Finally she managed to snake her way up the right elevators and down the right corridors where she found her mother sobbing hysterically in the waiting room.

"Caitlyn, thank God you're here."

Caitlyn threw her arms around her mother. "Mom, shhh, shhh, everything's going to be okay. I was so worried about you. Frank said. . . . I didn't know what had happened." Caitlyn squeezed her mother tight. "What did happen?"

"Eddie. We . . . were just about to get lunch. Suddenly his arm went numb. He said he had a pain in his chest and then . . . and then . . ."

"Why didn't you call me? Why did you call work but not me?" *Did you know how worried I was about you? What is wrong with you?* Caitlyn wanted to scream the words, but instead she just closed her eyes and held her tongue. This wouldn't be the first instance where her mother demonstrated completely skewed priorities. "The woman from work couldn't get hold of me, so she called Frank and told him you'd had a heart attack."

"I can't live without Eddie, Caitlyn. He's the love of my life."

"Shhh, shhh. I know, Mom. He's going to be fine. I have to call Frank and let him know where he can find us. He'll be here any minute. I'll be right back."

Caitlyn called Frank from a pay phone but got his voice mail. She left a message telling him where he could find them. She hung up the phone and lingered for a moment, still trying to calm her heart rate and erratic breathing.

She returned to her mother and sat next to her. Caitlyn put her hand on her mother's back and stroked it lightly.

Bridget was a thin woman who looked younger than her forty-eight years thanks to genetics, a good diet, and an obsession with Pilates and spin classes. She had honey-colored hair that she'd been highlighting blond for years. Caitlyn had always been awed by her mother's beauty and style. Even now with her eyes red and puffy, she looked elegant and stylish. Her black pants accentuated her long, slim legs. Her fitted pink cashmere sweater showed off her full bust to maximum advantage.

Bridget finally stopped sobbing. Caitlyn took her mother's hand in her own. As she did so, she admired her mother's acrylic french manicured nails that were just barely short enough to still pass for tasteful. For the first time, Caitlyn noticed the huge diamond engagement ring on her mother's left hand. Her mother had worn many engagement rings over the years, but this was the largest, prettiest yet.

"Mom, your ring, it's beautiful."

Still sniffling, Bridget looked at the ring and smiled.

"Platinum," Caitlyn said. "And the diamond, that's got to be, what? Two karats?"

Her mother nodded.

"Not too shabby," Caitlyn said.

"Thanks."

"You really scared me, you know. Frank said you were the one who'd had the heart attack. I was worried you were dead."

"Why did you think that?"

"I don't know. I guess your coworker misunderstood you, or Frank misunderstood her." Caitlyn exhaled. "Do you need some coffee? Some water? Something to eat?"

Bridget shook her head.

Caitlyn wasn't quite sure what it was she was feeling. There was relief and fear, but there was also anger. What if her mother *had* died? Caitlyn felt alone in the world as it was. She had Leah and Amy, sure but they lived halfway across the country. She had a few girlfriends in Chicago who were more drinking buddies than close friends. As nutso as her mother made her, Caitlyn loved the woman desperately.

Plus, Caitlyn thought bitterly, if her mother died, she would never know who her father was. The more she thought about it, the more irritated she became. All these years her mother had refused to tell her anything about her father. Every time Caitlyn had to fill out a form for a doctor's office about her family medical history, she could only answer based on the few people she knew about on her mother's side. Her mother's great-aunt had diabetes, her great-grandfather had spinal cancer, and Caitlyn's great-grandmother had died of suicide. That was it, her entire family medical history. What if on her father's side there were rampant incidents of breast cancer? What if Alzheimer's disease was prevalent? What if on her father's side of the family there were carriers for some rare disease she had never heard of, but was going to contract any day now? She would die a slow, hideous death, all because she didn't get the proper medical care that she needed in a timely manner. The more Caitlyn thought about wasting away from some rare illness, the angrier she became.

Without thinking, she said, "Mom, what if you *had* died?"
Bridget looked at Caitlyn with tear-stained eyes.

"Think about it. Do you really think it's fair for you to die without ever telling me who my father is? Really, Mom, no matter who he was or what the circumstances were, I want to know. It's not like I'm going to go out and try to track this guy down or anything. I just want to know. I think I have a right to know."

"The only reason you'd be upset if I died would be because you'd never know who your father was?"

Caitlyn rolled her eyes. "Mom, of course not. You know that's not it. I love you, and I'd be devastated if you died, you know that. It's just that lately, I've been really floundering. I haven't been writing. I don't have any guy in my life. I'm confused about who I am and where I'm going. I just feel like maybe if I could put this mystery to rest, it might help give me some direction."

"You're Caitlyn Blake. You're my daughter. My parents were Norwegian. My father's parents came to America at the turn of the century. My mother's great-great-grandparents came over a long time ago. What more do you need to know?"

At least Bridget wasn't getting mad at her—not yet.

"What if I have kids and they're mulattos, even though their father is white? My husband is going to think I cheated on him, though it's just that my father was black. That sort of thing can skip a generation, you know."

Bridget laughed. "Your father wasn't black, Caitlyn. Anyway, you don't want kids."

"That's not the point."

"What is the point?"

"The point is that I want to know who my father is. Tell me the truth. Is Eddie my father? Is that why you're so eager to have me get to know him? Is that what you meant by that comment about how we can finally be a real family?"

Bridget started laughing again.

"What? What's so funny?"

Before Bridget could answer, a male voice said, "Ms. Blake?"

Caitlyn and Bridget looked up at the doctor at the same time. He was in his early thirties, and there was something about his eyes and smile that made Caitlyn think of a used car salesman.

"Yes?" Bridget said as she jumped to her feet. "How is he? How's Eddie?"

The doctor held out his hand. "Ms. Blake, my name is Dr. Keyes. It's nice to meet you. Edward is going to be fine."

Dr. Keyes explained that Eddie hadn't actually had a heart attack, but that two of his arteries were ninety-eight percent blocked, meaning Eddie could have had a heart attack at anytime. The doctors had performed angioplasties on the two blocked arteries.

"He's recovering now. We're going to keep him overnight. He'll be able to go home tomorrow."

"Can we see him?"

"Follow me."

Caitlyn followed her mother, who followed the doctor. Caitlyn could feel that her mother was on the verge of telling her the truth. It was just a matter of time.

Chapter 28

Week Two

Leah had studied enough biology to know that mating was a natural animal instinct. So why did the entire human mating process seem so totally *unnatural?* Forced conversation, extra primping, too-bright smiles . . . The whole thing was exhausting.

She stood in front of the mirror wearing her white cotton bra and underwear and fussing with her short dark hair, trying to give it body using gel and silent prayers. She put on pale pink lipstick, which helped make her blue eyes appear more bright than usual.

She wasn't sure if it was from hanging out with Caitlyn or from heartbreak, but tonight she decided to go all out. She opened a package of nylons that she must have had in her drawer for years. As she battled to put them on, she remembered why she never wore skirts and nylons—she needed to be a yoga master to get the damn things on. At last she managed to pull them over her broad hips; then she slipped a dress over her pear-shaped figure. Downstairs she put on a raincoat and took out her umbrella and out she went into the cold rains that were inevitable in winter in Portland.

The drive to the sushi restaurant took only a few minutes. Leah loved the restaurant but didn't eat there nearly often enough. She'd asked her blind date to meet her there. If she didn't hit it off with him, at least she would eat well. Leah parked her car and walked inside. She shook the rain from her umbrella, then looked around.

The restaurant had a black lacquer sushi bar running along the area where the chefs worked. Lights hung down from the ceiling in bright colors of yellow, red, green, and blue.

Her date was waiting for her at the bar. She immediately recognized him from his picture and started toward him. He recognized her as well, and they smiled at each other. As soon as he smiled, she became transfixed by his teeth. She actually stopped in her tracks a few feet shy of him. Never in her life had she seen teeth quite as twisted and crossed and misshapen. One of his front incisors was practically jutting straight out of his mouth. She was fascinated.

She realized she'd become immobilized in amazement at his lack of dental luck and forced her feet to move once again.

"Ready to eat?" Snaggletooth asked.

"Uh, sure," she agreed.

The hostess sat them at a tiny two-top, and as soon as Leah sat down across from him, that was when she noticed: halitosis. His bad breath wafted over the small table in an inescapable miasma. She sat as far back from the table as she could, but the odor continued to hang in a fog between them. Nothing went with raw fish like breath that smelled of sewage. Charming.

They ordered dinner and sake and then looked at each other expectantly.

"How's the dating game been going for you?" he asked at last.

"To be honest, I haven't been playing it much."

"I've dated some nice girls, but none of them were quite right, you know?"

"Sure."

"I have a joke for you."

"Okay."

"How is a wife like a diploma?" he said.

"I don't know. How?"

"You spend lots of time getting one, but once you have it, you aren't really sure what they are good for."

Was that funny? Snaggletooth seemed to think so. He had a laugh like Horshack. He laughed so hard and so loud that everyone turned to stare in wonder. *I'm really not with him*, Leah longed to explain. *We only just met, really.*

"So, tell me about yourself," Snaggletooth said. "Have you lived in Portland all your life?"

"No. I grew up in Iowa. I went to college there. I majored in biology. I came to Portland after I landed a job with the Oregon Fish and Wildlife Department."

"Do you like your work?"

"I don't work there anymore. I actually *did* really like the job, but it didn't pay very well, so I tried to think of some part-time job I could do to make extra money. I started writing for a science magazine and ended up getting a full-time job writing for *Our World*. Have you heard of it?"

Snaggletooth shook his head.

"It's a science magazine written for lay people with an interest in science and medicine and technology. I work from home in my pajamas. It's a pretty good deal. How about you? What do you do for a living?"

"I'm actually currently unemployed."

"Oh?"

"Yeah. I got laid off about a year ago. I was an engineer for a telecom company. Ever since the market fell out of the telecom business, there have been lots of layoffs, you know? I'm not really sure what I want to do with the rest of my life, actually."

A year? He'd been unemployed for a *year*? And he had no clue what he wanted to do next? That didn't sound promising.

Their waitress, a pretty redhead wearing all black, brought them their amaebi (raw shrimp), maguro tataki (seared tuna), and magic mushrooms (with salmon). Leah focused intently on her plate, trying to avoid eye contact with Snaggletooth. She attempted to breathe through her mouth because when she inhaled through her nose, the odor of Snaggletooth's halitosis threatened to set her stomach churning.

"So tell me about your family," Snaggletooth asked.

At least he was showing some interest in her and not just talking about himself all night. The only problem was, she really didn't feel like telling him anything about herself. She just wanted to get home and have an emotional reunion with her couch and remote control.

"Well, I come from a big family. I have one older sister and five brothers. My dad owns a bar; my mom has always been a full-time mom for obvious reasons. Now my sister and brothers are spread out all over the country and have spouses and kids."

When Leah stopped talking, she realized the polite thing to do was to ask him about his family, even though she didn't particularly care.

They struggled through more getting-to-know-each-other talk, but the conversation was strained throughout the meal and never took off.

At the end of dinner, he offered to pay. A free meal would have been the one positive thing about the evening, but since Leah had no intention of seeing this man ever again in her life, she didn't think it was right to let him pay.

"That's nice of you, but really, you don't have to do that."

"No, I insist."

"No really, I don't mind . . ."

"Let me pay. Please, I want to."

"All right. Thank you. I'll be right back. I'm going to use the bathroom."

When Leah returned from the bathroom, Snaggletooth

stood. Leah glanced at the bill—fifty-one dollars. Snaggle-tooth had left four singles and a handful of change as a tip—that wasn't even ten percent! Leah thought quickly about how she could throw a ten down or at least a five without Snaggletooth noticing, but Snaggletooth helped her slip her coat on and began marching her out of the restaurant before she could get any cash out of her wallet.

"I'll walk you to your car," he said.

"That's really not nec—"

"I insist."

She mustered a smile, and together they walked to her parking space.

"Thank you for dinner," she said when they got to her car. Before she knew what was happening, halitosis-drenched Snaggletooth man was crushing his lips against hers. It was so unexpected—nothing about this night had been the least bit romantic, she hadn't flirted or fluttered her eyes or *any-thing*—that it took her a few moments to get her wits about her and wrest herself from his slimy hands.

"We'll do this again sometime soon, okay?" he said.

She just looked at him wide-eyed. "Mmm," she said. She jumped in her car, turned the ignition on, and pulled out of her parking space so quickly she could hear the rocks pop-ping out from under her tires as she peeled out of the parking lot.

She had put nylons on for this man! Never again! No man was worth nylons!

Leah went home, stripped out of her clothes, put on sweats, and collapsed on her couch. Listlessly she picked the remote control up from the coffee table and flipped through the channels. She stopped on the Discovery channel, which was running a program about lions.

"The female may mate approximately every fifteen min-utes when she is in heat for three days and nights without sleeping," the narrator said. "The penis of a lion, like all felines, has backward pointing barbs. In lions, copulation is often accompanied by snarling, biting, growling, and threats."

The specifics were different, but when you got down to it, Leah thought, life in the jungle really wasn't that much different from life in the city . . .

Chapter 29

Later that day

Caitlyn couldn't believe how good Eddie looked. To her, he didn't appear as though he'd just had a life-saving procedure.

A handsome older man, Eddie looked as if he was in decent shape. He had silver hair and icy blue eyes. He was in surprisingly good spirits.

"Oh, God, baby," Bridget said, rushing into his arms. He had thin tubes coming out of the top of his hospital gown. "I was so worried about you. You nearly gave *me* a heart attack I was so scared. Are you all right? Did they treat you okay?"

"I'm fine, darling. I'm fine."

Bridget finally released her arms from around his shoulders. She sat on the edge of his bed and clasped his hand.

"Caitlyn," he said, "it's good to see you again."

"Eddie, it's nice to see you again. I wish it could have been under better circumstances." She hugged him. He looped one arm around shoulders and gave a feeble squeeze in return.

"Honey," Bridget said. "what can I get you? Are you thirsty? Should I get you anything from home? Do you need a book? A magazine?"

"All I need is you, sweetheart."

As Bridget and Eddie talked, Caitlyn looked at the man lying before her. She didn't see any of her features in his, but he was sixty now. Maybe when he was much younger, he looked like her. Was it possible he was her father? Maybe he and her mother had been lovers years and years ago. He might well have been married. He might have broken it off with Bridget without even knowing she was pregnant. Not wanting to break up his marriage or sully his medical practice, Bridget might have run away from the small town in Tennessee where she'd grown up and come to Chicago. Fast forward thirty-two years: He coincidentally moved to Chicago and they passed each other on the street one day. He was divorced by then and she was divorced (again), too. They fell in love all over again . . .

"Oh, thank God!" Frank's distinctive voice pierced Caitlyn's ears. Reflexively, she smiled. Frank was out of breath and clutching his heart. "You, Bridget Blake, really know how to scare a man. Mitzie told me *you* were the one who'd had a heart attack. I guess there's a reason we call her Ditzie Mitzie. Although, my cell phone was breaking up at the time. *Maybe* I just misunderstood. Not that it's any better that *you* nearly had a heart attack," Frank said to Eddie. "It's going to be nothing but sprouts and skinless chicken breast for you from now on, Mr. Oliveri."

Oliveri. That sounded Italian. A Nordic mother and a father from Northern Italy. It would explain her dark blond hair and sincere adoration for pasta and buttery garlic bread.

Bridget, Frank, and Caitlyn stayed and made idle chitchat until the nurse stopped by and told them visiting hours were over.

"No!" Bridget cried, throwing her arms around Eddie if the nurse intended to take him away forever and sell him into on some remote island where he could never be seen again. "Please. Please let me stay."

"It's okay, baby," Eddie said. "I'm really tired. I could use the sleep."

"That's okay, that's fine. I'll just sleep on the chair right here next to you."

"I'm sorry, miss," the nurse began. She was an attractive young black woman wearing royal purple scrubs. "But . . ."

"Bridget," Eddie said, "go home. Get something to eat. Get some sleep. I want you to be all rested for when you come to pick me up tomorrow."

"Eddie, you know I'm not going to be able to sleep tonight."

"Please, sweetheart, for me."

Bridget looked into his eyes. "You're sure?"

"I'm sure."

"I love you more than anything."

"I love you."

After Frank and Caitlyn gave him hugs goodbye, they, along with Bridget, wove their way through the maze of corridors and out to the parking lot to Frank's Toyota Corolla.

"I'm *famished*," Frank said as he got into the driver's side after holding the front door open for Bridget. "I'm kidnapping you two and making chicken curry that's going to set your panties on *fire*." As Frank drove to the condo he shared with Byron, he talked the whole way. "I thought Eddie looked just *fabulous*. He was so lucky they caught it when they did. An angioplasty is *so* much less invasive than open heart surgery. You're going to need to stay on his case though. No red meat or fried chicken for him anymore."

"He's from the south," Bridget said. "He loves fried food."

Eddie didn't have any trace of a southern accent, but then again, neither did Bridget, and she'd lived in Tennessee for sixteen years. So he was from the south just like Bridget. Caitlyn wondered how many years after he'd knocked up Bridget that he'd moved to Chicago and lost his accent?

Frank and Byron's condo was a trendy one-bedroom place with a great view of Lake Michigan and Wrigley Field. Their place wasn't that much bigger spacewise than Caitlyn's, but it had been completely redone with granite countertops, stone-tile flooring, state-of-the-art track lighting, and art deco décor. Between the view and the brushed stainless steel refrigerator, stove, and dishwasher, they'd paid half a million bucks for the place.

Caitlyn always thought fondly of the nights she and her mother spent at Frank's place when Frank would cook dinner for them. As usual, the first thing Frank did was crack open a bottle of pinot noir.

"I know I'm supposed to let it breathe," Frank said, "but this has been a rough day, and I feel perfectly justified in pouring myself a glass and swallowing it down in a single gulp like a complete philistine."

He poured each of them a glass. Caitlyn and Bridget sat on stools at the counter and watched Frank as he chopped vegetables and chicken.

When Byron got home from school, he immediately went to Bridget. "Are you okay? Frank told me everything. You must have been scared senseless."

"Oh, I was, I was. But Eddie was brave enough for both of us."

"You know I would have come down there, but by the time I got the message, Frank told me Eddie was fine and that you were going to be coming home soon."

"Thanks, Byron."

Frank handed Byron a large glass of wine, and Byron sat next to Caitlyn. By the time the garlic naan and basmati rice and curry was ready, the four of them had almost polished off two bottles of wine.

As promised, the curry was spicy hot and delicious. The food and the wine relaxed Caitlyn.

"I've got to get to bed," Byron said. "I've been up since five. After three glasses of wine and nine hours of dealing with hormone-crazed teenagers, I'm wiped."

He kissed Caitlyn and Bridget good night and once again

told Bridget how happy he was that Eddie was going to be all right. After he'd gone into the bedroom, Frank said, "Well, there's no way I can let you two go home tonight in the condition you're in, and there's no way I can drive you. You two are just going to have sleep here. I'll get the pullout couch ready. Give me just half a sec."

With Caitlyn's help, Frank set up the pullout mattress. He got sheets and extra pillows from the linen closet and helped Caitlyn make the bed.

"Good night, my lovelies," Frank said, giving them each air kisses.

When Frank left them alone, Caitlyn pulled her sweater and jeans off. Wearing only her bra and panties, she crawled into bed. Moments later, her mother did the same.

"What a day," Bridget said with a sigh.

"Hmm," Caitlyn said, nodding. "God, that wine was good."

"It really was."

"I could almost go for another glass."

Her mother sat up. "I was just thinking that."

"Yeah?"

"Frank wouldn't mind if we cracked open another bottle."

"Of course not."

"Should we be bad girls?"

"Absolutely." Caitlyn hopped out of bed, grabbed another bottle of wine, uncorked it, and poured two large glasses. She climbed back on the bed feeling like a teenage girl at a slumber party. "Eddie is a hottie. You know, for an old guy."

Bridget smiled the hazy smile of a woman who'd had a few glasses of wine. "He is, isn't he?" she started giggling.

"What? What's so funny? Mom," Caitlyn said sternly. "Tell me."

Bridget's merriment quieted. She wiped the tears of laughter from her eyes. She took a long sip of her wine.

"Let me just say this. If I die, there is someone who can tell you who your father is."

"What if that person dies before you do?"

"Oh. I hadn't thought of that." She considered this for a moment. "You know, I don't understand why it's so important to you."

"Mom, it just is. It's important to me. Please, just tell me. I can take it. Whatever the truth is, I can handle it."

Bridget exhaled. She finished her entire glass of wine in a single sip. "Your father . . . your father . . ." She swallowed. "It's Frank, okay? Frank is your father."

Caitlyn shook her head, certain she must have misunderstood her. "What? Frank? Lotion store Frank? Chicken curry Frank? Frank whose house we're sleeping in?"

Bridget nodded.

"But Frank is . . . gay. He's very, very gay."

Her mother nodded.

"But how?" Caitlyn asked.

Her mother exhaled. "Frank and I grew up in a small town in Tennessee. Nobody talked about gay people. Back then, there was no Ellen DeGeneres or *Will and Grace*. Gay Pride parades didn't exactly find their way through our little town. All Frank and I knew was that we were different from the other kids. Frank and I were best friends since junior high. Back then I was skinny and gangly and I didn't have any tits. I had a mouth full of braces—other boys didn't want to have anything to do with me. Frank, on the other hand, was a good-looking guy. Sometimes I'd tease him about not going out with other girls, but he said the other girls were dull—he'd rather be with me.

"Frank was just about to go off to college in California when it happened. We talked about sex, and we decided we'd try it together. Right around that time, I got my braces off, and I was just starting to fill out. Boys were suddenly starting to notice me. But when you live in a small town, everything you do is under a microscope. Everyone knows everyone. I knew that if I started dating Ross Jenkins and Billy Hathaway, the rumors would start, whether they were true or not.

I thought experimenting with Frank . . . It would just be safer, for both of us. We thought we'd sort of . . . *practice* together. We loved each other, you know? Not like boyfriend-girlfriend romantic love, but we did love each other.

"So, one night, Frank stole a couple of six-packs from his father, and we rented a hotel room. We told our parents we were going to a movie in the next town. We tried it. Neither of us thought much of it. Frank went off to school; I started my junior year in high school. I didn't have morning sickness even once with you; I never felt nauseous. Maybe if I had, I would have realized I was pregnant a little sooner. When I didn't get my period for a few months in a row, I wasn't as worried as you might think. But my body started changing in other ways. I went to a doctor a couple of towns over, and sure enough, he confirmed I was pregnant. I knew it would kill my parents if I told them I was pregnant. I knew I couldn't stay in town. People would call me a whore and worse. But I wanted you, Caitlyn. Right from the start. I knew we were meant to be together."

Caitlyn wondered for a moment if she was dreaming. She took another sip of her wine. It tasted so real, she couldn't be dreaming. "What did you do?"

"I stole some money from my parents and told them I'd gotten a job as a dancer on a cruise ship. I'd taken tap and ballet for years and years, and even though I'd put on a bunch of weight and hadn't ever mentioned auditioning and hadn't taken a single dance class in months, they agreed that it sounded like a great opportunity—a way for me to make some money and see the world. With their blessing, I quit school. Instead of getting on a cruise ship, I got on a train to Nashville. I rented a rat-infested studio apartment. I bought myself a cheap wedding band from a pawn shop, earned my GED, and got myself a job as a waitress. When I really started showing, you wouldn't believe how my tips soared. Still, I didn't have that much money, and I didn't have any health insurance. That's when I met Don."

"What about Frank? Why didn't you just tell Frank?"

"I didn't want Frank to quit school. I knew he'd want to marry me, and I didn't want to marry him. I told him about moving to Nashville and getting a job. When Don asked me to marry him, I told Frank that I was pregnant and getting married. Like everybody else, Frank just assumed Don was the father."

Bridget held out her empty glass of wine. Caitlyn took the bottle from the end table and refilled her mother's glass.

"Don seemed really nice," Bridget said.

So did husband Number Two and Number Three. Number Four actually was nice, but that one didn't last either.

"He knew I was pregnant and accepted me just as I was. I thought I'd be happy and safe with Don. And for a little while, I was."

Caitlyn said nothing as she tried to absorb this windfall of information. Frank. Frank was her father. All this time, he was right there in front of her, part of her life.

"When you were born," Bridget said, "I'd never been happier in my life. Of course, in the months after you were born, that's when things with Don started going downhill. I had to pay so much attention to you, I didn't have as much time for him. As soon as you started preschool when you were three, I got a job and put every penny I could into savings so I'd be able to get away."

Caitlyn remembered the night they'd finally escaped. Her mother had woken her up in the middle of the night.

"What happened to your eye, Mommy? Caitlyn had asked. It wasn't the first time she'd seen a large purple bruise on her mother's face.

"Shhh. Grab Mr. Winkles. We're going on a little trip."

They drove all night from Nashville to Chicago. Her mother cried and chain smoked the entire trip. The only thing Caitlyn remembered her mother saying was, "Thank God he's not really your father. Thank God he's not really your father."

They got a ratty apartment, and her mother got a new job.

As soon as the divorce came through, Bridget legally changed both her name and Caitlyn's back to Bridget's maiden name, Blake. It wasn't long before Bridget met the man who would soon become husband Number Two. Bridget wouldn't allow any of her subsequent husbands to adopt Caitlyn, so Caitlyn remained Caitlyn Blake while her mother went from Bridget Bradshaw to Bridget Shapiro to Bridget Bloomwood and back to Bridget Blake.

Husband Number Two was transferred to Ohio for work. Caitlyn and her mother lived there for nearly three years. When Bridget and Number Two broke up, she and Caitlyn returned to Chicago, and eventually Bridget married Number Three. He was transferred to California and then to Houston.

Bridget blamed divorce Number Three on the heat. When she and Number Three split, she and Caitlyn returned to Chicago yet again.

"Frank and I stayed friends for all those years," Bridget continued. When I moved back to Chicago that last time, Frank asked me if he could come to visit. This was several months after his lover had died a slow, terrible death from ALS, Lou Gehrig's disease. The first week he was there, he met Byron, and he decided to stay. He bought the lotion shop and the rest is history."

"Why didn't you ever tell him the truth? Why did you refuse to tell me?"

Bridget swallowed. "Once you tell a lie, sometimes it's easier just to keep lying. I was worried . . . I didn't want to confuse or hurt you."

"Mom, I adore Frank. Why would it upset me that he's my father? Does he know? Did you ever tell him?"

She nodded. "I finally told him a couple of years ago, just before you started working for him. I swore him to secrecy. He wasn't supposed to tell you until I died He was thrilled to learn that he was your father. He already loved you as if you were his daughter."

"Why did you finally tell me the truth?"

He mother stared at her empty wineglass. "I don't know. I guess . . . I'm with Eddie now. Eddie makes me want to be a better person. I've spent so much of my life lying . . . I guess I'm finally done with it."

Caitlyn said nothing. She set her wine glass down and sank beneath the covers, pulling the sheets up to her chin. "Thank you for telling me, Mom."

"I know I haven't been a perfect mother, but I love you, Caitlyn."

"I know, Mom. I know."

Caitlyn closed her eyes but couldn't sleep. No wonder she had so many identity issues. She was the daughter of a gay man who hadn't yet realized that he was gay when he'd become her father.

The circumstances of her conception were far from romantic, but it could have been much, much worse.

Flamboyant Frank was her father. Caitlyn didn't see her mouth, nose, or eyes in his features, but at least now she knew where she'd inherited her sense of style, her *joie de vivre*, and her *je ne sais quoi*.

Caitlyn waited for the news to sink in. She'd been trying to solve this mystery for twenty-six years.

The truth felt comforting, like a warm blanket on a cold night. It just felt right.

Chapter 30

Week Three

Leah, dressed in her usual work uniform of sweats and a
T-shirt, went to her refrigerator and got a Diet Coke. She
pulled a frozen dinner of Lean Cuisine mac and cheese from
the freezer and popped it in the microwave. She boiled a hot
dog, and when the dog and mac and cheese were done, she
cut the hot dog into little pieces, mixed it up with the pasta,
and carted her meal upstairs to her study, where she ate sitting in front of her computer.

She never cooked unless she was dating someone and they
could cook together. If she was by herself and she tried to
cook anything that involved more than punching a few buttons on the microwave, she would forget what she was doing
and get caught up reading about some new scientific or technological breakthrough. She inevitably burnt whatever it was
she'd been attempting to cook. She had once left a pot of water
boiling on the stove for so long the bottom of the saucepan
actually burned away—Leah Albright was literally capable
of burning water.

After a few days of pouting about her disastrous date with
Snaggletooth, she still couldn't stop thinking about Jim. In an
effort to get her mind off him, she finally worked up the

courage to call Russ Evans, recruiter, the man she'd met at the airport who reminded her so much of her first love, David.

A giggling woman answered the phone.

"Hello?"

Leah hadn't expected to hear a woman's voice. Maybe it was his sister. "Hi. Is Russ there?"

"He's in the shower. He'll be out in a minute if you want to wait. Who's this?"

Leah though fast. "I'm an old friend. Are you his wife?"

The woman giggled again. "Not yet. Hopefully soon."

"That's great. I'm glad he found someone. How long have you been together?"

"Almost a year now."

"That's great. Well, I'll try Russ back later. It was nice talking to you." Leah hung up the phone feeling queasy. No wonder she was thirty-two and still single. Men were such astonishing shit bags. This Russ Evans creep had just wanted a regular fuck buddy when he was in Portland on business. Leah felt like an idiot for eating up all his lines about how he liked smart women. He must have been able to smell how desperate and lonely she was. And he'd reminded her so much of David and a time in her life when she actually had a life, when she was constantly going out with friends instead of always working, working, working.

She finished her dinner and typed furiously into her Word document. When she came to a point in her article where she wasn't sure what should go next, she just stared at her computer screen with her forehead furrowed and her lips twisted. Irritated with herself for not knowing what came next, she decided a break might help her perspective, so she checked her e-mail, quickly scanning it to see if there was anything important.

Leah's heart stopped when she saw she'd gotten an e-mail from jmaddalena51@aol.com. Quickly she opened the message.

To: leahalbright1111@ourworld.com
From: jmaddalena51@aol.com
Subject: Greetings!

Leah, I'm so sorry things were so rushed just before you left. I've been kicking myself ever since for not asking you for your e-mail address. Fortunately I was able to hunt down your e-mail address through the magazine.

I just wanted you to know that I had a wonderful time with you. I think you are an amazing woman. I wish we'd had more time together. I wondered if you might like to see me again? I've been toying with the idea of visiting my family sometime soon. Maybe I could come see you? Let me know.
XOXOXO,
Jim

A smile broke out across Leah's face as she hit Reply.

To: jmaddalena51@aol.com
From: leahalbright1111@ourworld.com

Jim, I'm so glad you wrote. I've been thinking about you ever since I left. I would absolutely love to see you again, anytime. My schedule is wide open. Just let me know. What have you been up to?

All evening Leah kept frantically checking her e-mail, hoping to hear back from him. Finally, at eight o'clock that night, she saw his e-mail address beaming up at her.

To: leahalbright1111@ourworld.com
From: jmaddalena51@aol.com

That's so great to hear. Actually, I wasn't planning on visiting my family—that was just a ruse. I have a week of vacation coming up and I wanted to spend it with you, if you'll have me.

Leah beamed. She couldn't *wait* to have him.

Chapter 31

Two weeks later

Leah felt panicky about Jim coming to visit. On the one hand, she had been fantasizing about sleeping with him ever since she'd left him in Mexico, so to say she was looking forward to that would be an understatement. On the other hand, there were so many things that could go wrong.

Leah hoped the weather would be nice for his visit. She had the illogical worry that if it was rainy and gray out, Jim would hate Portland and never want to leave Mexico, even though he'd lived in Seattle himself and knew exactly what the weather was like in the Pacific Northwest. Leah knew it was ridiculous to hope that Jim would come for a visit, fall in love with Portland, and want to move from a cushy job at a spa in Mexico, but that was her secret fantasy nevertheless.

When she'd been at the spa, he'd had his work, she'd had her friends, and they'd each had their own cottages to get away from each other for a time. What if spending one hundred and forty-four hours straight together killed whatever magic they'd had at La Buena Vida?

The day of his arrival was hot and sunny, and Leah sent up a silent thanks to the weather gods for working with her on this one.

She dressed in khaki shorts, a white V-neck T-shirt, and sandals. It wasn't the most flirtatious of outfits, certainly, but the plan was to explore the city, and she wanted to be ready for anything. She had spent a little money buying a swingy blue flowered skirt, a few cute tops, and a summer dress for romantic dinners, but during the day she anticipated hiking up mountains or going fishing.

She stood in the baggage claim area looking around anxiously. When at last she saw him coming toward her, her stomach flipped. His thick dark hair was pulled into a ponytail. He wore jeans, hiking boots, and a white T-shirt that stretched tight across the expanse of his muscular chest. He was better looking than she'd remembered.

He dropped his blue backpack and olive duffle bag on the floor so his arms were free to wrap around her as he kissed her. Leah got so lost in the kiss that she forgot they were in a crowded airport. At last Jim broke the embrace before they were arrested for public indecency.

"I missed you," he breathed into her ear.

"I missed you."

"So, what's on the agenda for the day?"

"Do you have any luggage to claim?"

"Nope. This is it."

"Well, you're the guest. Is there anything in particular you'd like to see first?"

"I'm all yours. I just want to see the city."

Leaving Jim's bags in her car, Leah took him first to a park so they could walk along the river.

"Do you want to get some ice cream?" she suggested, then blanched when she realized she'd just asked a nutritionist who worked at a health spa if he wanted to ingest pure fat and sugar.

"Sure."

"Sure?"

"You sound surprised."

"I just figured that ice cream isn't something a guy like you would eat."

"I don't eat it often, but how often do I get to see Portland on a bright, beautiful day, with a bright, beautiful woman on my arm?"

"Well, I have to say I'm happy to learn that you don't always eat perfectly. I dated a guy once who would never eat french fries or onion rings or pizza. It made me nuts. I don't trust guys who are too obsessed about their weight unless they are athletes or actors or something."

"It's all about moderation. A little ice cream every now and then won't kill you."

She got a scoop of banana ice cream with brownie chunks. He was a traditionalist, going for a straight scoop of dark chocolate ice cream in a cup.

"So how have things been going at work?" she asked as they walked.

"It's been the same as always. There haven't been any women going and getting themselves lost in the forest or anything exciting like that. Hey, a boat ride, you want to go?"

"Sure."

"Have you ever gone before?"

"Nope."

"How could you have lived here for ten years and never gone on a boat ride down the river?"

"It's kind of a touristy thing to do and I've never been a tourist."

The paid for their tickets and got on the flat-bottomed boat, sliding down a middle row to the end. "You take the outside," Leah said. "Just in case we get splashed. I'm wearing white."

"I'm wearing white, too."

"Yeah, but if your shirt becomes see-through, no one is going to care."

"If that's your argument, you should sit on the end for sure."

She gave him a light punch and laughed. "Shut up. Be a gentleman."

"All right, all right."

As they waited for the ride to begin, Jim asked her what she was working on.

"Well, I finished my influenza story and I just turned in my article about why people believe in pseudoscience. Now I'm working on a piece about the way the world fishes."

"The way the world fishes?"

"I don't mean recreationally but for food. The thing about fishing is that it could be a healthy, sustainable way to eat, except for the way businesses work. They don't care about being sustainable over the long term. They overfish an area until there are no fish left, which means there are no fish left to reproduce more fish. In some places we raise fish in what is essentially a fish farm, but it turns out that fish don't do well in confined spaces. They get diseased and develop lesions. It isn't pretty."

"Interesting."

She continued discussing what she'd researched about fishing in different parts of the world and how shrimp farms polluted the environment. He seemed genuinely intrigued by what she had to say. She loved that she'd found a guy who actually was interested in this kind of thing. She felt as if she'd won the jackpot with Jim—except her jackpot lived in Mexico.

Though Jim had taken the outside seat, it proved not to matter a whit. They'd been zipping down the river for only a few minutes when the driver purposefully stopped the boat so abruptly a giant wave of water drenched everyone on board.

"That cool you off?" the driver, a white-haired man in his fifties, said in a gravelly smoker's voice as he laughed. Clearly this was part of his usual shtick.

The passengers all laughed good-naturedly as water dripped from their hair, faces, and limbs.

"I look like I'm ready to audition for a part in an adult film," Leah said, pulling her T-shirt away from her skin so it wouldn't cling to her curves in quite such a pornographic manner.

"Yes, you do." Jim raised his eyebrows up and down. The gesture was done in a joking manner, but it managed to turn Leah on anyway. Why had they decided to start with sight-seeing when they should have just gone to her place and bonked until they couldn't walk?

It was a beautiful ride on a beautiful day, but Leah couldn't care less about the sights. She just wanted to get Jim home and out of his clothes. Leah tried to listen to what the captain was saying over the loud speaker as he described the history of the architecture they were seeing on either side of the river, but she was too busy looking at Jim. When the captain again stopped abruptly, soaking everyone on board, Leah shrieked and grabbed Jim's hand. He squeezed hers back and laughed.

She had forgotten how nice it was to have a strong hand clutching hers, even if she was soaking wet and her bra was showing and her nipples were standing straight as soldiers at attention.

Leah felt a thrill of excitement as the boat finally pulled into port and she and Jim were finally able to go to her place to wash the river off them. They stripped out of their clothes and climbed into the shower. Leah got under the hot spray of the water first, wetting herself down with clean water.

"I'm freezing over here. I'm pretty sure it's my turn." Jim said.

"You think so, huh?"

"I think so."

"What are you going to do if I don't move?"

"I guess I'll have to spank you."

"Promise?"

"I don't like to resort to corporal violence, but if that's what it takes . . ."

With both hands he gripped her butt. She shrieked, laughing, as he forcefully pushed his body tight up against hers and pressed his lips to hers. She lost herself in his kiss, in the feel of her breasts against his muscular chest, his strong arms around her.

In a flash he pivoted her so he was under the spray of the shower head and she was left out in the cold.

"Ah-ha!"

"You sneak."

"Guilty as charged."

Leah pretended to pout, but the truth was that his kiss left her lips quivering—she couldn't keep the smile off her face.

"I'm just kidding," he said. "We can share. Give me the shampoo and I'll wash your hair."

He washed her hair, kneading his fingers into her scalp. Leah moaned quietly with pleasure. His touch was gentle yet firm.

As she rinsed the shampoo out of her hair, he watched the water sluice down the curve of her breasts. Her gaze met his.

"There is an awful lot of filthy river water on you," he said.

"I know. You'd better clean me well."

He soaped her arms, her stomach, her chest, making her skin slippery wet. He paid particular attention to her breasts; then his fingers found their way between her legs. She gasped.

Then, suddenly, he stopped.

"What are you doing?"

"That's just a preview."

"Preview? What do you mean preview?"

"All good things come to those who wait."

"You bastard."

He laughed. "I'm a dirty boy. Gotta clean up first."

"I like you dirty just fine."

"Come on, help a guy out here."

She exhaled and gave him the evil eye, but she grabbed the soap and washed him. His penis was mostly hard, but when she put her soapy hand on it, it sprung fully to life. She stroked him, watching his breathing deepen. When he moaned, she stopped.

"All done."

"Ohh!" It came out as half moan, half laugh. "Touché, Leah Albright, touché."

"Last one to the bed is a rotten egg!" Leah shoved the curtain aside and raced dripping wet into her bedroom.

"Hey!"

Jim followed close behind and dove on top of her.

Leah laughed. "I won, I won, I won."

He kissed her. "What does the winner want as a prize?"

"I can think of a few things."

He put on a condom and entered her, but only barely. For a torturous minute he toyed with her before abruptly plunging himself deep inside her. She came almost instantly.

"Can you come again?" he said.

"I doubt it. I almost never come more than once."

"Let's try."

"Okay by me."

Leah was amazed when she came again. "Now it really is your turn."

"I'm thirsty and starving," Leah told him as they lay on the bed, a sheen of sweat glistened across his chest and face. He was on his back, trying to catch his breath. "I'll be right back."

She returned with a sweating liter of water. She drained a good portion of the bottle and passed it on to Jim.

"Let's get dressed so we can go eat," she said.

He nodded.

Leah put on her new skirt, a low-cut top, and sandals with small wedge heels. She wished Caitlyn were here to help her. Caitlyn would tell her the truth about whether she looked cute or like a total dork.

Leah went to the bathroom and involuntarily let out a squeak when she saw what having energetic sex with wet hair had done to her hairstyle.

"Jim, do you have a problem going out with someone who looks like she belongs in an early eighties punk band?"

She peeked her head in the door and saw that Jim's hair also looked like a bird's nest after a hurricane. She giggled.

"Here, we can wet our hair down and start again." She took the spray bottle she used to water her plants and wet her own hair down. Then she used it on Jim, except she used it like a water gun than a hairstyle tool.

"Cut it out! Hey!" he yelled.

"I'm just trying to be helpful," she said, deadpan.

"That's it." He lunged at her. She shrieked and laughed and tried to keep the bottle out of reach, but his arms were longer than hers, and with just a little wrestling, he snatched the spray bottle away from her and began showering her with water.

"No! Please! I have very few cute outfits!"

He kept right on going.

"Please! I mean it! I'll be good."

He tackled her onto the bed and began tickling her. "Ah! Stop! Police! Boyfriend abuse."

He stopped tickling her, and she realized she'd used the "B" word. *Fuck*.

She waited for him to correct her, to remind her that this was just a fling. She looked into his eyes and braced herself.

"Well, if my girlfriend would be a good girl, I wouldn't need to use tickle torture against her." He kissed her. Despite the fact they'd just finished having sex fifteen minutes earlier, she was instantly aroused again, and so, evidently, was he.

"Jim, Jim." Her words were muffled since his lips were pressed against hers. "I really am starving. We can eat and come back and . . ."

"Okay, okay, I'll be good."

As soon as he was off her, she grabbed the spray bottle and began her water assault again.

"Oh! You!"

"I'm sorry! I'm sorry! I know, that was terrible of me." She hid the bottle behind her back.

He kissed her again. "It's okay, I love you anyway."

Leah swallowed. He couldn't have possibly said what she thought he said.

"Uh . . . here's a comb," she said. "I'll be right back." She went into the bathroom and blew her hair dry. *Here's a comb? He says I love you, and you say here's a comb?*

She was so rattled, she had trouble putting on her lipstick and eyeliner. They hadn't known each other long enough to be in love, had they?

"How does Italian sound?" She asked him when she came out of the bathroom.

"Sounds great."

Over a red-and-white checkered tablecloth, they shared chicken parmesan and spaghetti with meatballs.

Jim told her about his big Italian family and what great cooks everyone was.

"Have you ever been to Italy?" she asked him.

"No. I want to. Have you?"

"Not yet." Before she could stop herself from thinking it, she imagined the two of them honeymooning in Italy. A few days seeing the sights in Rome, then just relaxing in the sun on the coast . . . She pushed the thoughts from her mind.

After dinner, she took him to Portland's famous Rose Gardens.

Walking into the gardens, they were overwhelmed by the strong scent of roses. They stopped at various flowers and inhaled their bouquet. Not all the flowers had a strong scent or even much of any scent. The Mr. Lincoln red roses had the most beautiful odor, but the Lagerfields were Leah's favorite. They were a pale white-violet color that looked not quite real, like a frosted rose on a wedding cake.

The gardens were a vibrant rainbow of colors. There were the rich corals of the Shreveports, the flamboyant pink of the Electron roses, the sensuous red velvet of the Precious Platinum, the lemonade yellow of the Sunsprites.

She tried to imagine these flowers at her wedding. She imagined clutching a bouquet of Lagerfields as she walked up the aisle. Jim would be waiting for her with a smile on his . . .

Leah looked guiltily away from Jim and pretended to smell a flower. She *never* fantasized about her wedding. Fantasizing about weddings was something girly girls like Amy and Caitlyn did. Leah's fantasies were of winning awards for her investigative reporting and being recognized for her professional success. But just now she could clearly see herself walking down the aisle to Jim.

"Leah."

Leah looked up from the flower she was smelling to see Jim training his digital camera on her. For a moment she worried he could somehow see into her thoughts. Then she remembered he'd told her he loved her first. It was all his fault that she was thinking like this. She smiled.

Every day Leah wished he would tell her he loved her again, and yet she was scared to hear the words because she wasn't sure what she would say in response. They spent the week hiking in the Falls, hanging out at the beach on the coast, tasting wine at wineries outside the city, and eating their weight in seafood. With each day that passed, she grew to care about Jim more and more. She was keenly aware of every minute passing, bringing them closer to when his plane would leave and take him back to Mexico. Neither of them spoke of what would happen once he left.

On the day Jim's flight was scheduled to take him back to Mexico, Leah took him to the Nob Hill area for lunch. They strolled around the neighborhood, doing a little window shopping. All the while, Leah thought about how he was going home in just a few hours, and they were in the exact same boat they were in before she left the spa. Once again they were going to be separated and they hadn't talked about what would happen next.

She wanted to tell him she loved him. She wanted to ask him to move here to be with her. But she had never been good with romance. She'd never felt comfortable expressing herself. So what she said instead was, "We should probably get going. You don't want to miss your flight."

He gave her a look she couldn't read. "Yeah. Sure."

His bags were already in her car. They got into her Saturn and drove almost all the way to the airport without saying a word. Just as they were approaching a bridge, Leah heard the shrill sound of a fire truck behind her. She followed the line of cars ahead of and behind her and pulled over to the side of the road just as the fire truck came barreling under the bridge. The bridge heightened the shriek of the siren until it was so loud the noise shook Leah to the core. She was struck in that moment by what a powerful feeling it was, the way humans all pulled together in times of crisis. She knew that getting out of the way of an emergency vehicle was the law, but people ran stoplights and stop signs all the time. Right now, all these strangers were working together to help that fire truck get to where it was needed to save people's lives.

Leah felt connected to the world around her, to other humans and to the earth itself. Leah was human, which meant the mating game was significantly more complex than it was for other animals. It also meant that everything else in life was more complex, too. And maybe that was a good thing. It kept things interesting. A lot more interesting than when she spent her days in front of her computer screen and her nights in the blue glow of her television.

She had no more time to waste. Without giving herself time to think or worry, Leah said, "Jim, I had a wonderful week."

"I did, too."

"I wish it didn't have to end." She glanced over and caught his smile.

"Me, too."

"Remember when we were having that water fight the first day you got here?"

"Yes."

Her heart pounded, but she forced herself to continue. "You probably didn't mean it, but, um, you said, well, the context was—"

"You mean when I said I love you?"

"Yeah, that's sort of what I was trying to get at. Anyway, what I meant to say was . . . Did you mean it?"

"I meant it."

"Oh. Because I think I love you, too."

"Really? I was sort of worried I'd scared you off after I said that."

"Scared off? I just had nonstop sex with you for six days."

"I know, but what choice did you have? I'm visiting from Mexico. I had no other place to go. What else were you going to do with me other than use me as a pleasure machine."

" 'Pleasure machine'? Where do you get this shit?"

He laughed.

"So . . . I want to see you again," she continued.

"I've been thinking about moving back to the States to be closer to my family. I think I'm ready to come back to the real world. Portland isn't that far from Seattle."

"You'd move to Portland?"

"Is that too weird? I know we haven't known each other very long."

"Wow." She shook her head, trying to absorb the news. This had been exactly what she wanted. So why did it feel so scary? "What if things don't work out for us?"

"I think we need to take a chance and believe they will."

"I don't want you to hate me if you uproot your life and things don't work out."

"I won't hate you."

"Promise?"

"Promise."

"I don't know, Jim. We really haven't known each other long at all. After the first rush of lust and attraction fades, it's very common—"

"Leah, Leah, stop."

"What?"

"Just stop. I love you for your mind, but sometimes . . . Look, not every single thing in this world can be explained away scientifically. It's true that it's possible that things might not work out for us. It's also true that we have something amazing and special and it's worth taking a risk to see if we can make things work. With some things in life, you just need to have a little faith."

Jim put his hand behind her head and pulled her lips to his. Leah was terrified, but for once in her life, she decided she was going to go forward with nothing more than blind faith to guide her way.

Chapter 32

Two weeks before Amy's wedding

D ressed in long-sleeved pjs, long underwear, and gym socks, Caitlyn pulled her hair back into a ponytail and padded the few feet from the bedroom to the kitchen to make herself some tea.

Frank. Frank Wright was her father. If her mother had married Frank, Caitlyn would have been Caitlyn Wright instead of Caitlyn Blake.

Caitlyn Wright. Caitlyn Wright.

It was a good, proper English surname. She rather liked it, although she didn't know if it would seem cheesy for a writer to be named Wright. Her mother had named her "Caitlyn" because the name meant beauty. The name had turned out to be prophetic. Caitlyn was a beauty.

Maybe, Caitlyn mused as she took the screaming teakettle off the stove and poured the steaming water into the waiting mug, the problem with her ongoing identity crisis stemmed from the fact that her real family name had been obliterated—her grandfather's name was George Blake Synnesvedt, and at one point he decided the Scandinavian surname was a burden and he became simply George Blake.

She brought her tea to her desk. She thought there might be a poem in this somewhere. She took a pen and scratched some ideas down. She was brainstorming when her e-mail pinged to let her know she had new mail.

To: chameleon0306@hotmail.com; amyharrington@attbi.com
From: leahalbright1111@ourworld.com

Caitlyn, I can't believe Frank is your father! All this time he was right there! I'm sorry you're still feeling confused about your life. I'm sure it's going to take a while for the news to sink in.

The thing is, Caitlyn, I've never understood why you think you have to come up with one definition of yourself and then stick with it for the rest of your life. All your life you've said you've been trying to figure out who you are, yet you never define yourself because you're worried you'll be locked in to that definition forever. That's not the way life works. You can completely reinvent yourself at any time if you choose, or, you can simply refine who you already are. It's an ongoing thing.

Here's something to think about—take it for what you will. People think that chameleons change colors to blend into their surroundings. Actually, chameleons change colors to communicate something, such as a willingness to mate. Their skin changes in response to temperature, lighting, and mood. When you change your hairstyle or job or clothing, you are communicating a desire for growth and change, and that's great—that's what life is about. But I think sometimes your changes are a way of hiding out. You talk about life as if it's just failures and successes, and that's not the way it works. Life is a series of opportunities to learn and grow.

I'll see you guys soon. I can't wait!
Love,
Leah

Caitlyn logged off her e-mail and sat a moment, thinking. She liked the idea she could refine who she already was. Maybe she did know who she was. Maybe she was a flighty poet who liked to change her hairstyle a couple times a season. She was a poet who'd had writer's block for much longer than she cared to think about. She was a single woman who had more experience dating than any one person really should have.

Caitlyn sipped her tea and opened her notebook. She scratched some notes down, then wrote and rewrote. After a while, she read over what she'd written.

What's in a name?

All through high school and college
When I had to fill in the Scantron bubbles
I thanked my great-grandfather
George Blake Synnesvedt
For his good sense
In dropping the Synnesvedt
Who has got that kind of time?
Surely the taut, five-letter efficiency of Blake
Gave me a minute or two advantage on tests
Over the Lymberopoulouses and the Neelameghams
Or, God forbid, the Potochniak-Montgomerys

We are a nation, after all, of fast food microwaved
and kept hot under searing lamps
Chosen for us before we even get there—
These restaurants, they already know what we want
And save us the hassle of waiting for fresh food
Who has got that kind of time?

I do appreciate not having to spell out a ten-letter sur-
name

Every time I order tickets to a play or
Make a doctor's appointment
But I miss my ties to my Norwegian roots
That link with ancestry and custom

There's tradition in this loss of tradition
We are a nation, after all, of Goldsteins who became
Golds
Markovics who became Marks, Snedlditetikas who be-
came Smiths
All those pesky umlauts and accents erased
All that cumbersome religious and cultural history
wiped out
With a quick slash of a pen
Simplified, streamlined
Hidden, covered up like a cat concealing its waste
Swipe, swipe, swipe
Shh, don't tell

History, ethnicity, tradition
Who has got that kind of time?

Caitlyn smiled. Then she looked at the clock and realized that if she didn't hurry, she was going to be late to work. She hopped in the shower, got dressed, and went outside into the cold to catch the "L."

Work passed quickly. She felt good. It felt good to write again. She wasn't even sure what she'd written was any good. It had just felt right to be thinking that way again. All day the words tumbled through her mind. She kept thinking of things she wanted to reword and move around. When there were no customers, she jotted down little notes to herself.

Caitlyn got home that afternoon and stopped by her mailbox. Because she was a writer, she was always getting important things in the mail, namely acceptances and rejections. So, as she'd done for years, she stood right there in front of her mailbox and sifted through the envelopes. When she came to one that said University of Chicago on the return address label, her heart stopped. Quickly, she slid the envelope open.

Dear Ms. Blake,
    We thank you for applying for the Hayes Grant. We had many fine applicants; the choice was a difficult one. While you were not selected to receive this year's grant . . .

Caitlyn stopped reading. *While you were not selected. While you were not selected.* Ouch. God she hated being rejected.

Suddenly, the light, airy mood she'd been in all day vanished. Dejectedly, she went to the elevator and hit the Up button. She stomped into her apartment, dropped the mail on the floor, threw off her jacket and shoes, and collapsed on her bed in the fetal position. She'd had so many fantasies about spending six months in Paris going to art museums and writing poetry at cafes. Maybe she would have met a handsome Parisian who would become her husband. And now she would never have a chance to meet her soul mate because the committee who decided the Hayes Grant recipient had no vision, no taste . . .

For a good hour or two, Caitlyn sulked. Why did she have to be a poet in a world where no one read poetry? Even among the eleven people on the planet who did read poetry, she still faced endless rejection. Why couldn't she work in finance like Amy? Every business on the face of the earth needed someone to calculate the finances. Amy would never be out of work. Amy would never have to live through the constant rejection that Caitlyn faced. Even when Caitlyn's work was published, she was still subject to endless jabs from critics.

Oh, God. Amy. Amy's wedding was coming up fast. Caitlyn bolted upright. She had promised to write a poem and to help Amy and Eric craft the script for the judge who would marry them; plus she was supposed to help with the vows they would exchange.

Caitlyn had been honored when Amy asked her to help them out. It was rare that poet's talents were in demand. If Caitlyn had been a doctor, her friends would constantly be asking her medical questions. If she were a mechanic, she could help her friends fix their cars. As a writer, it wasn't often she could actually be useful. Wedding vows were a big deal.

Caitlyn opened her notebook and jotted down random ideas about love. At first, it was frustrating work. Though in college she'd constantly declared to her friends that she was in love yet again, she knew maddeningly little about true love. She didn't have much experience with it.

Though the work was hard and slow going, it was also therapeutic. Thinking about love and friendship, Amy and Eric, Amy and Leah, she forgot, for a moment, just how disappointed she was in not winning the grant. In this moment, she felt good. In this moment, she was a writer who was writing again.

Chapter 33

The Big Day

"Where are my shoes? My shoes!" Caitlyn frantically ran around Amy's house, lifting the long satin skirt to avoid tripping. The hairdresser had spent far too much time on her hair for her to go sprawling and have all of her carefully arranged curls and bobby pins come flying out.

"You're more of a basketcase than the bride is," Leah yelled as she helped Amy arrange her veil. Then, to the mirror Amy was looking in, she said, "Actually, you're not a basketcase at all."

"Oh, no, I am, I just hide it well."

"You look gorgeous."

Amy's hourglass figure looked stunning in her ivory dress, which had a satin halter sheath with a beaded V-neck empire bodice and fishtail skirt.

Amy smiled. "Thank you. So do you."

The periwinkle dress did look beautiful against Leah's blue eyes.

"Found 'em!" Caitlyn called from downstairs. "Hey! Guys! The limo's here!"

"Ready?" Leah asked Amy.

Amy exhaled. "I guess so."

Caitlyn and Leah fussed around Amy as she climbed into

the limo and arranged her skirt along the plush gray leather interior.

"Oh, my God, I'm so nervous!" Caitlyn said as the driver pulled out of the driveway.

"You're nervous? Think about the bride over here," Leah said. "She's getting married."

"You're so lucky. You'll always have a date for weddings," Caitlyn said.

"I thought you didn't believe in marriage."

"Now that I've been single for a couple months, it's looking pretty good. Leah, I'm sorry Jim couldn't make it."

"It's okay. He'll be out of his contract in two months and will move in with me and we'll be together all the time. Assuming we don't kill each other."

"That's a big step," Amy said.

"Not as big as the step you're about to take."

"I'm nervous. My palms are starting to sweat," Amy said.

"Everything will be fine," Leah assured her.

"It's got to be more than fine. It's got to be perfect."

"Nothing is ever perfect," Leah said.

"Except my wedding."

Later, Leah would have to concede that as weddings went, Amy's came close to perfection. She and Eric got married at the same place they held their reception. The stunning reception hall had a large ballroom with elegant chandeliers, and the bridal party descended down a wide, winding staircase, then down the aisle to the judge who married them.

The vows, which Caitlyn had helped them write, brought a tear to everyone there. Afterward, people sat at the round tables covered in periwinkle blue tablecloths waiting for their meals.

Caitlyn stood and clinked her fork against her champagne flute to get everyone's attention.

"We're here today to celebrate the marriage of our friends Amy and Eric. Earlier this year, Amy told me that she was worried she wasn't leading an exciting enough life. The thing is, anyone can jump out of an airplane or hike through the Amazon or hunt big game in the Australian Outback. The biggest risk a person can take in life has nothing to do with extreme sports or racing a motorcycle or going rock climbing. It has to do with opening yourself up to loving someone and being loved. If you sprain your ankle or break your wrist, give it a few weeks, and you'll be fine. With love, if you get hurt, the pain lasts much longer. Sometimes years, sometimes forever. Amy isn't afraid of love, or of commitment. She's a bigger risk taker than she realizes. In life, the important thing is to know what is worth risking. Today we're here to celebrate Amy and Eric doing something that statistically, is pretty risky. I'm here to say, Amy, Eric: fasten your seat belts, it's going to be a wild, wonderful, amazing ride."

Caitlyn held up her champagne flute. "I'd like to make a toast. To Amy and Eric. To love and to friendship. To taking risks." Caitlyn looked at her friends, and smiled.